Unlikely Beast

A Novel by

John Lavrinc

Unlikely Beast

A Novel by

John Lavrinc

Bookstand Publishing
www.bookstandpublishing.com

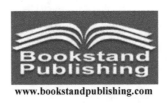

Published by
Bookstand Publishing
Morgan Hill, CA 95037
4769_3

ISBN 978-1-63498-921-3

Library of Congress Control Number: 2020907853

This book is dedicated to my wife, Kelly, who put up with me for all the weeks it took me to write it, also, for allowing me to share events in our life that became small parts of the book.

-Chapter 1-

I'm writing this in the event of my descent into total madness; I remember the first time I became a killer. A disciple of Satan, the Dark Lord. I remember all the specifics about that night. I was sitting by the Colorado River in Laughlin, Nevada, looking up at all the millions of stars twinkling in the dark sky. Little did I know how much my life would change that fateful, and very dark, starry night. It was Wednesday, March 16th, 2016.

The biggest question I've asked myself about that night is how could I take someone's life from them? It was such an easy thing, too! Way too easy! One minute I'm boring Jack, and the next minute I'm a confused killer, with blood on my hands, standing next to a cold, dead body. I used to be the most unlikely person to harm anyone, or anything, for that matter. To this day, if there's a spider or bug in the house, I'll trap it in a glass and take it outside instead of stomping it with my foot or squishing it with a tissue and flushing it down the toilet. I even open the window to shoo the flies out rather than splattering them on the glass. I never even swore before becoming a killer. Not one curse word. My Ex-wife, Susan, told me one time, that was one of the things that attracted her to me. She always introduced me as "Jack, my thoughtful gentleman." She told me a few time's that her friends were jealous of her for having such a wonderful gentle husband. A few years ago, I started cursing a lot. Cursing like a sailor. I find all of this extremely ironic, now.

I wish I could blame Susan for everything I've done. All the bad things I've done. She did, after all, divorce me after we'd been married for 15 years. 15 years! About 9 years of wedded bliss and then 6 years of hell heading towards pure hell, but it was pure hell for both of us. It'd be easy to forget about our unhappy union, our fucked-up life together, and blame her for making me the demon that I've become. But, to tell you the truth, I was happy when Susan filed for divorce. I don't think it had any bearing on the path my life has taken. I can't blame her. She and I had become just roommates, basically, for a long time. Grunting at each other, each day, like a stone age couple and always getting in each other's way. We each had moved into our own bedroom years before the divorce so, basically, we were already separated, and we just went on with our lives that way. A separated, unhappy couple living as roommates.

I've always suspected that boredom and a lack of physical activity between us drove her into the arms of one of the guys at our gym, a guy named Mark. I say "our gym" loosely, because I rarely went, and when I did, I always ended up standing around with another out of shape, boring guy like me, named Steve, mostly just bullshitting and killing time until our wives were done with their Zumba or Aquacise class. I showed up to the gym earlier than usual one cold October morning and saw Susan talking with Mark in the parking lot. Her Jeep was running, and he was leaning in the window close to Susan, and when she happened to glance in my direction, I knew. I saw it in her face.

Although she denied anything was going on between her and Mark, a lot of things changed. She would disappear on the weekend for hours, texting me she was "having lunch with the girl's," or she would tell me she was "volunteering" here or there, and every time Mark's name came up during one of our arguments, she would angrily tell me, "Mark and I know each other from the gym, for Christ's sake, Jack! Get over it!"

We began to fight on a regular basis, but she never left me. I could never figure out why, she just didn't.

Thanksgiving 2015 was horrible. We started out fighting over God knows what and ended up on opposite ends of our little home, Susan upstairs with the dog and me downstairs with the fucking cat. I never even cooked the turkey breast I had bought. I ended up throwing it out later that day, mostly just to piss her off. We both had toast and jelly for Thanksgiving dinner. Susan said to me "Just another fucked up day in the Martin house." We avoided each other for a week or so.

Christmas was equally as bad. The tree was never put up and we both told friends how much we hated Christmas and wished the whole holiday would go away. Neither of us bought a present for the other and I don't even think we said "Merry Christmas" to each other the entire day. Just another fucked up day in the Martin house.

The Monday after Christmas, Susan left about an hour early for the gym which seemed odd, but I didn't think much of it. I had already decided to forego the gym for lack of interest and lack of stamina. After I heard the garage door close, I got up, still in my pajamas, and carried the trash to the curb. All at once a skinny little red headed, pimply doofus jumped out of his car and threw a stack of papers at me yelling "you've been served!" Several emotions passed over me, some sad, but I was also thankful and relieved. Susan deserved better than me by then. My anxiety issues and bouts of depression caused me to be an ass to her. We waited too long, no, I waited too long to try and fix our marriage. We never did go to any kind of couple's therapy. We would have just been sitting there mouthing the words, anyway. Nothing would ever be the same as it was the first nine years of our marriage.

My neighbor Dave Holloway who, along with some of my College buddies, is one of my very few good friends, saw what happened and came over to console me. He told me his wife Jen was aware, somehow, of what was going to happen that specific day and she had told Dave and a few other neighbors about it. I looked around, standing there in my P.J.'s and saw a few of the neighbors watching everything occur while peeking from behind their curtains. I can't even explain how fucked up that moment was for me.

I drove to the gym and looked for Susan in the pool and in the Zumba room, but she was nowhere to be found. I drove through the parking lot three times but never saw her Jeep. I'm not sure what I would have said to her had I found her there anyway. I haven't really seen her in the flesh since that day. We haven't even talked on the phone, either. I know what you're thinking, reading this, but no, I didn't kill her and bury her in the back yard like my co-worker Rick suggested I had done. I mentioned I was happy about the whole Divorce thing, however, a few days later, that happy feeling left me when my house was completely emptied while I was at work, and I mean "emptied." Evidently Susan, and probably Mark, had rented a truck and felt free to rid me of everything in my little, piece of shit house. She even took the dog and cat. I could give a shit less about the cat but I kind of liked the dog.

Oh well, she's Mark's problem now. I almost feel sorry for the fucker! Talk to me in a few years big guy!

I apologize for the R rated language and for jumping around in my narrative, I haven't been myself since March 16th of 2016.

Let me tell you about myself. My name is Jack Earl Martin. I was born in Hoffman, Minnesota on February 10th, 1975. Hoffman is a small farming community in Grant County along the Chippewa River. My folks told me there was a major blizzard the day I was born, 48 inches of snow fell on our small town in 24 hours. Needless to say, the town shut down because of it. My Dad, a typical Minnesotan, still loves to tell me, "Dat der was a whopper of a storm, dontcha know. I thought you was gonna come before we made it to the dern hospital." I love my dad, but he could be a character out of that movie "Fargo." I used to be embarrassed by the way he talked, but after being away from home for so long I find myself, at times, homesick for it. My mom grew up in Peoria, Illinois but, listening to her today you'd think she was a native Minnesotan, too.

I'll be Forty-Two in about two weeks. Holy Buckets! Another thing my dad often says. My asshole Doctor told me at my last physical, that I had the body of a Sixty-Two-year old. Oh, he's a funny fucker, let me tell you. Someday I may just sucker punch that old Bastard for saying that to me, or maybe just for making me sit in his shitty exam room for an hour every time I go there.

I wasn't all that popular in High School or College, for that matter, the few years I attended College, that is. I had a few friends but, really, kept to myself. I used to say, "Half the friends I have don't really like me and the other half I don't really like them." Susan used to hate it when I said that. She, on the other hand, was very popular in High School and, also, in College. We went to the same College, by the way, Susan and I, the University of Colorado in the wonderful town of Boulder Colorado. Susan was a cheerleader, star volleyball and softball player and was considered quite the catch. She was voted most likely something or other, I don't remember. How I ended up with her is still a mystery to me.

Susan's major was Creative writing, with a minor in Law. My major was Mathematics, with a minor in shot gunning cans of beer, and smoking weed. We were in a few classes together but had never spoken to one another. It was in an Abstract Algebra class that we finally met and talked. I've always been good at math it just came very easily to me. As a result of this our Professor, Brookheart or Brackhart or something, it really doesn't matter, paired Susan and I together one day and quietly asked me to help tutor her. She was very attractive, and I had started secretly eyeing her, so I quickly agreed to help. She smelled so good the first time I tutored her I could barely concentrate on the math lesson. You know how freshly laundered sheets smell after they've hung in the warm sun for hours? Just like that.

She was fun to be with and I became attracted to her right off. It took her several tutoring sessions to start to warm up to me. But eventually, we just sort of clicked. We dated off and on for a few months and eventually ended up moving into a tiny apartment together, right next to the foothills on West Pearl Street, in Boulder. Beautiful setting, but a very small, and expensive apartment.

The explanation we gave to friends and family was, we had moved in together mostly to share expenses. But, by then I think we both knew that this was the beginning of our life together. After a few, great, years together, Susan Marie Johnson surprised me, on a drizzly Tuesday afternoon, by showing up at my work and asking me to marry her. Apparently, 2000 was a leap year, and women can propose to men during a leap year, which happens every four years, I was told. It was the first I had ever heard of such a thing. I assumed she made the whole thing up. Now I know that Leap Year is a real thing. This year we are in, 2016, is also a leap year. Unusual things tend to happen during a leap year and this one is no different.

It took me a full week to give her an answer, I don't really know why. I couldn't imagine being without her. She was the only woman I wanted to wake up to every morning and every night she was the last woman I wanted to see before I went to sleep. We always made sure to say "I love you" to each other at least a few times a day and I'm certain she meant it. I know I certainly did.

We eventually married at the Boulder County Courthouse, in downtown Boulder, on June 1st of 2000. There were no family members present, just my best friend Randal Jay and two witnesses that I had to pay, $10 each, for being there. She was Twenty-Five years old and beautiful! I still remember how incredible she looked that day in a form fitting baby blue chiffon dress she had bought at a local thrift shop. Even if she had worn a designer dress made specifically for her by a French seamstress, she wouldn't have looked lovelier. I had borrowed one of Randal Jay's suits, basic black and a bit big on me. But it worked. The ceremony was quick and simple, and I was the happiest I had ever been in my entire life. Randal Jay said to me "I can't believe you ended up with that gorgeous woman, you must be hung like a bull." He always had a little crush on her and admitted it to me that day.

Susan cried big tears after the ceremony and her makeup dripped down her cheeks. I used a white handkerchief, I found in the pocket of Randal Jay's suit, to wipe her tears away. She always told everyone those tears, were tears of joy but years later she admitted to me, during an argument, the tears were because she really wasn't sure she had wanted to marry me. I had a steady job, but it was a shitty one. I had been working for Sanders Brothers Construction Company, out of Longmont, Colorado. I got the job, as a part-time laborer, while I was still in College. Mostly I worked just weekends until I finally dropped out of C.U., at which time I became a fulltime laborer. It was a steady job, and the pay was okay. Mostly, I made my money selling weed to the students who lived in our apartment building. Susan's Dad, Ken, never really liked me, he thought I was beneath his daughter. And I quote, "Susan definitely could have done better. Why would she settle for that big sissy Jack? He's just a damn laborer. He couldn't even finish College." This is verbatim. I was standing on the back deck, outside the kitchen window and I heard him, he was talking to his wife in the kitchen. I never told Susan because I didn't want her to think less of her father. Her father was raised in a ranching family in Kansas, somewhere. I think the town was Ford, but it may have been Ford County. I just remember hearing the word Ford when Ken talked about his ranch. I do know the name of the ranch. It was the J.P. Johnson Angus Ranch, named after Susan's Granddad, Joseph Peter Johnson. Ken inherited it from J.P. and to his credit, turned it into one of the most profitable and prestigious ranches, not only in Kansas but, in the forty-eight contiguous states. In 1996 he sold everything on the ranch and all 8,340 acres of it for just over Fourteen million dollars. Susan got $250,000 dollars from Ken when we got married. Ken always makes sure to remind me every time he sees me that the money he gave her is hers and hers only. He's such a prick to me.

Her only sibling is a younger sister, Sheri. Sheri's a religious nut who feels it's her responsibility to tell every person she meets that Jesus loves them. One time she even prayed for me, and, placed her "healing hands" on my knee after I tore the MCL in it. Years later I heard her tell Susan how her prayers to Jesus had healed my knee, but it was, actually, repaired by an arthroscope in a very sterile, and very bright, Surgery room at Boulder Community Hospital and, to my knowledge, Jesus was not involved.

Susan's folks, moved to Cherry Creek, in Colorado, after our wedding so they could be close to her and the grandkids if we were to ever have any. Their house is enormous. Six-bedroom, four car garage, swimming pool. Incredible! John Elway, former Denver Bronco quarterback, was their next-door neighbor for a while. I very rarely went with Susan to her folk's house, and never, ever, by myself. But when I was forced to go for whatever reason, usually during the holidays, I would mostly sit in the back yard and smoke cigarettes, which pissed off Susan's father Ken. I always made sure a few butts ended up in his pristine lawn. I'm chuckling now, thinking about it.

In the summer of 2003, I got a job as an Assistant Manager at Champ's Sporting Goods in Broomfield, a small community in the northern suburbs. I was finally making decent money, so we purchased a two-bedroom, 1700 square foot brick bungalow at 4218 Everett Court in Wheat Ridge, about eight miles west of Denver. The house sits on a dead-end road along with five other homes, three homes on the East side facing three homes on the West side.

Years ago, when there were no homes here a man named John Long owned the parcel of land which was about seven acres in size. He had inherited the land from his father who grew wheat on it for many years. John Long had five children, three boys and two girls and decided to build six small brick homes, one for each of his kids and one for himself and his wife Theresa. The houses were all but done when John Long died in 1952, of alcoholism. John's wife Theresa had to sell everything to pay all the bills John had racked up. John's oldest son Ezekiel, (Zeke) bought one of the homes and lived there with his wife and three children for nearly thirty years. My house is one of the original small brick homes that John Long built. I think it was going to be one of the daughter's homes. It was in great shape when Susan and I bought it, and the price was way under Market price. The owner before us had a run in with the next door neighbor and just wanted out so he, basically, gave the house away to us. We used $15,000 of the quarter million Susan's Dad gave her as a wedding gift, as our down payment. Her dad, Ken, would shit himself if he ever found out about that. I should call and tell him he'd probably have a stroke and die because of it.

The house sits on nearly an acre, I had always had big plans for that big chunk of land. I wanted to have a huge garden and become self-sufficient, but that never happened. I'm basically a lazy person and most of my big ideas never happen. We finally just had a landscaper put in a simple inexpensive yard and went with that. Susan liked the house when we bought it, but it hadn't been her first choice. I told her we could live here for 5-10 years, have the house "scraped" off the land and build a brand new, bigger home in its place. One she could help an Architect design. Every homeowner on our street has done just that. Scraped the original, 1950's brick home off, and built large, modern homes in their place. Our little brick bungalow is the last of the original homes John Long built. The two homes beside us to the North are in excess of 4000 square feet. Bradley's house right next door is about 4650 square feet and Dave's house next to that one is about 4100 square feet, or was, anyway. That's a story for another time. The three homes across the street are smaller, probably 3500 square feet each, but very nice, modern, custom built homes. One of them, I believe John Long's home, has a large half-acre pond with bass in it. Susan and I always envied our neighbors homes. Now that it's just me, I'm fine with this little house. I doubt I'll ever do anything to change it.

We tried to have kids for several years but obviously one of us doesn't have the right plumbing, or something, because the whole "kid" thing never came to fruition. Thinking about it now, it was probably for the best that we never had any kids. Kids should never have to deal with Divorce.

At any rate, to catch you up, I am a newly divorced man with no females in my life to speak of. I'm fine with that, though. Women are a lot of work, and I don't have the energy for it. I still work, occasionally, at Champ's Sporting Goods, in Broomfield.

My life has always been cyclical. Ebbs and flows. As a child my life was wonderful, full of great memories. As a teen life became tougher for me, I had unrecognized bouts of distress and anxiety. Because it was unrecognized, there was no help for me. In College, things came easy for me. I made good grades and made a few great, long lasting friendships. As a young adult, I found myself without direction. I had a shitty, dead end manual labor job and life was glum. I met Susan and life became brighter, she was the love of my life, but our marriage began to slip and life with her eventually went sour and ended. As a newly divorced man, I found life full of fun and happiness again but eventually that life, too, has come to an end and here I am an unlikely beast, full of remorse and regret.

Since the divorce, I have started having issues again. Shitty anxiety issues that cause me to wake up sweaty, confused and claustrophobic in the middle of the night. I've had these issues for as long as I can recall. These issues tend to come and go depending on certain things. I've read several books on the subject trying to figure it all out. Most of the books say anxiety or depression is due to a chemical imbalance of some sort in the brain. This may or may not be true, depending on what book you read. I do know this however, other things, things like the dog dying or a fight with the wife or wondering if she's fucking some guy from the gym can also cause these issues to rear their ugly heads. Many nights I've had to bolt outside into the darkness in order to flee the stifling feeling that comes from nightmares and bad thoughts I have had. Dave, my neighbor, has caught me a few times on his surveillance cameras bent over gasping for air, standing there in nothing but my boxers. I'm sure Dave's wife Jen and all her nosey neighbor friends have seen the recordings and find it all a big joke, but, believe me when I say, it's not a joke! Susan never really understood it when these issues happened to me, putting me in a depressive state. I think she always thought I was faking an anxiety attack to get attention or something. But I have never faked anything. These feelings, these anxiety, laced nights were, and still are very real.

It seems that nearly every night, lately, I have been plagued with very detailed and brightly colored nightmares that involve evil, horrible people either chasing me or searching for me while I try to elude them and stay hidden. There are usually knives or guns or some type of weapon in these nightmares. Sometimes I have some sort of weapon but mostly the chasers have the weapons. One time some type of saw was being used on me and everything around me was stained by a bright scarlet red liquid. It was a horrible, very graphic nightmare! I vomited for an hour after jolting awake that night. Just writing about it now makes the hair on the back of my neck stand up.

All my recent anxiety problems are a result of my newest killing ways. My ex sister-in-law, Sheri, would say that an evil spirit has entered my mortal body and taken over, and that crazy bitch would be right.

I see the Angel of Death, sometimes, in the faces of customers in my store or walking among the people in the streets and on a few occasions, I have even seen him standing in the shadows of my bedroom watching me. These are not apparitions, they're as real as real can be.

I have become Satan's wicked helper. All my thoughts, lately, come directly from Him. I know this in my soul. I read the bible as a teen, trying to find some direction, but it's full of contradictions and things that do not make sense, so I quit reading it. But in the Bible, John 3:8 says "The one who does what is sinful is of the Devil." I've ended people's lives for Him, I am of the Devil. I am the Devil. This part of the bible is prophetic.

Most days my stomach is in knots and the pain is unbearable. My hands shake intermittently and without warning, and in the last few months my hair has gone from small traces of gray to totally gray, nearly white. Yesterday I noticed a bald spot starting on the top of my head. I feel I have aged 10 years in the last few horrible months.

I dialed the local police department a while ago. Literally in the last hour or so. I was intent on telling them the truth about who I am and what I've done. It's time to end this insanity, but a voice inside of me made me slam the receiver down before they answered. The same voice that seems to control me, at times lately.

I've seen news clips, on TV, about the people I've killed, and I know the authorities are looking for me even though they don't know my name or anything about me. When I'm out among the masses, I watch every set of eyes closely, looking for someone, anyone, who might recognize me for the unlikely beast I have

become. I'm truly sickened by the horrible things I've done, but I don't know how to stop any of it. Killing seems to be my true calling in this shitty life I live, and I know, someday I'll pay for my indiscretions on this Earth. It's just a matter of time.

-Chapter 2-

Jack Martin woke to an empty house Sunday morning. He stretched, rubbed his eyes and glanced at his watch. 9:43 am, February 6. Holy cow, he thought, in a week I'll be thirty-six! Susan had left a cryptic note on the kitchen counter. ***Jack, pack a bag for 2 days. Don't forget your bathing suit.*** "Now, what the heck?" Jack wondered aloud. Susan was, obviously, taking him on a trip, somewhere for his birthday. He packed his bathing suit and various other clothes in a small satchel and jumped in the shower. When he got out, toweled off and entered the kitchen, Susan was there packing a picnic basket with various snacks and beverages.

"Hi, hon." Susan kissed him on the cheek, "Are you ready for an adventure?"

"Yah, always. What's going on?"

Susan handed him a small, wrapped present. "For your birthday."

Jack looked at her and started unwrapping. Inside the box was a toy wooden train. His puzzled look prompted his wife.

"We're taking the train to Glenwood Springs for your birthday. Happy Birthday, early!" Jack stepped back. Susan always gave great gifts, but this was fantastic!

He was blown away. "Wow! Thank you!" was all Jack could say.

Susan filled him in, "We leave Friday morning and come home on Sunday, your birthday. I got us a room at the Colorado Hotel."

"Very nice, Susan."

They both loved Glenwood Springs. Neither of them had ever been on a train trip so that would be a new adventure. Jack could not wait.

The couple had spent their honeymoon in Glenwood Springs just eight years earlier, when they were very poor but so much in love. Jack had booked the "Lover's Room" at the "Blue Jay Motor Lodge", an older motel, several blocks from the hot springs, that had seen better days. The room was not what Jack had expected, but Susan was fine staying there, "We're just going to sleep here Jack, it looks clean. We'll spend most of the day in the hot springs, anyway. It'll be fine." But Jack wasn't happy. The place he booked was a dump. He gathered his new bride and their bags, and they drove to the Colorado Hotel, one of the nicest hotels in Glenwood Springs. He left Susan in the car while he went in to see if there was an available room. When he returned, he was carrying a key and a bouquet of flowers. "No bride of mine is going to spend her wedding night in a worn-out place like the Blue Jay Motor Lodge," he told her.

Susan was very happy. "My thoughtful gentleman." She said to him. She loved telling people that story whenever the subject of their wedding day or honeymoon came up.

Their neighbors, Dave and Jen Holloway had agreed to watch Tiger, Jack and Susan's new puppy, while they were in Glenwood Springs. Dave and Jen Holloway owned an accounting and tax business called 'Bean Counters Accounting'. Jen had named the business and always laughed when she told someone the name. When she told Jack and Susan the name Jen had snorted quietly while she laughed. Dave and Jen never had any children and changed the subject if someone asked them about it. They were good, God fearing people who attended church regularly. Jack found them way too square, but Susan thought they were very nice people. Dave had a "state of the art" security system with at least six cameras at various places around his house. If you wanted to know what was going on in the neighborhood you went to Dave. He had everything recorded. Dave and Bradley White, the neighbor between him and Jack, were always feuding and had been for a few years.

"Bradley White is a 'roided up douchebag. Pardon my French," Dave had said to Jack when he and Susan first moved in. "He's the reason you got your house so cheap."

"What do you mean?" Jack asked.

Dave continued, "The guy who lived here before you, Martin was his name, was gay. Bradley used to call Martin a fag all the time to his face, trying to get him into an altercation, but Martin was too nice of a guy. He would just ignore Bradley and go in his house, your, house." Jack turned and looked at his house. "One day, last fall we heard someone screaming for help and saw Bradley just pummeling the heck out of Martin on this very lawn."

Jack looked down at his lawn, "No shit." he pulled out a cigarette and lit it, then looked back up at Dave, who continued "Jen called 911 and I ran out and tried to break it up. I ended up with a broken nose"

"Oh Geez!" Jack gasped and took a puff of his smoke.

"Yeah" Dave continued, "and poor Martin was in the hospital for almost a week. He was barely breathing when the cops got here."

"Mercy!" Jack exclaimed, looking down again at his lawn where this had happened, "Did the guy die?"

"No, never died. He moved in with a friend in Denver. A moving company came one day and emptied the entire house. Jen and I got a Christmas card from him. He thanked us for being such good neighbors but never mentioned what had happened that day, and there wasn't a return address on the envelope."

"What about Bradley, was he arrested?" Dave looked a bit pained as he explained the rest of the story. "I pressed charges, and Bradley spent a night in jail. We settled out of court, but that was it. Martin never did press charges, I guess he was scared Bradley would hunt him down and do something bad, maybe kill him." He watched as Jack took all this in.

Jack finally said, "Good God, what have we gotten ourselves into?"

Dave sighed and said, "I installed all my cameras a few days after that day."

Jack looked at Dave's cameras, and then back at his own house. Susan was doing dishes in the kitchen and she smiled and waved. "Don't tell Susan about this, please." Jack took one last drag on his Marlboro and flicked it into the street.

The train ride to Glenwood was incredible. They had a wonderful breakfast in the dining car and sat for hours in the observation car watching for animals and enjoying the mountain scenery. Susan reached into the picnic basket she had packed and brought out a bottle of Pinot Grigio and two plastic cups. They sat there drinking the fruity and slightly floral tasting wine. Jack put his face close to the window and exhaled causing a big condensation patch to form. He took his finger and drew a heart, and in the heart, he wrote S & J. Susan smiled and kissed his cheek. Jack was such a wonderful husband. The train ride was so relaxing that Susan fell asleep for a full hour in Jack's lap. Jack enjoyed everything about the train ride. He told Susan "I don't think I could ever be happier." While in the back of his mind he couldn't quit thinking about their new neighbor, Bradley White, and what he had done to the former owner of their home.

The train arrived in Glenwood Springs at 1:45 PM, about 25 minutes late, and Susan had a car waiting to take them to the Colorado Hotel. "You just sit here I'll take care of checking in this time" she told Jack when they entered the lobby. Jack sat in a large comfortable antique chair by the roaring fireplace and waited. He looked around at the expensive carpeting and drapes and all the antique furniture. This place is beautiful, he thought. Their room, a suite, was also beautiful. "Newly remodeled", Susan quoted the man at the desk. It had a living room and a bedroom with tall ceilings and wonderful antique furniture throughout. The bed had a thick and irresistibly soft comforter. Jack hugged his incredible wife and they toppled onto the bed kissing. Jack was a very gentle and attentive lover and always made sure his wife was completely satisfied each time they made love. He didn't disappoint her on this day.

Later that afternoon they changed into their swimsuits and walked to the Hot Springs and soaked for a few hours. The sun was starting to set over the mountains. Orange and pink stripes crisscrossed the blue sky slowly turning to a deep gold and crimson radiance against the now black mountains, and eventually the entire sky was dark with just a trace of dark pink sprinkled about. The night sky came on clear and with thousands of twinkling stars. Jack and Susan sat in the hot pool and stared at the sky in awe.

Jack asked Susan, "What did I ever do to deserve this great day?"

"Remember our honeymoon? When you refused to allow your wife to stay in the dingy little motel? I'm just paying you back."

The next day Jack rented a car and they explored the town of Glenwood Springs. When they were here on their honeymoon the couple had no vehicle and had to walk everywhere so they were very limited as to what they did and saw. With the rental car they were able to find a quaint little diner on the South end of town, beside the Frying Pan River. They sat on the outside deck and listened to the burbling cold, clear water as it slowly ran downhill and watched as a fly fisherman caught two small green trout with orange underbellies. They had a fantastic breakfast of huge proportions.

When they got in the rental car Susan puffed her breath out and said, "Whoo, oh my gosh, I'm stuffed!"

Jack agreed by saying, "Uff-da!" They stopped and bought two nice bottles of Champagne and a package of plastic wine glasses. They decided instead of exploring more of Glenwood Springs they would return to the Hotel and explore each other some more. Walking up the front steps in front of the hotel they noticed a big fire pit with a roaring fire and six Adirondack chairs around it. Another couple was sitting enjoying the fire and it looked very inviting to Susan.

She said to Jack, "Let's go sit by the fire and have our champagne."

They introduced themselves to the other couple and the other couple did the same,

"Hi. I'm Kris and this is my husband Craig" The woman said. The other couple was a few years younger than Susan and Jack, probably just under 30, Jack estimated.

Craig shook Jack's hand firmly and said, "We're here for Kris's birthday, what about the two of you?" Jack looked at Susan and they both laughed.

Jack explained to the couple, "My incredible wife brought me here for my birthday, as well." All four of them laughed.

Kris said "February 12th," pointing at herself.

Jack said "February 10th," and pointed at himself.

Kris said, "Aquarius. Analytical and easy going."

Susan agreed, "Easy going for sure," She said as she put her arm around her sweet husband.

"Not so much with this one." Craig pointed his thumb at his wife. Kris playfully punched her husband in the shoulder.

The four of them sat and talked for over an hour. Jack opened the Champagne and shared it with the other couple. Susan raised her glass and toasted Kris and Jack's birthdays. The younger couple shared the snacks they had brought with them to the fire pit, Triple Cream Brie and

Manchego cheese with Croccantini crackers. Craig and Kris told the other couple that they lived in Fruita, Colorado, about ninety miles west down I-70 where they owned a very small winery.

Jack was impressed, "Wow, that is such a cool thing, winery owners."

Craig explained, "We're a very small operation, just Kris and I and six part-time employees. Last year we only produced about 130 cases. So far, we've only made two varieties of red wine, a Petit Verdot and a blend called 'Night of the living Red'."

Susan loved the name, "Very clever," she said, and Jack echoed, "Yah, very clever."

Craig smiled and continued, "Next year we hope to add two white wines, probably a Chardonnay and a Muscat Blanc we're going to call 'Sweet Mel Blanc' for the guy who gave Bugs Bunny a voice. We're aging the blend we've made, and we won't start selling it for at least a year."

Kris told the other couple they had always wanted to own a winery and used the money from their wedding to put a down payment on the winery in Fruita. The subject of their respective weddings was open now and Susan told the other couple about their simple wedding, she in a thrift store dress and Jack in a borrowed suit in front of a judge at the County Courthouse with no family and only one friend. She said that they had honeymooned right here at this hotel and were happy to be back. Kris described her and Craig's vows. They had flown with their parents and some family to Germany, Kris's family was of German descent and Craig was part German. Craig and Kris weren't necessarily religious, so they had a civil marriage in the local "Standesamt" before a German registrar and afterwards during the reception a local chimney sweep showed up with horseshoes and four-leaf clovers for the approximately twenty-five people present. "Chimney sweep?" Jack asked. Craig explained to Susan and Jack that the chimney sweep represented good luck and good health for the newlyweds and thus far, in their six years of marriage they had enjoyed both. Craig and Kris had traveled all over the world and done all types of interesting things together. The couple had gone to Costa Rico, one time, specifically to surf and after a day of surfing, they hiked up the Turrialba Volcano, which happened to be active and they toasted marshmallows on the hot lava. Craig said their hiking boots melted from the heat emanating from the earth. Craig showed Jack and Susan photos of the event on his phone, Kris with a big smile holding a dark brown gooey marshmallow and Craig holding his melted boot towards the camera while steam from the heat swirled around his head.

Jack sat back from looking at the photos and said, "Wow! You two have done some wild stuff, you're very interesting people."

Kris thanked Jack and said to him, "Well, I think the two of you make a great couple, and Jack, I love your accent. Minne-so-ta?" She stretched the word out as a native would do.

Jack was surprised. He told Kris, "I guess I didn't realize I still had an accent. But you're right. I was born and raised in Minne-so-ta." Jack exaggerated the word, also.

Susan squeezed Jack's arm and told Kris, "His accent only shows up when he's back at his folk's house or sometimes if he's really relaxed, like right now."

Craig spoke up and said he and Kris had reservations at an Italian restaurant under the bridge called "Luigi's Bistro" and suggested their new friends join them. He said he would make a phone call and change the reservation to four instead of two. "Shouldn't be a problem." He said, "Absolutely the best lobster ravioli you will ever eat in your entire life." Craig looked at Kris and she nodded her head in agreement.

"We've driven the ninety miles from Fruita, a few times, just to have Luigi's lobster ravioli."

Jack and Susan looked at each other and said that sounded great to them. The four of them decided to meet in the lobby at 6:00 that evening. Jack and Susan had four hours before they were to meet Craig and Kris for dinner, so they went to their suite and changed into their suits and flip-flops and with a soft warm robe wrapped around them, they walked over and soaked in the soothing and therapeutic Hot Springs for a few hours.

When Jack and Susan came downstairs just before 6:00 pm, Craig and Kris were sitting in the lobby by the fire waiting for them. The two couples walked to dinner across the bridge spanning the Colorado River. Susan and Kris side by side followed by Jack and Craig. Dinner was fantastic, the service was five star and, Craig was right, the lobster ravioli was the best Susan and Jack had ever tasted. The two couples ordered Tiramisu for dessert even though Susan and Jack had never heard of it. Craig had been a dessert chef in a very nice restaurant in Las Vegas after graduating college and explained it to them.

"It's a variation of a dessert made in Italy in the 1930's called 'Zuppa Inglese'. Now it's known as Tiramisu which, I think, translates to 'Pick me up'. It's basically three or four layers of lady fingers soaked in either Rosolio or sometimes espresso with whipped eggs, sugar and Mascarpone cheese flavored with cocoa in between the layers."

Susan couldn't wait, "Sounds yummy."

The silky coffee flavored Italian delicacy was delightful, a perfect ending to a perfect dinner. The check came and Jack and Craig each reached for it. Craig ended up with it, but Jack was determined to at least pay half. Craig held his hand up like a cop at a street crossing and Kris told the couple, "We're paying, this was our idea."

Jack and Susan thanked the other couple and Jack threw two twenties on the table for a tip. Everyone was happy. The foursome walked back over the bridge, it was a little chilly, so Craig and Kris walked in front of Jack and Susan, each couple snuggled together against the cool river air. Once inside the lobby Jack suggested drinks by the fire, his treat.

"What would everyone like?"

Kris and Craig just wanted some type of red blend wine and Susan said that sounded good. Jack went to the bar and ordered a nice bottle of 2010 Orin Swift Napa Red Blend. An hour later after the wine was long gone Craig and Kris decided to call it a night. They were going mountain biking the next morning and planned on leaving around 7:00 am. Jack and Susan decided to stay by the fire and share another bottle of red wine, their train didn't leave until after noon. They all stood, Susan hugged Craig and Kris hugged Jack, the two women hugged, and the two men shook hands. Jack and Susan sat down again and watched Craig and Kris as they got on the antique elevator and disappeared to their room.

The next afternoon the eastbound train was right on time and sat idle for ten minutes while the small queue of travelers boarded and found their seats. Jack dropped two bags at their reserved seats and joined Susan in the observation car just as the train started moving. It snowed hard the first half of the trip home. Fat lazy flakes drifted past the train windows piling up on everything. "Isn't it beautiful?" Susan asked fixated on the white flocked pines, rocky steep cliffs and dark blue flat river. They sat there staring out the window at the everchanging landscape pointing out different beautiful views and the occasional herd of elk or deer. Five miles West of the Moffit Tunnel a small herd of deer ran across the tracks in front of the train, but a small straggler wasn't quick enough, and the train hit it. No one on the train realized this had happened until the train slowed and finally came to a stop.

The Conductor came on the overhead speaker. "Afternoon folks this is Conductor Michael Reynolds, we are going to be delayed for a while. Unfortunately, we, uh, hit a deer and we had to come to a stop so our people can go outside and check for damage. I am not sure how long this will take, but we ask that you be patient. I'll let you know if there is any damage that would keep us from continuing on to Denver."

Everyone on the train groaned and started talking about either the inconvenience of it all or the poor deer laying battered and bloody under the Iron Beast.

A man sitting near Jack and Susan said, "Someone's having Venison tonight for supper." Several passengers around them laughed out loud. Susan didn't think it was funny and leaned as close to the window as she could, trying to see the poor deer. Her eyes filled with tears and Jack put his arm around her. After half an hour the train started moving again. The passengers clapped and cheered.

The speakers crackled, "This is Conductor Michael again. As you've, uh, figured out by now the deer has been cleared from under the train, but it knocked a few electrical lines loose and it took a while to repair those lines. Luckily all the parts we needed were on the train. Again, I apologize for the delay. Uh, since the weather is better on the East side of the Continental Divide, we should be able to make up some time. Right now, our estimated arrival is 1 hour and forty minutes later than expected. We should arrive approximately at 7:55 pm. Thank you for your patience."

Susan said, "He never said if the deer was dead or not."

Jack looked lovingly at his wife but said matter-of-factly, "Trains are huge and very heavy devices. The average mule deer is probably about 120-130 pounds. I'm afraid the poor deer passed as a result of the accident." Susan teared up again. Jack apologized for making his wife cry. "I'm sorry my love." He put his arm around her again, and she leaned her head on his shoulder.

The train finally pulled into Denver's Union Station a full 2 hours late at 8:15. A cold breeze met them when they stepped off the train with their bags. They both grabbed the collars of their coats and leaned into the breeze heading towards the terminal. Susan was relieved that it wasn't snowing yet. As planned, Dave and Jen Holloway were waiting for them in the lobby to shuttle them home. Jack saw right away, from the look on their faces, that something was wrong.

Dave was the first to talk, “Hey guys, welcome home.”

Jen started crying and turned away. “What’s going on?” Susan asked, walking to Jen.

“Oh my God, Susan. I don’t know how to tell you…,” Jen dropped onto one of the wooden benches, “It’s Tiger.” The tears were really flowing now.

Jack rushed past Dave to Jen. “What’s the matter with Tiger! Where is he?” But Jen just looked at him without saying anything.

Dave finally said, “We think one of Bradley White’s dogs killed your little Tiger!”

“Killed? What are you saying? Tiger’s dead?” Susan blurted the questions, practically screaming.

Jack looked at Dave and demanded, “Dave, what happened to Tiger?!”

Dave’s face scrunched up a bit and his lip started to quiver, “I’m sorry buddy. Yesterday, we found Tiger in our backyard barely alive, he was all chewed up and bloody. I took him to the pet emergency room, the one on 38th, but they couldn’t do anything for him. They had to put him down. We have little Tiger’s body at home.” Jack looked at Susan, she was bawling now. He sat his wife down next to Jen and he sat also and wrapped his arms around her. The three of them sat crying and watching the people walking by with their luggage.

Jen had let Tiger out with their dog Chipper so the two of them could do their doggy business. It was a nice February morning, sunny and fifty-eight degrees. It had snowed the day before and both dogs were rolling around in the fresh snow, loving life. Chipper was afraid to be out too long, having been scared at some time in his life by something or someone, so he was scratching at the door within minutes, wanting to be let back in. Tiger loved the snow and stayed outside refusing to acknowledge Jen when she let Chipper in and called for Tiger to come in, as well. Dave, an avid sports fan was watching the sports news on TV.

Commissioner Gary Bettman was threatening to cancel the NHL season if there was no resolution to the labor dispute between the NHL and the NHLPA by 11:00 am that day. Dave glanced at the clock on the mantle. "Well, looks like we may not have Hockey the rest of the year, Jen!" There were several shrill cries and growling noises from the backyard and both he and Jen stopped and listened. "What the heck…?" Dave asked and leaped up and ran to the back door with Jen on his heels. The back yard was silent. In the corner, by the fence, was a wet scarlet body lying in the virgin white of the fresh snow.

Jen screamed, "Oh my God, Tiger!" The small dog was still alive but struggling to breathe.

"Get the car, Jen!" Dave screamed as he scooped up the wounded pup.

Jen drove like a maniac to the pet hospital, quietly repeating, "Oh my God, oh my God!"

Allegedly one or possibly both of Bradley's Rottweilers "Patten or Autie" had jumped the fence and viciously attacked poor little Tiger as he rolled around in the snow with not a care in the world. The dog, or dogs, satisfied that the smaller dog was dead, then jumped back over the fence to their own yard. Dave walked around and asked some of their neighbors if anyone had seen what had happened that morning, but no one had seen a thing. Patton and Autie stood at the front fence of Bradley's house and growled and barked at Dave as he walked around talking to people. The neighbors, as well as Dave and Jen were afraid of Bradley's dogs and always walked a bit faster when walking by his house. Dave had always thought that Chipper was so timid because he was also terrified of the big dogs next door.

Bradley White was a U.S. military history buff. He had named his pedigree dogs after two of his favorite U.S. Generals. "Patten" for

George S. Patten, Commander of the 7th army during World War 2 and "Autie" for George Armstrong Custer, Commander of the 7th Cavalry, who, along with 210 soldiers was annihilated by a superior force of over 2000 Sioux and Cheyenne Indians at the Little Big Horn in Montana Territory.

Jack had gone storming over to Bradley White's house immediately after arriving home from the train station, despite Dave and Susan's concerns about confronting their beefy neighbor. Susan had physically tried to hold Jack back, to no avail. "Bradley White killed our dog!" he tearfully screamed at her as he tore free. Jack pounded several times on the door, but no one answered. The house was completely dark. Two days later when Jack saw Bradley arriving in a cab with a suitcase, he told Susan he would be right back. He had calmed a bit in those two days, and told himself he needed to go over and just reason with his neighbor.

He walked up and said to the muscleman, "I think your dogs killed my dog."

Bradley put down his suitcase and looked at Jack. "And you are?"

"I'm your neighbor. I live right next door to you." Jack said, a bit frustrated.

Bradley looked Jack up and down and sneered at him, "Well, little man, before you accuse me or my dogs of doing anything, you better have the facts. My housekeeper called me in Atlanta and told me about your dog. It's a shame what happened, but my Rottweilers are highly trained and very disciplined and would never harm anyone or anything without my ordering it. Some other dog, or dogs must have killed your little mutt."

And with that he turned and went into his house leaving Jack standing there dumbfounded. Susan was in the kitchen, on the phone with the police, when Jack came back in the house.

An officer with the Wheat Ridge Police Department, Officer Al Scherff, arrived within the hour and listened to Dave and Jen, explain what they saw and what they thought had happened. He assured all of them he would walk over and have a discussion with Mr. White and then call Jack and Susan to let them know where everything stood. He wrote down the couple's phone number in a small book he had in his breast pocket. Jack watched as Officer Scherff knocked on Bradley White's door, was greeted by Bradley and invited into the house. Bradley glanced at his neighbors watching everything and scowled.

"That guy's in for it now." Jack spit at the window.

Dave laid his hand on his friend's shoulder. "Don't get your hopes up too high, Jack. Brad's gotten out of trouble with the law before. Remember Martin?"

The two men looked at the neighbor's house. "Poor Martin!" Dave sighed.

Officer Scherff never returned to talk with Jack and Susan and they never received the promised phone call. The next morning, first thing, Jack called the Wheat Ridge Police Department and asked what was going on in the investigation regarding the death of their dog Tiger.

The female voice on the other end put Jack on hold and several minutes later she came back on the line and asked, "Sir, are you still there?"

"Yes, I'm here."

"Please hold while I patch Officer Scherff through."

There was some clicking and the sound of a phone ringing and Officer Scherff picked up the receiver. "Mr. Martin?"

"Yes," Jack answered and began the speech he had run through his mind while he was on hold, "My dog was mauled by the neighbor's dogs and died as a result of the attack and I was wondering what you found out after talking to Bradley White."

"Mr. Martin, let me start by apologizing to you for not getting back sooner. I talked with Mr. White and his housekeeper yesterday and they both insist the dogs that killed, um," He checked his notes, "Tiger, the dogs that killed him were strays and the housekeeper, Anne I think is her name, told me Mr. White's dogs were both kenneled at the time your pup was attacked."

"But, what about the paw prints?"

"I'm sorry sir, there just isn't enough proof that Mr. White's dogs were the culprits. If you could go around and talk to your neighbors, maybe someone saw the dogs that attacked your dog. Without an eyewitness we really can't do anything. Again, I'm so sorry."

Jack hung up the phone and looked at Susan. "They're saying they can't prove anything, not enough evidence. I'm so sorry love." Susan started to cry and Jack hugged her tightly.

That afternoon, Jack buried Tiger in the back yard. Susan couldn't bear to watch so she went to her parent's house for a few hours. Jack wrapped Tiger in a baby blanket the pup used to sleep on. He was extremely cautious when he filled the small grave, and marked it with a big square granite stone he found in the yard. Jack stood up and looked towards Bradley White's house and decided eventually Bradley White would get what he had coming to him. Karma, was indeed, a real bitch and Bradley White would eventually meet that bitch.

The next day ADT Security installed a security system in the Martin home along with seven cameras around the outside perimeter. Jack took the day off work to be there when it was all installed. The technician spent well over an hour teaching Jack how to zoom in and out, how to record and how to fast forward and reverse the recordings. He also showed Jack the buttons to push to lock and unlock the front door and the button that controlled an intercom so Jack could converse with the person at the front door from the basement. Jack immediately sat down and started monitoring Bradley White's house. He sat in the small room, in the basement, watching the TV monitors for several hours. He watched Jen leave and an hour later she came home and closed the garage door. Went for groceries, Jack thought. He watched Bradley's girlfriend, Kami, pull into the garage, walk out and pick up a newspaper and return. The garage door closed.

Jack said out loud, "That girl should put some clothes on she looks like a prostitute." Several neighbors came and went but the whole day watching the monitors was very boring work. Bradley didn't show his face that whole time. At about 7:30 pm, Jack finally gave up and went upstairs to be with his wife.

The next evening after Jack got home from work, he walked through the kitchen and past Susan in an apron cooking dinner. He gave her a quick peck on the cheek and told her it smelled great and headed downstairs. Bradley was in his yard doing something by the fence. Jack sat and stared at the screens. Bradley continued working on various tasks around his yard. Jack was a mild-mannered person, but he loathed Bradley for killing their dog. He decided then and there he would spend most of his free time watching his neighbor.

Susan called down, "Dinner's ready." Jack reluctantly stood, turned off the monitors and headed upstairs for dinner.

The next night when he got home, Bradley was in his garage and Jack was anxious to get downstairs and start recording his neighbor while he was visible to Jack's cameras. He wasn't hungry and told Susan the same thing.

"What are you going to do? Watch Bradley some more?" She asked.

"That jerk is in his garage and I want to record him for a while. I won't be too late."

"Famous last words."

"No, I'll be up in time for bed."

But he stayed in the basement until after 11:00 pm. He knew Susan would be mad about him sitting in front of the TV monitors for so long. He went upstairs but the whole house was dark and silent, so he went back downstairs and slept in the spare bedroom. Hopefully Susan would understand why he was spending so many hours in the basement. She was not happy the next morning despite his apologies, she gave him the silent treatment and left for work early. That night when he got home, he bypassed his wife and went directly downstairs. He didn't even pretend to be interested in what his wife was doing or cooking, in fact Jack hadn't eaten dinner for a few days now. He sat in front of the TV monitors and drank beer and smoked Marlboros.

Susan finally came downstairs and confronted her husband, "My gosh, Jack! You've got to give all this spying stuff up," Jack didn't know what to say. Susan continued, "You thought Dave was some lunatic for watching the neighborhood all the time and now you're just as loony as him, sitting down here in your little Spy versus Spy room!"

Jack knew what Susan was referring to, he had read Mad magazine as a kid. Jack's dad always thought Jack resembled Mad magazine's Alfred E. Neuman because as a kid Jack's hair was a reddish color and his ears were a bit too large. Since then, Jack had grown into his ears and his hair got dark and was streaked with gray.

Susan thought the gray made her husband more handsome, but right now she was mad, and she got louder. "Jack! Earth to Jack!"

He snapped back to the present and frowned at his screaming wife.

Susan yelled at her husband, "Tiger's gone, Jack, and we'll never know what truly happened to him."

Jack had heard enough, he yelled at Susan. "That fucking piece of shit next door is going to screw up again, eventually, and I'll have it recorded."

Susan stepped back. She had never heard her husband curse before. Never in all their years together. It was a little unsettling. At that moment she realized her husband was starting to change. She loved him but he had to come back to Earth. She wasn't going to live with the stranger he had started to become, and she really didn't like the four-letter words. This was not the Jack Martin she had said "I do" to. "This basement smells like an old ashtray!" Susan said and turned and stomped up the stairs.

-Chapter 3-

Within a month Jack packed up all his clothes and everything of his in their bedroom and moved all of it into the smaller bedroom downstairs. He and Susan had different hours, what with all the monitoring and such, and frankly, things were starting to change between them. She had also started complaining about Jack smoking so moving downstairs seemed like the best thing for them both. Occasionally Susan talked Jack into going to a movie or out to dinner but neither of them enjoyed themselves. Even though he was there physically, she knew his mind was back at home, at the Spy versus Spy room full of TV's. Intimacy between them was always great, awesome in fact. Lately not so much. She suggested marriage counseling. He told her there wasn't a problem with their marriage. Marriages had ups and downs and they were in a down period now. As soon as Bradley did something, some offensive thing to them or to one of the neighbors he would have it recorded, and the authorities would have to do something. His goal was to put Bradley White behind bars, that's where he belonged. Once this happened things would return to normal in their marriage, again. The next day, after thinking about it for several hours, Jack decided it was not worth it to damage his marriage in order to watch the damn neighbor. He came upstairs. Susan was eating a bowl of oatmeal and checking her e-mails. She grunted a "Good morning" to him without looking up from her laptop. Jack meekly told her she was right. He was going to end the nonstop monitoring of the neighbor and try to get back to a normal life with her again. Susan was dubious but Jack assured her he was done watching the neighbor. Susan was overjoyed. She hugged him and kissed him on the mouth.

After a few months of bliss, on a warm, lazy Saturday afternoon in the Spring, Jack walked through the door with a large wrapped box with a bow on it.

"It's for you, Love." He told Susan handing her the suspicious box. The barking coming from the box ruined the surprise and she excitedly tore the paper off and opened it.

"You didn't," she looked at him happily.

"Yah, I did." He replied coyly. The little black and white puppy jumped from the box, into her lap, and excitedly started licking her on the face.

"Oh Jack!" She squealed, "He's so cute! I love him, and I love you!"

Jack had a huge smile on his face and announced to her proudly "His name is Roscoe! I named him on the ride home."

"Well", Susan said "We may have to rethink that name."

"OK" Jack replied. He liked the name Roscoe, but he didn't care. It was just nice to see his incredible wife so happy. He sat and watched her with the new puppy. She was so beautiful, and he was such a lucky man to have her in his life.

It took a few days of discussing names before they settled on "Oreo" for the little black and white furball. Dave and Jen had come over to see the new puppy and when they first saw him Jen exclaimed "Oh my gosh, he looks just like an Oreo cookie!" And the rest, as they say, is history. Susan pulled out Tiger's bed and toys from storage and the new pup settled in as the newest Martin family member.

"Oreo Roscoe Martin." Jack announced to Susan and handed her a red collar with a bone shaped tag he had specially made that had that specific name on it.

"Whatever", she said, giving up and putting the collar around Oreo's neck.

Despite everything being hunky dory between them, Jack, still, remained in the basement and Susan slept upstairs. They were each used to the living arrangement and had different hours, after talking about it they agreed they would keep it the same. They still visited each other, three or four times a week, to make love or sometimes just to cuddle. It reminded them both of when they were dating, it was kind of fun. A bit of roleplaying Jack thought. The puppy didn't like the basement stairs, so he slept with Susan in her room on the main floor and for some reason, even though Jack didn't care much for her, the cat, "Snickers" decided to sleep in his room downstairs. Normalcy, to some extent, had come back to the Martin home. Susan liked the fact the cat preferred the basement. She moved Snicker's litter box downstairs and decided Jack would take care of Snickers from now on and she would take care of Oreo. "That seems fair," Jack told her.

Susan's Mom Audrey called one sunny Saturday morning while Jack and Susan sat having breakfast. Susan saw the name on the caller I.D. and grabbed the phone before Jack. Jack had seen the name and was frowning at his wife.

"Hello Mother, how are you this beautiful morning?"

Audrey answered Susan "Hello sweetheart. I'm fine thank you. It is a beautiful day! Your Father and I thought we might come over and see our new 'Grand puppy.' But we didn't want to just show up. Your sister is here with Miller and they'd like to come over as well. Would that be okay?"

Susan looked at Jack, he could hear Audrey and was shaking his head no. Susan gave him a pleading look and he finally said quietly. "Whatever. I may have to go into work for a few hours though."

Susan smacked him on his rear end, and he smiled at his wife a big toothy smile. Susan mouthed the words, ***Thank You*** to him. "Yes

Mother, we should both be here all day." Jack was shaking his head no again. Susan chuckled and continued, "What time were you thinking?"

About an hour later, the doorbell rang and Oreo ran to the door and started jumping against it while barking his most ferocious bark, except his tail was wagging a mile a minute.

Susan walked to the door and said to the puppy. "Oh Oreo, you're such a tough guy. It's grandma and grandpa Johnson. They've come to meet you."

Audrey came in first and scooped the puppy up and Oreo commenced to licking her on the ears and face. "Oh Susan, he's adorable." Ken came in holding a big basket with dog toys, dog treats and dog clothes. It had a ridiculously huge red bow that hung over the side of the basket. Susan was thrilled her parents had shown up. Jack grinned and bared it until Susan's younger sister, Sheri showed up with her new beau, Miller. Jack decided he would retire to the basement and away from his in-laws and said so to his wife. Unfortunately, his father-in-law heard him and decided to join Jack downstairs.

"This puppy business is pretty ridiculous." He said to his son-in-law. "If you don't mind, Jack, I'll join you downstairs. The Rockies are playing the Dodgers and I have money on the game."

Jack wasn't all that excited but said, "Sure Ken." He led the way down to the basement. He was certain neither of Susan's parents had ever been down here before. They had come over the week after he and Susan had closed on the house and moved in, but they weren't impressed with the little brick home and they certainly weren't interested in seeing an unfinished basement. Since then, about a year ago, Jack had taken out a loan and had hired a great contractor that Dave Holloway had recommended to finish the basement.

What they ended up with was fantastic and Ken said the same when he got downstairs and looked around "Jack! This basement is fantastic! This must've set you back some?" He said it as a question. "Oh, you know, it wasn't too expensive, and I did some of it, myself", he told Ken proudly. In reality, Jack had just helped by sweeping and vacuuming the mess at the end of each day, when the workers left, but Ken didn't need to know any different.

Jack pointed at the refrigerator. "Go ahead and grab us some beers and I'll get the game on, who'd you say? The Dodgers?"

Surprisingly, the afternoon with Ken in the basement went very well. Ken sat in Jack's recliner completely involved in the Rockies, Dodgers game. Jack sat on the couch smoking a cigarette and was just happy to have a couple beers and get away from Susan's Mom and Sister, as well as Miller. He sat and thought about that name. Who names their child Miller? He shook his head. Wasn't a miller a type of moth that fluttered around the lamp or TV at the most inopportune times? Jack wasn't interested in the game on TV. He was not a Colorado Rockies fan. He wasn't sure why his Father-in-Law would be either. The Royals were across the Missouri River from Kansas. Yes, it was really Missouri, but it was closer to where Ken grew up than Denver where the Rockies played.

He decided to ask Ken, "Do you not follow the Kansas City Royals? Seems like that should be your team, not the Rockies."

Ken answered Jack without turning from the TV. "I grew up a Saint Louis Cardinals fan, actually." Ken continued, "You know the whole thing with the 'Jayhawkers' and the Missourians?" He asked while waving his hands. "My father and I never cared for anyone from Missouri and that includes the Kansas City Royals."

Jack was still a bit confused but decided to let it go, the less he and Ken talked, the better they got along. Jack still followed his childhood team, the Minnesota Twins, who were in a dogfight with Detroit for the lead in the American League Central. Joe Mauer was batting .360 and Justin Morneau had 13 homers and 68 RBI's. With half the season done the Twins were well on their way to winning their division, the American League and hopefully the World Series. Dave and Jack had started watching the "Twinkies" a few times a week together. (Twinkies was a nickname the Minnesota fans had given their team when they were horrible, way back when.) Dave, Jack's neighbor was a Los Angeles Dodgers fan but enjoyed watching the Twins with Jack. Dave was a sports fan, any sport, and enjoyed spending time with Jack no matter what sport they watched on TV. He considered Jack one of his better friends despite only knowing him a few years. Dave always brought a six pack of Rolling Rock beer when he came over to Jack's, even if he only drank one or two of them. Every time Jack would say, "grab your beer" when Dave got up to leave, Dave would reply, "No, leave it in your fridge. That way I'll always have beer here if I need it." Jack preferred Grain Belt but never mentioned that to Dave.

Jack went to the fridge and grabbed two more Rolling Rocks. He offered one to Ken.

"Thanks Jack, I appreciate it." Ken said, with sincerity, taking the green can from his son-in-law. Ken looked around and noticed the room with the TV monitors. "What's up in there?" Ken asked Jack.

"Your daughter calls it my Spy versus Spy room", Jack told Ken, "She doesn't like it much. It's been a problem between us, to tell you the truth. Just keeping an eye on things, you know Ken. Just being safe."

"Spy versus what?" Ken seemed confused.

Jack tried to clear it up, "You know, Ken, from Mad magazine. Spy versus Spy?"

Ken frowned and shook his head no. "No Jack, I don't know what you're talking about, but I agree with you, you're right, you can never be too safe. May I see how it all works?"

The TV monitors blinked on and showed Jack and Susan's property in its entirety. Ken was impressed and a little too interested, Jack thought. The Rockies game was over, they had lost to Los Angeles 0-1 in a pitcher's duel.

"I guess you lost your bet, huh Ken?"

"Yeah, it was only Fifty bucks, no big deal. You have quite the set up here, Jack."

The two men stared, silently, at the TV screens. Ken asked Jack for a demonstration of how everything worked. Jack showed his Father-in-law how he could zoom in and out and how detailed the cameras were. He zoomed in on a tag on the wooden fence out front. They could clearly read the name of the company that installed the fence. Jack told his Father-in-law that he could record days at a time, and he explained how he could control the front door lock as well, just by pushing a button. The two of them sat there with the blue light from the TV monitors illuminating their faces. Ken finally exclaimed "Whoa! Look!" pointing at a specific screen, "What is your neighbor up to?" Jack looked where Ken was pointing. There behind his fence stood Bradley White nonchalantly throwing something into Jack's back yard. "What's he throwing over the fence, you 'spose?" Ken drawled.

Jack just shrugged his shoulders. They both headed up the stairs and hurried out into the back yard. Susan and Audrey were curious about what their husbands were rushing out to see so they followed the men out the back door. Bradley was nowhere in sight, but there by the fence were several piles of fresh dog feces.

"Hah!" Ken said, "That's a hell of a neighbor you have there. Does he always clean up after his dogs by throwing their waste into your yard?"

Jack just stood there and wasn't sure how to respond. "I, uh, I don't know. The neighbor and I don't really get along very well. He's kind of a jerk."

"I should say" Ken grunted.

Susan's Mom turned to Susan and asked, "Did your neighbor just throw his dog's poop into your yard?"

"Apparently so Mother." Susan answered Audrey.

Ken spoke gruffly to Jack "You need to talk to that ass."

"Yah, probably so." Jack said.

"Probably so." Ken repeated. Everyone headed back into the house. Jack stood shaking his head. He stayed behind to clean up the mess.

Susan's Father insisted that Jack call the local Police Department and tell them about their neighbor tossing dog poop over the fence into their yard. At first Jack said no, and tried to downplay the whole thing, but he knew once Ken was involved there was no getting out of it. He reluctantly agreed and dialed the phone number printed on the little police car magnet, on the refrigerator, to the Wheat Ridge Police Department.

Officer Scherff was on patrol with a new rookie, Eli Ortiz, when the call came in. "10-11 at 4218 Everett Court, caller claims his neighbor is throwing dog waste into his yard. Come back."

"I know that address," Scherff told Ortiz. "Tell her we'll take it."

Ortiz grabbed the microphone, "Dispatch, this is 325, we're 10-76, 5 minutes away."

"Copy 325, 10-76, 5 minutes. The complainant's name is Martin, Jack Martin, he'll meet you outside."

Ortiz sounded very professional and ended with. "Roger dispatch."

Scherff was impressed with his new partner, "Nice job, Eli. We'll make a cop out of you yet."

Ortiz got a huge smile on his face. He turned east on 44th Avenue and headed towards the Martin house on Everett Court.

Scherff had filled his partner in on the problems between the two neighbors on the way there.

"These two guys have a history. Jack Martin, the guy we're contacting, claims that his neighbor's dog or dogs killed his pup a while ago. It's a volatile situation that could end badly someday."

"Did the neighbor's dog kill Jack Martin's dog?"

"Most likely, but there just wasn't enough proof and there were no eyewitnesses."

When the patrol car arrived Jack and his Father-in-Law were standing outside waiting. Jack had told Ken he would handle this, but Ken insisted he should be there, too, after all, he was a witness to the crime. Crime? Jack shook his head. This was nothing compared to when Bradley's dogs killed Tiger. That was truly a crime, one that Jack would never forget. Ken was making too much of this. It was just dog poop, after all. Bradley had left or wasn't answering the door. Probably the latter, Jack thought. There wasn't much that could be done, so Officer Ortiz left a note on the neighbor's door that read: ***Mr. White, please call the Wheat Ridge Police Department and talk to Officer Scherff or Officer Ortiz as soon as humanly possible.*** Ortiz left his business card with his phone number on it.

"That's it? That's all you're gonna do?" Ken asked the two uniformed officers.

Ortiz stepped up "Unfortunately that's all we can do if Mr. White isn't home. We'll contact him by phone or hopefully, he'll contact us. A report will be made so it's all on record should it happen again."

Ken was not happy. He got louder and said "That big bastard is in his house, right this minute, watching this and laughing his rear end off. He never left, we would have seen him leave, right Jack?"

Jack felt awkward and didn't want the subject of his Spy versus Spy room to come up in front of the Police. He said, "We may have missed him leaving Ken, it took us a while to come upstairs and get into the back yard."

"Poppycock!" Ken grunted, and decided his son-in-law was a weak sissy of a man who was destined to be pushed around the rest of his life. Why his daughter had married this weakling was beyond him. Ken turned and stomped into the house. Jack thanked the officers and they got in their cruiser and left. Bradley White stood in his living room looking at the neighbor through the curtains with a huge smile on his face. "Fucking pussy." He said out loud.

Bradley White wasn't seen at home for days. Jack didn't check the recording but had been watching the monitors for some time. He knew Susan would get mad at him if he stayed too long downstairs. He was certain Dave would be watching their offensive neighbor for him, so he went upstairs to spend time with his wife. They had started playing a game called 'Hand & Foot' with Dave and Jen. Usually once a month at least. Jack asked his wife, "Up for a round of Hand & Foot?"

"Sure, sounds great. I'll get the cards." She liked the game a lot. She very seldom lost to Jack, he never understood why she did so well against him. At Dave and Jen's, it was always the boys against the girls and the boys very seldom lost. The two of them had a nice evening sitting there playing cards by a roaring fire and listening to Soft Rock on the stereo. Oreo laid on Susan's feet all night and kept them warm for her.

Finally, after three days, Dave texted Jack. ***He's home!!!*** Jack was making a cup of tea to soothe a scratchy throat. He hurried to the dining room window that faced the White house. He could see the note and card from Officer Ortiz still stuck in the handle of the front door, unread. Susan was volunteering somewhere for the day, so Jack went downstairs, into the Spy versus Spy room and settled in to spy on Bradley White. The warm glow of the monitors soothed Jack. His plan was to just watch for 3 or 4 hours and then come upstairs and hang out until Susan came home, but he had taken some cold medicine about an hour earlier and after watching the monitors for a time, he laid his head on the desk and started snoring immediately. He slept all through the night like that.

Susan woke her husband the next morning by slamming the door. Jack bolted awake. His neck was killing him. "What the hell, Sus..." He never got her name out.

"Not again, Jack! For God's sake, give it a rest! Brad White is a jerk. That much is true, but he's turning you into a crazy person."

"I'm sorry!" Jack apologized to his wife, "I never meant to be here all night. Just a few hours, but I fell asleep, I think because I took some Nyquil." He stopped and thought of Bradley calling him 'Little Man'. He disliked Bradley so much he said to his wife, "He killed Tiger, Susan. The man is a self-centered ass!"

"He didn't kill Tiger, Jack. Some dogs killed Tiger. We don't even know if they were Brad's dogs or some strays. It may have been coyotes for all we know. Brad wasn't even..."

"Yes, I know Susan," Jack interrupted her "Bradley wasn't even home at the time!" Jack was starting to get angry, "Fuck! You need to face reality!" He told Susan emphatically.

"No Jack, you need to quit being a crazy person! I'm not going through this again! I'll divorce you first!"

Jack stopped and stared at Susan. Divorce?! Divorce?! What the hell was going on?

Susan saw Jack's puzzled look and said, "That's right Jack. You heard me. I am not living with a crazy person." She slammed the door, again, when she left.

That was the first time either of them mentioned divorce. It certainly wouldn't be the last time. By the time they got divorced it was mentioned so many times by each of them it had become a normal part of their daily lives. Instead of saying 'I love you' each day it was 'I'll divorce you' each day.

Bradley White was downstairs in his game room playing Call of Duty: Advanced Warfare. He loved this game, he got to kill people. He imagined the people he was killing in the game were his wimpy neighbors. His present girlfriend Kami was in Las Vegas with her sister and would be gone a few more days so Bradley decided to just hang out at home for the week. His assistant Cielo would run his gyms while he was away. She did a better job than him anyway, he told himself, he should just stay away from his office and let her run the business, profits would most likely go up. He, actually, thought seriously about taking Kami on a long vacation, maybe Cabo San Lucas or Cancun. Someplace warm and sunny with an ocean and beach. Cielo could stay at his home while he was gone. He knew Cielo lived with her parents in a shitty rental house. His assistant would feel like a queen in his huge home, she could bring her boyfriend to stay with her. The phone rang and the muscleman checked the caller I.D. ***Wheat Ridge P.D.*** "Yeah, I'm gonna answer that one. Not!" he said out loud and returned to killing his neighbors on his TV.

Susan was out doing errands or something, Jack wasn't sure. She left without a word, and without leaving a note. It was Saturday, five days after their fight, and he had taken most of the previous week off work due to a bad cold and, also, anxiety issues. He had anxiety issues as a teen and never really got any help for it. He just lived with it. His folks didn't understand why he would spend days in bed.

"He's sick, I guess" his mom told his Dad one time, "He won't let me take him to the doctor."

His Dad just shrugged his shoulders and said, "He's a teen, all teens are lazy and moody. Give him time. Maybe he'll go with us dis afternoon to da meat raffle at the VFW. He always likes when he wins somethin'. And den tomorrow I'll take him up North to da trailer, do some fishin'."

Because of everything that was going on in his life, Jack had that feeling again as an adult, laying in his bed, coughing in the basement. The anxiety from fighting with his wife, fighting with the neighbor, dealing with Ken and now a cold on top of it all had put him in a depressive state. He started to hate his job, also. Jack woke up hungry, but he was depressed and unable to get up and fix something to eat. It was easier to just stay in bed. Snickers was happy about the whole situation. She was in bed with him, laying at his feet, purring like crazy. Jack heard the garage door open and cringed. He felt more comfortable, recently, when Susan was gone. He was starting to not care where she went or what she did all day, so long as she stayed away and let him sleep. His life was starting to unravel, and he didn't like it. Susan liked it even less. He heard her storming down the stairs to his bedroom.

She flung the door open. "Get up!"

"What?" Jack slurred. He was confused.

"Get up Jack! What is going on with you? It's after 5 o'clock in the evening!" She said the last three words at a louder volume as if being louder would make it easier for Jack to understand her.

"I don't know, uh, I just, uh, I have issues Susan." He stammered.

"Uh, uh, uh issues!" She mocked him. "What kind of issues are we talking about? The anxiety thing again? Do you still love me Jack?! Because I'm starting to question my love for you!"

Jack looked at Snickers who was not happy about all the screaming. She was poised to jump off the bed and he helped her by pushing her with his foot. Snickers ran into the next room. Jack looked at Susan. He didn't know what to say, so he didn't say anything.

"You need help, Jack! For God's sake go to the Doctor and get some pills or something. Your becoming unbearable to live with!" Thirty seconds passed with the two of them staring at each other, not speaking.

Finally, Jack broke the silence and admitted, "I don't have an answer for you." Susan stormed out slamming the door behind her.

-Chapter 4-

Susan drove into the parking lot of the gym and parked in the first spot she saw. She was early and had to wait for the first Aquacise class to end before hers began. She had recently changed jobs, she would soon start working as a Legal Secretary at DiSanto and Anderson P.C., a small law firm in Broomfield about 9 miles north of home just one mile from Jack's work when he worked. She had been extremely nervous when she interviewed with Walt Anderson, one of the firm's partners. But after looking at her resume' and talking to Susan for half hour or so, Mr. Anderson had told his secretary to send all the remaining interviewees home, he had found who he was looking for. Susan was thrilled, she went out and spent several hundred dollars on a new wardrobe for work. Jack wouldn't be very happy about that but, frankly, she didn't care. He was such a stranger to her recently. "Not the wonderful guy I married", she told her friends at Aquacise class that morning. After class, because Susan didn't start her new job for a few days, she and her older friend Jane went to I-Hop and had breakfast together.

Susan used Jane as a shoulder to cry on. "Jack is having some problems and I'm not sure how to help him. I'm not even sure I want to try and help him. We might end up divorcing."

Her older friend, Jane, who was from Ireland, said she and her husband, John, had problems occasionally. "It's just the way it is anymore, Susan. People get married and a few years later, poof, they're divorced. It happened to me, before John, I was married to a lovely man named Sean. Sean Ryan. But Sean drank far too much and tended to stay at the pub far too late, and on occasion he wouldn't come home at all. Finally, I had had enough, I told him 'Feck off Sean', pack up your things and get your arse out of this house!' I hired a good lawyer and filed for divorce. I got the house and half his Social Security. Last I heard he was living in some assisted living place in Denver. He used to be such a handsome man while we were married. Let me tell you, he's no oil painting now, and the man is so broke, he hasn't got a pot to piss in, either." Susan smiled at the quaint way her friend spoke. Jane was born Sinead Gabriel Flynn in 1937 in Limerick County, Ireland. The nickname for Sinead in Ireland is Jane and that's what she preferred to be called ever since Sinead O'Connor tore up a picture of Pope John Paul ll on Saturday Night Live back in 1992. "I don't want any association to anyone who would disrespect the Holy Father in that way." Jane had explained to Susan when they first met.

Susan said to her Irish friend "Well, Jane, I'm telling you right now, if my husband Jack doesn't change his ways soon, I'm telling him to 'feck off' and get his 'arse' out of the house, as well."

They both laughed at that. Jane was nearly twice Susan's age, but despite this the two women were best of friends. Jane loved to gamble and went to the casinos, at least twice, sometimes three times a month. Susan drove her friend most times because Jane's husband, John, wasn't much of a gambler. Susan wasn't a big gambler either, but she enjoyed their trips to Black Hawk. She thought of it as more of a social thing, she enjoyed her friend's company so much. Occasionally she would win money but mostly she left about $50 there. To Susan, that was a cheap evening spent having a good time with a good friend. Jane always seemed to win. "The luck of the Irish!" Jane always told Susan as she stood counting all her winnings.

Bradley White was searching the internet for a contractor to install a nice gym in his basement. He wanted his home gym to be like one of the gyms around the Denver area that he owned. A few years ago, Bradley had started with one small gym in a leased building on the main street in Longmont. From there, he had built the business up and now owned four gyms around the Denver metro area. He named his gyms "Beast Mode Fitness." The name fit him, he thought. Bradley had become a professional weightlifter, right out of College. He was a mountain of a man, 6'3" 285 pounds. Kami lifted for a while, also. She was very toned and very fit. She was a stripper, in a men's club, and had been for a few years. Kami lived with a roommate in Aurora because Bradley wouldn't allow her to move in with him. He didn't even allow her to leave anything at his house. She had to pack a bag when she came over and when she left the bag and all her stuff had to go home with her. She left a toothbrush one time and Bradley threw it in the trash and warned her not to do it again. Kami's attraction to Bradley was purely physical as was his attraction to her. They were both shallow and very self-centered people. Nearly every neighbor on Everett Court either disliked or was frightened by Bradley White. He had had some sort of disagreement with all of them at least once each since moving in. He was not a good neighbor and could not care less about that.

Susan gathered her gym bag and headed into the gym. From the corner of her eye she saw a very attractive man doing sit ups. She was running her eyes all over him when he looked directly at her and smiled. Embarrassed that she got caught staring at a perfect stranger, she turned away and went into the Women's locker room. She couldn't stop thinking of him all through the Aquacise class. She made it to work ten minutes early, made herself some coffee, and settled in for the day. She met one of the ladies from Zumba class for lunch and had a nice afternoon proofreading legal documents for Walt Anderson. Around 4:30 pm she started dreading going home to Jack. She was not in the mood for his stupid bullshit. Had he even made it to work today? Probably not, she told herself. She was aware he never made it to the gym but, that wasn't so odd, working out was not a priority for him, lately. Her thoughts went back to the guy doing sit ups. She had asked around and found out his name was Mark and he was single. Not that that mattered, she was a married woman and had other problems she should be focused on. But it was fun to daydream a little.

Jack wasn't home when Susan finally got there around five thirty. He had walked to Dave's house so he didn't have to face Susan when she got home from work. She didn't understand anxiety and depression. If she caught him sleeping or just sitting around, she might start screaming at him again. Jack's truck was there but when Susan checked his bedroom, and his Spy versus Spy room, he was nowhere to be found. "Must be at Dave's, I guess" Susan said aloud. Snickers looked at her from the bed. "What do you think, Snickers? Is daddy at Dave's." Snickers ignored her.

The next morning Susan decided to skip her Zumba class and just work out in the gym, maybe a recumbent bike or a treadmill. She pondered them both but after seeing Mark doing pull ups next to the recumbent bikes, she decided her best choice today was riding a bike. She had been pedaling for about ten minutes when Mark walked up and asked her something. She saw his lips move but never heard him. She pulled her ear buds out and looked at Mark. "I'm sorry", she apologized, "I had my ear buds in, were you speaking to me?" Mark smiled. Susan couldn't take her eyes off his beautiful set of pearl white teeth.

"I'm sorry." Mark finally said, "I was wondering if you worked in Broomfield, I think I saw you there one day in the Plaza West Building. Was that you?"

"Plaza West?" her head was spinning. Was that the name of the building she worked in? "I just started that job in Broomfield about a week ago. I'm sorry but I can't remember the name of the building." She could feel her face flush.

Mark tried a more specific question "Do you work at DiSanto and Anderson?"

Susan shook her head yes. "Yes, I do. You saw me there?" She was still a bit flustered.

"Yes" Mark said and smiled at her again. "I'm sorry, I hope I didn't startle you. I know Walt Anderson, he's a good friend of mine. We play poker once a month. I'm a lawyer as well. Walt and I have tried a few cases together."

"Oh wow!" Susan said, stepping off the bike and straightening her workout suit. Susan told Mark, "Walt hired me, he's such a nice guy!"

"Nice guy", Mark repeated and finished it with, "Horrible poker player!"

"Really?" Susan seemed surprised.

Mark was sorry he had said that about Walt and said, "No, I'm just kidding. Don't tell Walt I said that about him."

"OK", Susan said to Mark and made a motion across her mouth like she was zipping it shut. Oh my God, she thought to herself. Did I really, just do that? That had to look stupid. She stared at the floor and felt a bit uncomfortable.

Mark finally extended his hand, "I'm Mark Griffin, by the way, and you are?"

"A bit flustered", Susan admitted finishing his sentence. She took his hand it was soft and warm. "I'm sorry. I'm Susan, Susan Martin."

They both smiled at each other and Mark said, "Well Susan Martin, it was certainly nice finally meeting you." They both smiled at each other and Mark turned to continue his workout. Susan went into the locker room, showered and dressed for work.

When she got a break at work that morning, she called her friend, Elaine who did Zumba on Thursdays with her. Elaine answered on the second ring. "What's up, Darlin', why weren't you in class?"

Susan didn't know where to start. She told Elaine about finally meeting Mark, the gorgeous guy at the gym. "He's a lawyer and he knows my boss. He saw me the other day at work. Oh my god, he's so good looking."

"Yeah, did you forget to tell him you were married, Susan?" Elaine waited for an answer from her friend. Susan glanced down at her ring finger, she had pulled her ring off last night and put it in the jewelry cleaner. "Oh my gosh! I wasn't wearing my wedding ring today at the gym. He probably thinks I'm single!"

Elaine laughed a devilish laugh. "You think? Is that a bad thing or a good thing?"

Susan stared out the window. "I don't know." She finally answered.

To avoid seeing Mark again, Susan stayed away from the gym for a week. She still left at the regular time, but instead of working out she went to Starbucks and had a Butterscotch and Coffee Frappuccino and read a romance novel while she sipped her drink. Jack would never find out because he never went to the gym anymore. He just moped around the house and slept a lot. Things weren't good at home. She and Jack had drifted apart. At least he had given up on watching the neighbors for hours on end. She had, also, given up trying to motivate him, that just ended up with the two of them screaming at each other. Marriage counseling was out, too. She no longer felt it would help them recover even a snippet of what they once had. Their wedding anniversary came and went without either of them mentioning it, just another shitty day, she thought to herself.

When Susan started going to Zumba class and Aquacise again, she noticed little things about the other ladies. She saw them whispering to each other, while sneaking looks her way, and if she happened to come in and they were giggling or laughing they would stop immediately. She was sure she was the subject of their conversations. On a Thursday, she had forgotten her fit bit in her gym bag and when she went back to her locker to retrieve it, she heard her name mentioned. She walked to the end of the lockers and eavesdropped on two women talking as they got dressed. They were talking about her and Mark, debating whether she was fooling around on "poor Jack" or something to that effect. Oh my God, she put her hand over her mouth. Everyone thinks I'm screwing Mark behind Jack's back.

"Well, aren't you?" Elaine seemed surprised after her friend pulled her aside in Zumba class.

"Of course not!" Susan was emphatic. "Jack and I are not good, but he's still my husband. I loved him, once."

"Once? But not now?" Elaine inquired.

Susan thought about it, "I don't know, I really don't have an answer for you, Elaine." The Zumba instructor admonished the two ladies and told them to pay attention.

The summer of 2015 went by in the blink of an eye, with little change in Jack and Susan's married life. Jack still had anxiety issues but kept them under control by staying away from Susan and going to work nearly every day. He only drank occasionally, maybe three times a week and usually only on the weekend so it wouldn't interfere with going to work. He smoked a lot less, also. Somedays he would only smoke two cigarettes. Susan went to the gym religiously. She loved her job at the law firm. Walt Anderson had given her a healthy raise in June. She had started writing a novella about her friend who had died of Cancer. It was an inspirational tome set in San Diego, and writing it took a lot of her grief away. Everything on Everett Court was good. Bradley and Kami spent several weeks in Cabo San Lucas, then stayed in a rental in Palm

Beach Florida well into October so Jack's Spy versus Spy room went nearly unused. Bradley's assistant, Cielo stayed at Bradley's house with her boyfriend, the whole time Bradley was away, so they could watch his dogs for him and care for his house. Everyone on Everett Court liked Cielo, she was a way better neighbor than her boss. When she walked the neighborhood as exercise she would stop and talk with anyone who might happen to be walking the dog or working in the yard. Her boyfriend, D.J., owned a plumbing business and got a lot of work from most of the neighbors, including Jack who had D.J. replace his water heater and all the toilets in the house. "Well, staying at Brad's has worked out well for you. You've gotten a lot of work from the neighbors." Cielo nonchalantly mentioned one Sunday afternoon while they sat snuggled up watching the Broncos game on TV. "It's been fantastic, but it may have helped that my work van was sitting on the street like a giant billboard." D.J. told his girlfriend.

The leaves were changing colors and Wheat Ridge was blanketed in various shades of gold, red and green. The aspens in the mountains were a brilliant gold color and their leaves rustled in the wind with a swishing sound. Susan, the literary genius said the swishing sound was called psithurism, as in ***Enjoy the psithurism of the golden leaves in the breeze***. Jack loved the Fall season. Warm days, cool nights. Football, especially football. His beloved Minnesota Vikings were in Denver playing the Broncos one afternoon in early October. Dave had invited Jack to join him, Jen and Jen's friend Bev at the game. Dave and Jen got tickets, occasionally from clients and just happened to have an extra ticket for the Broncos, Vikings game. Their neighbor Jack, the huge Viking's fan, was their first choice to ask to join them. Jack was thrilled, as was Susan who wanted to work on her book and savored spending the whole day without her husband. Jack dressed in his #28 Adrian Peterson purple and gold home jersey and was at Dave's house thirty minutes early.

"You know you're gonna catch hell from the Bronco fans today." Dave told Jack pointing at Jack's Viking's jersey.

Jack answered him, "Don't care."

The game was a letdown for Jack much like his life lately. Adrian Peterson had 81 yards and one touchdown, but the Broncos hung on for a 3-point victory. Jack had bought everyone beers all afternoon and was trashed by the end of the game. The ride home was quiet, but Jack heard Susan's name brought up in the backseat where Jen and her friend sat talking. He cocked his head to listen and heard Jen's friend, Bev, ask Jen "Is that the woman who's fooling around on her husband with the guy at the gym?"

Dave turned the radio up and Jen quickly changed the subject, but the damage was done. Jack was drunk but his hearing was not impaired. Apparently, Susan was fooling around with someone at the gym, that's why she was gone so much on the weekends, Jack thought. She probably was fooling around on Jack while he had been at the Broncos game today. He decided right then and there he would start going to the gym again.

Jack started going to the gym as religiously as Susan. He would leave the house about ten minutes after Susan and head to the gym to lift weights or walk on the treadmill. On a cold Monday in late October 2015, Jack had just gotten out of his truck in the gym parking lot and saw Susan and Mark talking. Susan was in her Jeep and Mark was leaning in the window talking to her. Mark was saying something to Susan and his breath showed up as small white puffs as he spoke to her. Jack felt awkward. Should he just get back in his truck and leave? He was starting to do just that when he saw Susan look at him. She looked guilty as hell. He realized at that moment that what he had heard was true. His wife was fucking Mark from the gym. He climbed in his truck and drove to a local diner and had breakfast. He didn't know what he would say to his wife if he went home and she showed up. It would most likely end in a fight and he was not in the mood for that. Jack studied his shiny gold wedding ring Susan had bought it for him when they lived in the small apartment in Boulder. He pulled it off and put it in the truck's ashtray.

Fall arrived in all its glory and the fighting between Jack and Susan escalated. Not a day went by without some sort of argument. They fought over money, they fought about Susan's family, they fought about the neighbor. The least little thing would blow up into a, full-fledged, screaming match. He started to dislike the person he once adored, the woman he couldn't wait to see after work each day. Everything between them was slipping away like the sands in an hourglass, and just like an hourglass, eventually their life together would be empty. Jack sunk into a deep, dark depression. He quit going to work. He started to drink more and more often. His boss at work, Rick, liked Jack, he thought he was a great worker. He accepted that Jack was sick, he had been an alcoholic at one time, also, and understood the sickness. Rick promised Jack his job would be waiting for him after he got well again. "And I know you will be well again." Rick told him in confidence. But Jack doubted he would ever be well, again. Life for him was insufferable. Completely and totally insufferable.

-Chapter 5-

In early November Audrey Johnson called her daughter and asked her what the plans were for Thanksgiving in just over a week, it was almost here, and she was getting concerned. Usually she and Susan had Thanksgiving dinner planned for several weeks ahead of time. She and Susan alternated hosting the meal each year. Whoever wasn't hosting brought wine and dessert. Last year Audrey had spent days planning a huge meal for her family. She roasted a huge turkey with all the usual accoutrements. Susan brought two bottles of Pouilly Fuisse', a pumpkin pie and a cherry pie. Jack loved cherry pie and preferred it over the traditional pumpkin. Sheri never hosted, she just brought green bean casserole every year along with whoever she was dating at the time. This year Susan was the host and had hinted to her Mom she was going to make a Prime Rib dinner instead of Turkey which was a nice change of pace, but Audrey hadn't heard from her daughter and was starting to panic. She knew Susan and Jack were having problems and hoped their problems didn't affect a lovely Thanksgiving meal together. Susan and Jack had just had a whopper of an argument and Susan was not in the mood to talk to her Mom when Audrey called. "Hello, yes of course, I don't know Mother. I was going to roast a Prime Rib. I know Daddy would rather have that than turkey, but Jack and I just aren't doing well. I'm not sure we'll even have Thanksgiving this year." Audrey was disappointed but understood, and she certainly didn't want any drama ruining a nice meal with the family. That had happened a few times over the last few years. It would just be her and Ken and Sheri and Miller this year. Audrey hung up from Susan, after telling her daughter she hoped everything worked out for them and called Sheri to see if she could bring more than her usual green bean casserole. "Maybe a nice Kabinett and a pie of some sort?" She asked her youngest daughter.

Jack woke up around 8:30 am on Thanksgiving morning. He was in a good mood because Susan had told her Mom that since they were having marital problems, they weren't going to host this year. That suited Jack just fine. He was so happy he went out and bought a small turkey breast. He decided he would cook it on the smoker and do twice baked potatoes with maybe some steamed asparagus. He informed Susan that he would do the dinner for just the two of them. Susan told him that would be nice, she liked that he was cooking and hoped, maybe, they could have one nice day together. She had no desire to cook, for anyone. Jack was brushing his teeth when he decided he would make Susan and himself a nice breakfast to begin Thanksgiving day. Susan was still sleeping when he came upstairs. Snickers followed him, rubbing against his leg. The small black and brown, Calico cat wanted food, but Jack was going to feed himself and Susan, first. He turned on the stereo and put on a country station. He knew Susan listened to country music in her Jeep each day driving to the gym and to work. Jack opened the refrigerator and stared at its contents trying to figure out what he could make them. He pulled out the bacon, four eggs and two potatoes, and started to make a nice breakfast.

Susan woke to the smell of bacon, Jack must be making himself breakfast, she thought. Oreo was standing by the door wagging his tail. He wanted out to go potty. Susan ignored him and jumped in the shower. She was all soaped up when Oreo started barking.

Susan yelled to Jack, "Jack! Oreo needs out to go to the bathroom!" There was no answer. "Jack!" Still no answer. "Damn that man." Susan hissed and hurried through her shower and stepped out. She wrapped a large, fluffy towel around her body and another, smaller, towel around her head and went to the bedroom door to let Oreo out. Oreo was standing by a small pile of dog poop looking guilty. Susan stormed out the door and to the kitchen.

Jack greeted her with, "Good morning, I'm making us a nice breakfast. It'll be ready in about twenty minutes."

Susan was pissed and said, "It would have been nice if you could have let the dog out while I was in the shower, he crapped on the carpet in my room."

Jack looked at the pup and said, "Oreo! Bad boy! Did you poop on Mommy's carpet?" Oreo stood by his empty dog bowl, oblivious that he was in trouble.

Susan was mad, "I called for you to let him out!"

Jack shrugged his shoulders, "I'm sorry, I never heard you." He told her.

Susan turned and started back towards her room. "You need to get some paper towels and that spray you use on the carpet and come clean up Oreo's mess."

Jack was dumbfounded, he followed Susan into her room. "I'm not sure why I have to clean up after your dog. Can you enlighten me?" He pleaded with his angry wife.

Susan turned on the hair dryer and got louder so Jack could hear her over the noise, "I was calling you to let the dog out to go to the bathroom, I was in the shower. You can't let the damn dog out?"

Jack was stunned and hurt. He went back into the kitchen and turned off the burners on the stove. He took the pan that had eggs in it and dumped them in Oreo's food bowl. He pulled out the trash and dumped the hash brown potatoes into it. He started to throw out the bacon, too, but decided against that. He put all six slices on a paper plate for him to eat after he cleaned the damn dog's poop from the carpet. Later after the carpet was clean, the dog had been let out and fed and watered and the cat had been fed and watered, he took his bacon and went downstairs to sulk. Susan called down to him around 11:00 am, "What's going on with this turkey breast?" Jack knew it should have been in the smoker by now.

He yelled back, "Don't know, I'm not cooking it and if you aren't cooking it, I guess we'll have toast for Thanksgiving dinner!" He left it at that.

Susan muttered under her breath, "Bastard!"

Jack muttered under his breath, "Bitch!"

They stayed away from each other all that afternoon and into the evening. Finally, around 7 pm, Jack stomped up the stairs, grabbed the uncooked turkey breast, walked out the back door past the chair where Susan sat reading and threw the Turkey breast in the trash can. Susan watched him and when Jack came in from the backyard, she said, "Another fucked up day in the Martin house!" Emphasis on the words, fucked up.

It went this way through the remainder of November and into December. Christmas had become a dreaded holiday in the Martin house. Jack was cheap and lazy and refused to spend a fortune on Christmas, and putting up the tree, and all the lights and bullshit, was just a bunch of unnecessary work as far as he was concerned. Susan had a very good friend from College who had died of ovarian cancer two years before on Christmas Eve, so Christmas just brought back bad memories of her lost friend. Since then she disliked the holiday as much as Jack. When someone wished them a Merry Christmas, they both said in unison. "Bah, Humbug!" Susan never sent any Christmas cards in 2015, the first time that had happened ever. New Years, however, usually brought the two of them together. They always booked a room at the Hotel Boulderado, a late 1800's Hotel in Downtown Boulder, and had done so for about twelve years, but during an argument in October, they decided to give that tradition up, as well.

Two days after Christmas of 2015, Jack was still in bed trying to decide if he wanted to go to work when he heard the garage door open and then a few seconds later, close. He looked at the clock, 6:05 am, seems a bit early for Susan to leave he thought but whatever. Lately he liked it better when she wasn't home. He got up and carried the trash to the curb in just his pajamas and bare feet. Oreo went out behind him and did his doggy business while Snickers sat on the windowsill and watched everything. All at once a red headed, pimply faced kid jumped out of a beat-up 1972 Pinto, ran up to Jack and tossed a pile of papers at him and yelled "Jack Martin? You've been served!" Jack stood there stunned while Oreo stood barking at the strange man. Jack looked at Dave's house, Dave and Jen were watching from their kitchen window. Dave was embarrassed that his friend saw them watching and immediately came over and said to Jack, "Sorry, buddy. Are you okay?"

Jack nodded yes.

Dave told him "Jen knew this was going to happen, somehow. I don't know if Susan told her or what. Jen told me about it, last night, I probably should have called you. I don't know. It's probably for the best."

He and Jen had noticed when they visited their friends lately Jack and Susan argued a lot or were snippy with each other. Jack looked around at the other houses across the street. There were a few other neighbors peeking out of their windows watching. Dave was his friend but at this moment he felt as if he had no friends.

He looked Dave in the eye and said, "This is fucked up." Jack leaned down and gathered Oreo, turned, went back into his house and closed and locked the door.

Dave, who felt horrible at that moment turned and walked back to his own home.

Jack stood in the small living room hurt and confused. I guess this decides it he thought, no work for Jack today. He went down to his bedroom and climbed in bed and pulled the covers over his head. After sleeping for a few hours, he woke up and laid there thinking about everything that had happened earlier that morning. He knew it would eventually come to this. He and Susan each deserved happiness and there would never be happiness for either of them, as long as they were together. They were like oil and water, now. Jack weighed the pros and cons and decided he would be happier as a divorced man. He didn't even care if he found another woman to share his life with. Things would be easier if he stayed single. Women were just a pain in the ass.

"Don't get me wrong" he said to his friend Dave, a few weeks after he was served divorce papers. "I'm not turning gay, or anything. I just don't care to have a woman in my life right now. Maybe a few years down the road, that will change, but right now I just don't need a woman."

Jack didn't see Susan through the whole divorce process. She had retained a lawyer months ago because she knew divorce was inevitable. Jack showed up to the divorce hearing by himself, without a lawyer. Susan's weasel of a lawyer showed up in a two thousand-dollar Giorgio Armani suit and was an asshole through the entire process. If it was up to him Susan would get everything and Jack would be standing on a corner with a sign begging for food. Because of Colorado's divorce laws, though, it was pretty cut and dried. Jack didn't like change, so he said he would like to keep the little house on Everett Court. He would pay Susan whatever he needed to keep it. The judge ruled he should pay Susan half the equity of their house, which was just under $60,000 plus the $15,000 she put down that her father had given her plus another $5000 because of the difference in annual income. There was no alimony awarded, Susan made way more than what Jack did. This baffled Jack. Shouldn't Susan have to give him alimony? The judge didn't see it that way. All the furnishings were to be either sold and the proceeds split or if the two parties agreed, they could divide the contents how they saw fit. Jack just laughed and shook his head at this. Susan had already come over with a big truck when he was at work, probably with Mark, and they had taken nearly everything in the entire house. She left Jack's recliner downstairs, his bed and most of the stuff in the basement, but the main floor was empty. She took all their living room and dining room furniture as well as all the master bedroom furniture. She did leave the silverware, dishes, a few pots and pans and all the food in the small pantry. She also gathered up Snickers and Oreo and all their food and toys and took them with her. Jack didn't really like the cat, so that was fine, and Oreo was a gift to Susan so she was right to take him, but Jack wished she wouldn't have. He liked the little black and white pup. Jack opened the refrigerator. Susan had left him all the beer Dave had brought over, nineteen green cans of Rolling Rock still sat on the shelves. So, he sat in his recliner in the basement and drank all nineteen cans. He fell asleep in his chair and slept there all that day and into the night.

Susan legally changed her last name back to her maiden name, Johnson, and quit wearing the wedding ring Jack had bought her. She went to a jeweler on 44th, in Wheat Ridge and had it melted down and made into two very nice earrings. She bought a two-bedroom, 1800 square foot condo in Golden with the money Jack gave her for the house in Wheat Ridge. It was bigger and newer than the house in Wheat Ridge. That house had never been her choice, anyway, so letting Jack have it didn't bother her. The apartment was right in the foothills and had a beautiful view of the mountains off the deck out back and you could see the Denver skyline from one of the front windows. The realtor was smart, she took Susan to see the top floor condo right when the sun was setting. It was a typical Colorado sunset with a lot of oranges and reds next to a backdrop of dark blue mountains. The realtor and Susan sat on the big deck and shared a bottle of Merlot and Susan decided then and there she would take it. She hired some college kids from the School of

Mines, and they moved everything from storage into her new Condo. Susan bought new dishes and some other things and made it her own little home. Snickers and Oreo loved it there. There was a bike path right out the front door that went around North Table Mountain, so Oreo got walked a lot and he loved that. The condo had a bay window and Snickers sat in it most of the day watching all the comings and goings throughout the neighborhood. Susan joined the recreation center by the School of Mines campus and continued her workout regimen there. She missed seeing her friends from Zumba and Aquacise but made new friends in Golden. Joan from Aquacise and Elaine from Zumba both visited often and the three of them occasionally went out for meals together and Susan still drove when she and Jane went to the hills to gamble. Susan's work was a few miles further but lately Susan had been seriously thinking of taking up writing full time, and if she did, she would give Walt Anderson two weeks-notice, and become the writer she always dreamed of being. She had journals full of stories and poems she had written over the years and knew she could sell at least some of them. Susan Johnson's life was good.

Jack started to pick up furniture here and there to replace the furniture Susan and Mark had absconded with. He got most of the replacement furniture at garage sales or thrift stores and within a few weeks his house was full again, albeit with less quality stuff than what he and Susan had. The yard and all the vegetation on the property was ignored so within weeks Jack's house became the ugly house of the neighborhood. Jack's life consisted of, waking up at 7:00 am, shit, shower and shave, punch in at work a few minutes before 9:00, work till 5:00, with one, hour long, lunch break, which was usually Arby's, Taco Bell or McDonalds, (they were all close), drive home, watch a few hours of TV, either drink his dinner or go without, fall asleep in his chair, get up sore from sleeping in said chair, go to bed about 11:00 pm, toss and turn all night, get up at 7:00 am and start all over again. Same old, same old. Just like Bill Murray in "Ground Hog Day" he thought. Jack had a younger brother, Joseph, "Joey" in the Palm Springs area. He loved his brother, but rarely called him, about four or five times a year Joey would call Jack to say Hi and just talk. Jack's Mom and Dad called about as frequently as Joey but Jack rarely called them. He did go to visit his parents, in Minnesota, at least once, sometimes twice a year, but only during the warmer months very seldom in the colder months. His parents lived in Brainerd, Minnesota but had a small trailer on Rabbit Lake in Crosby about a half hour drive east of Brainerd. It had 122 feet of shoreline and a small dock with just under two, wooded, acres. Years ago, Jack and his Dad had gone halfsies on a 14-foot, Lund Bass boat with a 75 horse Evinrude motor. Jack loved it up there on Rabbit Lake he always caught his limit of fish and ate fresh fish nearly every day. Jack's folks went to the Wood tick Races in Cuyuna, the next small town, every year, without fail. Jack went with them nearly every year since he was a teen back in the '90's. Susan had attended nearly every year since she and Jack were married. She loved it as much as Jack and his folks. It was always fun. Jack always brought his own wood tick, one he had found on his folk's property, but in all those years his tick never won a race. He always ended up out of the competition early, but that was fine. He and his dad would sit at the long wooden bar with all his dad's friends until late and drink Grain Belt out of the tap while Susan and Gladys sat at the trailer and crocheted or read. Jack always looked forward to this time with his dad each year.

Since their divorce Susan volunteered, part-time on Saturdays, at the local retirement home in Golden teaching a writing class to the seniors living there. She had done some volunteering when she and Jack were together, and she loved doing it. Some of the older people were very talented writers and she told them they should be submitting their work to a publisher. Older people, in Susan's opinion, had a lot of wonderful, insightful things to share with the world. One of the older men there, Warren, a man in his early nineties had a small crush on Susan and during the Spring and Summer months he brought her flowers he grew outside in his little garden. Beautiful fresh cut bouquets of Marigolds, Geraniums and Shasta Daisy's with Lavender sprinkled in. She was thrilled with her new life, post Jack.

Jack's life, in contrast, became tedious and boring, but that was okay with Jack. He only left the house to go to work or occasionally to go eat at a local Italian restaurant called Rossi's. He avoided his neighbors and pretended he hadn't seen them when they waved to him. Dave Holloway was the exception, of course. Besides Randal Jay from College, Dave was Jack's best friend in the world. Jack hadn't seen Randal Jay since his and Susan's wedding. They talked once or twice a year on the phone. Randal Jay or R.J. as Jack called him, got a six-figure job right out of College with Apple and in a few years was one of the big wheels in the Cupertino, California headquarters, still making six figures but nearer to seven figures. R.J. moved to San Mateo and lived there in a luxury high rise right on the Southern part of San Francisco bay. He dated a lot of women but was never married. Randal Jay was the guy Jack always wanted to end up as. He was wealthy beyond his means, knew important and influential people and owned beautiful expensive cars. R.J. was James Bond to Jack and dressed just like 007. Jack sat and wondered what his friend from College was up to now. He should just buy a plane ticket and fly to San Francisco and visit R.J. one of these days. Randal Jay would be thrilled to see Jack he was certain of this. As if there was some form of mental telepathy between the two friends, the phone rang and R.J.'s name was on the caller I.D. Jack was flummoxed at the sight of his friend's name on his phone. He snatched the receiver off the base and excitedly said "Randal, my man!"

-Chapter 6-

The Airbus 220 banked sharply to Starboard and nosed into the wind. The guy beside Jack grunted but continued to snore lightly. At least Jack hadn't ended up next to someone like the dingbat in the row in front of him who kept talking about her three dogs. "Her babies!" She kept saying to the man beside her while showing the man pictures of the dogs. Jack didn't like talking to strangers on a plane. More times than he could count he had faked being asleep so the person next to him would leave him, the fuck, alone. On one occasion he had fake coughed the whole time the plane was boarding, and everyone left him alone and found another seat. Mostly, though, he had just worn his noise cancelling headphones but had forgotten them this trip. Susan on the other hand enjoyed meeting new people and talking with them. By the end of the flight she and the person sitting beside her knew everything about one another. Jack wouldn't miss that. His roommate from College, Randal Jay, had called Jack about a week ago to ask if he would like to go to a College reunion, of sorts, in Laughlin, Nevada of all places.

"Heck no, of course not!" was the answer, "I'm not much for School reunions."

Randal Jay decided to come clean, "It's not an official College reunion, actually." He said to Jack. "Kenny Ford and Bob Longfellow are meeting me for a long weekend of gambling and debauchery, and they thought you should come, too. Kenny was the one who said it wouldn't be a Colorado University reunion without your grouchy ass."

"No thanks, R.J., I appreciate the call but,"

Randal Jay interrupted him, "Come on man, it'll be fun! I'm going from March 11th through the 14th. Bob and Kenny, I think, are only going for a few days."

"Some other time, maybe." Jack said.

Randal Jay would not be deterred, "We're staying at the Highwater Casino. It's an older place so the rooms are dirt cheap. You remember Crazy Bob, don't you?"

"Of course, yes." Jack answered his friend.

He thought about it, when was the last time he had talked to Crazy Bob? It was July of 1998. He had seen Bob in Brainerd, Minnesota at the Crow Wing Co-op, of all places. Bob grew up in Brainerd, but he and Jack never met until College when Randal Jay had introduced them. "You two sound like brothers you really should meet each other." R.J. told the two one time at a bar across the street from their dorm. Bob and Jack became friends but not like the friendship Jack and Randal Jay had, and Kenny? Well Kenny was just a guy that showed up to the many keggers held in the dorm. Nice guy but again, just really an acquaintance. "So, what are you doing up north, den?" Bob had asked when he saw his old friend at the Crow Wing Co-op that day. Bob still had a distinct Minnesotan accent.

Jack shrugged, "Just up at the camper, doing some fishing."

"You're folk's camper on Rabbit Lake?"

"Yah, what're you doing up here? I thought you moved to the cities."

"I did, I live in Saint Paul now. I just come up to visit my Aunt Karen. You should meet my crazy Aunt Karen, Jack. She's a hoot!" "Hey, what are you doin' tonight?"

Jack looked at the boxed Traeger smoker in Bob's shopping cart, "I guess I'm coming to your place for smoked meat, of some sort."

Bob lit up, "You're darn tootin' you are, buddy! Smoked Walleye at my Aunt's place. I'll give you da address."

That had ended up being a great day for Jack. Hanging out with Bob and his family at Bob's crazy Aunt Karen's place right on Serpent

Lake. Jack got drunk and decided it would be funny if he started talking with a thick Minnesotan accent like his Dad. "Oh, yah Bob, I'd love to go spear fishin' but der's a hockey game on da tube der. Da Wild are playin' da Bruins."

Bob said to Jack.

"Uff-da! You sound just like my Uncle Pete, dontcha know! Come over to da house der and have hot dish with us."

Exaggerating his accent even more. Jack replied. "Yah, sure, you betcha!"

They both laughed their asses off. They ate smoked walleye and Aunt Karen's famous lutefisk and ended up watching shooting stars in the night sky while sitting around a small campfire passing a bottle of Jack Daniels Black label around until it was gone. The next day Jack sent a huge bouquet of flowers to Bob's Aunt Karen with a note. **Aunt Karen, Thanks so much for the nice meal and company. It's folks like you that make this world a better place**. He signed it, **Jack (Bob's friend)**

"Jack!" Randal Jay yelled into the phone, "You still there?!"

Jack snapped out of his memory, "Yeah, yeah, I'm here. I'm sorry." Randal Jay said, "Jesus dude, I thought you fell asleep or something."

Jack said, "No, I was thinking about the last time I saw Bob." He paused, let out a big sigh and finally said, "I don't know R.J., seeing you and Bob, again, would be nice."

"Is it money? Because I'll buy you the damn airplane ticket."

"No, not at all, I just don't do much, you know, since the divorce."

"Oh yeah, the big D. Come on you fucking pussy, I'll pay for a hooker for you. I'm sure you haven't been laid in over a year!"

Jack's face flushed. Randal Jay had a sailor's mouth on him that was embarrassing at times. Jack thought for a second. He did have three weeks of vacation that his boss, Rick, kept reminding him of, and lately his work ethic had gone South, he might as well go South also. He chuckled at his own joke. "What the heck! You know what R.J.? I'm in, I'm not sure why. but give me the details."

Laughlin / Bullhead Airport was overflowing with people. Crazy Bob and Randal Jay were waiting at the baggage claim. Jack grabbed his suitcase and followed them to a limousine waiting outside. "This is ours?" Jack asked. "Yah buddy, you betcha!" Bob grinned from ear to ear. "Nuttin' but da best for us! Come on, get in." There was a small bar in the back along with a nice stereo and a disco ball. R.J. rolled a joint while Jack made drinks. "R.J., I know you like the foo-foo drinks," Jack said and handed him a White Russian. Bob said, "White Russian works for me", so Jack made one more then he poured three fingers of Beam over a couple ice cubes for himself. R.J. lit the joint and passed it around. They cranked the stereo and turned the disco ball on. By the time they arrived at the Highwater they were all a little lit, especially Jack who was on his fourth Jim Beam. They checked in and went up to their rooms and promised to meet in the casino in half an hour.

Jack was in his room when the phone rang, he picked it up and slurred some sort of greeting. Randal Jay was confused, "Hey buddy, Bob and I are waiting for you in the lobby. What the hell's taking you so long?" Jack suddenly remembered he was to meet his friends in the casino, he was drunk and apologized to his friend, "Sorry R.J. I'm on my way."

"Well hurry it up, Bob's antsy to get gambling."

Jack hung up the phone, grabbed his wallet and card key and headed downstairs. When he entered the casino, R.J. was standing by himself and made a beeline for Jack.

"Dude, I just met a dealer from the casino here, her name is Amber Beever. She wants to play blackjack with us, she's in the bathroom.

Jack looked around, "Beaver?"

"Yes, Beever with two "E's."

R.J. saw the attractive dealer walking towards the blackjack table and grabbed Jack by the arm and guided him towards her.

"R.J., where's Bob?"

"He gave up on you, I think he's playing the slots. Look, Jack, this girl is hot, straighten yourself up. Are you drunk?"

"Yes, very much so."

Amber got a big grin on her face when she saw Randal. She looked past him at an obviously drunk Jack and asked, "Who's this?"

"Amber, Jack. Jack, Amber"

"Nice to meet you, hon."

Jack took Amber's hand and put it to his mouth and kissed it. Amber put both of her hands on her chest and said, "My, my, quite the gentleman!" She thought a few seconds and quoted something she had heard, "Being male is a matter of birth, being a man is a matter of age, but being a gentleman is a matter of choice."

Randal Jay leaned close to Jack and said, "Keep it up and this girl is yours." He smiled and slapped Jack on the back.

They all sat down at the blackjack table. Amber knew her stuff, Randal was impressed.

After an hour of playing she was up a few hundred dollars as was Jack. Randal was holding his own. Amber leaned over to Randal and whispered, "I've got a big, fat joint in my pocket, wanna go smoke it?"

"Absolutely. Dealer can you color us up please?"

Amber liked Randal Jay, he was good looking and obviously had money. He was sporting a blue Dulce & Gabbana tailored suit and looked damn good in it.

Amber said, "Come with me," she headed for a door clearly marked "Emergency Exit Only." The two men followed her as she disregarded the warning sign and went through the door. She took them to a makeshift sitting area outside the casino and offered them a seat. Jack was visibly drunk and plopped down in the nearest chair. Amber and R.J. remained standing. Amber pulled the joint out, lit it and passed it to R.J., he took a big hit of it and looked up as he let out the smoke. The sky was starting to turn different shades of pink and orange and was promising to be a fantastic sunset.

Later that evening, Kenny Ford and his wife and three kids showed up. Jack was blotto by then. He vaguely remembered bear hugging Kenny and meeting his wife, but, didn't recall any kids. The whole evening was a blur, but Jack seemed to remember a nice looking, red head and smoking weed with her and R.J. by the river.

"I should do this more often," he thought that evening while showering. "I'm having a great time!" It was March 9th, it would be a full week before the fateful day.

The next morning, Jack met R.J. for a buffet breakfast at "Captain Jack's" in the basement of the Highwater Resort. Somewhere, last night, someone had given him a stack of free buffet vouchers and he had called his friends to have them join him. R.J. was the only one he could get a hold of, so here they sat. "Hung over?" R.J. asked.

"Yes, I am, most of yesterday was a blur, but I know I had fun."

R.J. started laughing, "Fun? Shit! I guess so. Do you remember meeting Amber? Amber Beever?"

Jack pondered the question, "Beaver?" he asked and frowned.

"I kid you not", R.J. roared, "We hung out, last night, with a dealer from the Highwater named Amber Beever! B.E.E.V.E.R. You really don't remember?! You tried to kiss her, and I thought she was going to deck your ass!"

Jack pondered what his friend was saying. "Was she a thin, red head with nice tits?"

"Yep, that's the one," R.J. chuckled, "She's the one who bought us this breakfast."

"Okay, I do remember her. She's the one who gave me the breakfast buffet vouchers? She must think I'm the biggest jerk in the world."

R.J. sat back in the booth and looked around, "You ARE the biggest jerk in the world, Jack."

Jack thumped his head on the table. R.J. jumped up threw a $10 bill down and turned back to his friend.

"Come with me, we've got plans." He headed for the escalator. Jack pulled a wad of bills out of his pocket and also threw a $10 bill on the table. Apparently, he had done well last night at the Blackjack table. He stuffed the huge wad of bills back into his pocket and ran to catch up with Randal Jay.

The Laughlin Ranch Golf Club is considered one of the best golf courses in Nevada. Jack, Randal Jay, Bob and Kenny arrived in a silver Cadillac SUV that Kenny had rented for the trip with his wife and kids. Three attendants met them in the circular drive. One of the attendants whisked them into the bar and told the bartender, "Get these gentlemen some drinks, please. Are any of you hungry?" he asked the four of them.

Bob was perusing the menu and said, "How 'bout four a dem rib eyes, medium for me."

The other three agreed. "Medium is good." They said in unison. Jack decided he would limit his drinking today and ordered an Arnold Palmer.

An hour later after an incredible lunch, the foursome was teeing off on the immaculately manicured golf course. The Laughlin Ranch Golf Course was incredible. Emerald green rolling hills backed by beautiful purple green mountains in the middle of a sandy desert. Here and there on the golf course were Saguaro cacti, flowering Ocatilla and millions of yucca plants. There were geckos running around dodging the golfers and their golf balls. Fluffy white clouds floated here and there in the baby blue sky. Jack looked up at the blue sky and back at his cohorts and savored the day. He shot a respectable 86, and although he had the worst score of the four of them, he was very pleased with himself. "OK boys, what's next?" Jack asked the other three men when they pulled out of the golf course parking lot.

R.J. twisted in the passenger seat and looked at Jack and Bob. R.J. knew people at the Riverside Casino and had set it up so the four of them could be in a televised Holdem tournament together after their golf game. "There's a Holdem game at the Riverside in a few hours. I've already signed the four of us up. Two hundred dollar buy-in."

Bob exclaimed. "Geez! A two hundred dollar buy in? Not me, I'll stick to $5 Blackjack."

Kenny said he and the kids were going to spend the day at the pool, he had promised them, but they all knew Kenny was cheap and was using his kids as an excuse to get out of spending two hundred dollars. His wife wouldn't approve of Kenny spending that much money to play cards anyway.

Randal Jay stared at Jack who was fumbling in his pocket trying to extract a big wad of cash. Jack finally got it out and counted the bills to himself. He was holding just over $1700. R.J. grinned at Jack. "What about you Mr. Gates? You in?"

Jack grinned back, "I guess I'm in."

R.J. turned back around in the passenger seat and addressed Kenny. "Well, alrighty then! Driver, drop my friend and me at the Riverside Casino and step on it!"

Jack and Susan used to play in a regular game just a mile from their house, years ago, until they started fighting so much and decided to quit. Susan had seen the poker game listed on an app called "What's Happening" and responded by text to a guy named Mike. She texted Mike that she and Jack might be interested in playing some time. Mike texted right back and invited them to join the game that evening. Jack and Susan had played a few hours before Jack realized Mike, the host, was Mike Sanders, a backup wide receiver for the Denver Broncos. Susan, not really a Bronco's fan and certainly not a football fan was oblivious. The second time they played poker with Mike, Jack asked her on the way home if she knew what Mike did for a living.

Susan pondered the question and said "Well, he's certainly in good shape, maybe he owns a gym or something."

When Jack told her that Mike played for the Denver Broncos she was floored. She immediately googled Mike Sanders and couldn't stop talking about him for hours. The next Monday everyone at Aquacise knew about Susan and Jack playing poker with Mike Sanders, Wide Receiver with the local NFL team, the Denver Broncos.

One hundred people played in the tournament. R.J. and Jack drew seats at different tables, but they kept an eye on one another. This was a big deal for the Riverside Casino and Poker Room. There were stage lights and TV cameras around the Poker room and two men in tuxedos sat in a soundproof booth and did commentary for the TV audience. Everyone was told the whole thing would air on ESPN in about six weeks. Jack was very nervous, he had never played poker on television before, but eight hours later Jack finished in third place. He was dealt two Aces, 'Pocket Rockets'. The cameras zoomed in, so the TV audience knew what he was holding. He had first action and bet 30,000, six times the big blind. The guy behind Jack folded. The only other player was a skinny Vietnamese kid named Kwan. The kid never hesitated matching Jack's bet. The flop came Ace, King, Queen, rainbow. Jack had a set of Aces. He checked, trying to trap the kid. The kid, it seemed, fell right into his trap betting 250,000. Jack pondered the bet mostly for drama, he had the kid, he was certain of it. Jack pushed all in, roughly 1.3 Million, the kid snap called him. What the heck? Jack thought. They showed their cards. Jack had his set of Aces and was hoping for a boat or another Ace for the quads. The kid showed 10, Nine suited. Jack was ecstatic, he did the math in his head. He was a 67% to 33% favorite with 7 outs Kwan only had 4 outs. Randal Jay, who was knocked out of the tournament early, yelled from the audience, "Yeah Baby!" The crowd stood and got loud as well. The Turn came 2 of clubs. No help for either of them, except now Jack had 10 outs and Kwan still only had 4 outs. Jack did the math, he was now a 79% to 21% favorite. The dealer was wearing an earpiece. Someone in the ESPN trailer told him to slow down to excite the crowd. The audience got louder anticipating the last card. The river came Jack of Spades, giving Kwan a gut shot straight. The kid thrust his fist into the air and the crowd roared. The two commentators stood and talked excitedly into their microphones. The people in the ESPN trailer high fived each other. They couldn't have scripted it better this was great TV. The ratings for this tournament would be huge. Jack was dumbfounded, the River had beaten him. He stared at his lowly set of Aces. He turned and looked back at R.J. in the audience who put his hands in the air, like whatcha gonna do? Jack shook the kid's hand, and said, "Good luck, kid!" into his opponent's ear. R.J. came over the rail and hugged his friend. A guy with a headset on steered Jack and R.J. over to the side and told them, "Wait here, don't move." After three boring hands, the crowd was getting restless. They wanted to see who would end up with the $10,000 top prize and the coveted gold bracelet that came with the money. Kwan ended up winning the final hand, he fell on the floor in astonishment as his family and friends climbed the rail and mobbed him. John, a 62-year old, also from Colorado, was whisked over to where Jack and R.J. stood. Kwan sat alone at the table as two busty, scantily clothed, young women dumped $10,000 dollars on the table in front of him. The Vietnamese kid was all smile, from ear to ear as photographers took photos. Jack won a cool "Three Grand". The three winners each fanned their money and posed, as photographers from "Card Player's" magazine took their photos. Randal Jay slapped Jack on the back. "You were so lucky today. You're just like Robert Johnson."

"Who?" Jack asked, confused.

"You know, the Blues dude who sold his soul to the Devil to become the greatest guitarist of all time. I believe the Devil helped you today and now he owns your fucking soul!" Jack frowned thinking of the Devil and then smiled at his friend.

The next morning Kenny and Bob found R.J. and Jack sitting at the bar in the Highwater. They were both sitting there with shit eating grins on their faces. The bartender was making them each a Bloody Mary.

"Come on you two" Kenny said, "Bob and I are heading to breakfast down river at Flora's. Best steak and eggs in Nevada! I shit you not, and I'm buying." He proudly announced.

R.J. looked at Jack and whispered to him, "We better go, the world must be coming to an end, Kenny's buying!" Jack and R.J. both laughed out loud, R.J. even snorted, he laughed so hard.

Kenny looked puzzled. "What? What did he say to you Jack?"

Jack just shook his head, "I'd tell you Ken, but it would just piss you off, and it's too nice of a day to be pissed off." They waited for their drinks and joined Kenny and Bob outside where a water taxi was idling, ready to shuttle them to Flora's. Kenny was still confused about what R.J. had said to Jack.

R.J. said, "Forget it dude." He and Jack roared with laughter. It was beginning to be another fantastic day for Jack and the rest of them. Randal Jay started telling Kenny and Bob about the tournament.

"Jack won $3000 for third place."

"Holy crap!" Bob said, $3000!"

"Yep' that's what I said."

Kenny slapped Jack on the back, "Nice job!"

The food came and the four of them dug into their breakfasts and didn't talk again the entire meal. Finally, the waitress dropped the bill on the table between the four of them. Kenny grabbed it, but Jack shook his head no and threw two crisp hundred-dollar bills on the table. They all got up and left, laughing and joking all the way back to the water taxi.

In the morning Kenny, his wife and kids said goodbye to Kenny's three College buddies. Kenny's wife congratulated Jack on his big win and promised to watch it all on ESPN. Jack thanked her and watched as Kenny and his family got in the silver Cadillac SUV and headed North. Bob promised to keep in touch with both Jack and R.J., then got in a waiting taxi and headed to the Airport, turning around and waving as he left.

"Well", Randal Jay said to Jack after their friends left, "Just you and me, buddy. It's my last night, I fly out tomorrow morning on the Red Eye. Whadda ya think? Hookers and Fireworks tonight?"

Jack thought for a minute, "Geez, I gotta be up about five Grand and I'm sure you're ahead,"

"I am."

"Well, I'm not much for fireworks but we're both single and over 21. Heck, hookers sounds great!"

R.J. grinned from ear to ear, "Jack, my friend, let me handle everything. I know people here."

That evening Jack showered and dressed in some clothes he had bought that afternoon in the chic clothing store in the lobby of the Riverside Hotel next door. He had also gone to the small gift shop in the same lobby and bought a four pack of ribbed condoms. He looked in the mirror and said to himself, "Jack, my friend, you look marvelous. It's been a while since you've been laid. Tonight, may just be the best night you've had in a long time. You deserve it after all the bullshit that's happened to you." There was a knock on the door, so Jack slid the condoms off the desk and pocketed them as he went to open the door. Standing in the hall was R.J. in a tailored grey suit with each arm around a gorgeous female, Jack estimated they were in their early twenties.

"Holy cow!" was all Jack could think of saying.

R.J. looked at Jack sheepishly and winked. "You ready to have some fun?" The two young ladies giggled, and Jack pushed the door all the way open and invited the three of them in.

Most of the night was a very nice blur. One of the ladies had brought a small bag of cocaine with her. She opened the bag and cut the white chunks up on the glass table and formed the resulting powder into a dozen small lines. Jack snorted a few lines and then continued drinking to excess. R.J. and the blonde, Sandy, snorted a few lines each and disappeared with a bottle to his room.

Jack was left with a lovely, dark haired beauty who said her name was Demi. "Like Demi Moore?" Jack inquired.

"No", she said, "Like Demi Lovato."

Jack felt old, he had no idea who Demi Lovato was. It was March 14th.

Jack woke up naked and alone in his room the next day. He didn't remember much about the previous night but knew he and Demi had fun. "Wow!" He yelled thinking of all the fun he'd had this week in Laughlin and especially last night with Demi. He squinted his eyes and glanced around and noticed a cart with what appeared to be breakfast on it. He got up and looked closer. There was a note that read, **Thanks for the fun evening. Thought you might need some nourishment, Demi.** That was nice of her, Jack thought and glanced at the bill laying on the cart. Demi had charged two breakfasts and a bottle of 2007 Piper-Heidsieck Champagne to Jack's room. The Champagne was $500 and it, as well as the other breakfast, had left with the dark-haired hooker. Oh well, Jack thought, still well worth it. He added a very generous tip to the bill and signed it.

After eating breakfast Jack looked at the clock, 10:30 am. Randal Jay was at home in San Mateo by now. Jack's friends were all gone. They left to continue their lives and he already missed them. He had, almost two full days before his flight home to Colorado, so he sat and counted the bankroll in his pocket. The Gambling God's had been good to him. He counted $5895 dollars. This was an indescribable trip, he thought to himself. It's like R.J. said, I've sold my soul to the Devil, he smiled and looked at his reflection in the mirror.

An hour later, after a shit, shower and shave, he sat down at a Blackjack table and spread $1500 on the felt.

The dealer, called out "Changing fifteen hundred" and asked Jack how his week was going so far. Jack looked at the dealer's name tag. It read John, Kingman, Arizona.

"Well John, from Kingman, Arizona," Jack smiled smugly, "My week has been incredible."

John, the dealer said to Jack, "I remember you from a few nights ago. When I left the table, you were up about a Grand. What'd you end up winning that night?"

Jack squinted at John and said, "You know, I remember you now, I was a bit drunk to tell you the truth. We made some money that night, didn't we, John?"

"Yes, we did, my friend. I appreciate the nice tips."

Jack thought for a minute and said, "I've been so lucky this week. I think I won about, maybe $1600 that night."

"Nice!" John stated but still wasn't convinced Jack recalled everything about that night. "You and your friend played at my table and Amber, one of our high stakes Texas Holdem dealers was with you."

"Yes," Jack agreed, "I remember that. I need to talk to that young lady, I think I may owe her an apology."

John was shuffling the cards and told Jack. "Well, she usually shows up a few hours before her shift and plays Blackjack or Pai Gow Poker. She should be here in about four or five hours."

-Chapter 7-

Flavio "Chucho" Valdez fired up his Harley Davidson Fat Bob and yelled at the house, "Victoria, if you ain't out here in 10 seconds I'm gonna fuck you up. I don't got time for your shit today, Bitch!"

Victoria Ramirez, at least several months pregnant with his child, ran out carrying a small bag and jumped on the bike, right behind the angry Mexican.

Chucho spit on the ground and said, "Don't fuck up my day you fat cow." He shifted the bike into first and shot out onto the paved street heading South. Chucho and Victoria, along with Victoria's older sister Celina and her husband Rudy, were meeting several other Vagos Club members in Laughlin for a big party at the Highwater Casino to celebrate Chucho's big day. He had just been promoted to President of the Chino, California Chapter of the Vagos Motorcycle Club. Flavio Valdez had given himself the nickname "Chucho" as soon as he joined the Chino Chapter. The name meant Jesus and Flavio felt as if he were the same as the Jewish Carpenter who had twelve disciples and hundreds of followers. The Chino Chapter of the Vagos only consisted of about a dozen members at present but Chucho envisioned a day when he, also, had hundreds of followers.

Based in San Bernardino and founded in 1965, the Vagos Motorcycle Club was one of the few remaining 1%'er Clubs in the world. Chucho had picked the Highwater in Laughlin because they still allowed Motorcycle gangs to wear their "colors" while in the Hotel and Casino. Las Vegas, by comparison, had recently passed laws trying to dissuade Motorcycle gangs from visiting after the Bandidos and the Sons of Silence had shot it out at the Sands Hotel, around 1995, and twelve people were killed during the shooting melee. Chucho preferred Las Vegas to Laughlin but the Highwater was one of the few casinos left that still welcomed Motorcycle gangs and Chucho was going to take advantage of it while it lasted so he decided to party with his people in Laughlin. They usually came to Laughlin at least once a year. Victoria, hanging on to her boyfriend, laid her head on his back and quietly sobbed. Her mommy Maria, had cried, also, when she found out her baby girl, Victoria, was pregnant by the gangster biker.

"How can you bring a little baby into that horrible situation?" She asked her daughter. "That baby will end up a drug dealer or worse yet, a murderer like it's Papi! Mija, you've got to leave that Devil, Chucho Valdez. You and that baby will both end up dead by his hands."

Victoria knew her mommy was right. She had met Flavio Valdez when she was eleven and he was Twenty. She was too young to date him at that time and he thought she was just a pain in the ass always wanting to be around him. His family was from the same neighborhood of Corona, California as the Ramirez family. Victoria had fallen in love with him right away, way before he became the Beast sitting in front of her heading south to Nevada on highway 15. They had run with the same crowd that whole time but had been boyfriend and girlfriend for only about a year. Flavio reminded her of her Papi, they both had the same build and people looked up to Flavio like they did her Papi. Victoria's Father was a member of the Vagos Motorcycle Club, also. He had died when Victoria was about nine, shot in the back at Froggy's Bar in Gardena, California. He had stopped at Froggy's because it was pouring big droplets of rain outside and he was on his '45 Knucklehead getting soaked. He shook the rain from himself and sidled up to the bar and ordered a Budweiser in the bottle. The bartender, Rocco, knew Hector Ramirez. "Teto" was a regular at this bar, coming in nearly every night, always with at least two or three other Vagos. Teto was never there alone, this was unusual, Rocco thought. The burly bartender brought the ice-cold brew and set it in front of the biker. Teto took a big gulp of his beer and looked back towards the bartender. Rocco had ducked behind the bar and Teto knew exactly what was coming, he had thought about this moment since his teens when he became a member of the Vagos. Before he could get turned around to face his murderer, he was shot in the back. Teto stood at the bar refusing to fall until he heard the cowardly shooter turn and run, and then he collapsed to the floor. Rocco jumped over the bar and carried the wounded biker outside to wait for EMT's to arrive. They whisked the gangster biker to the nearest hospital, which was Memorial Hospital, a few miles away. There were forty people in the bar when Teto was shot in the back, and not one of them saw what had happened or who had shot him. Hector "Teto" Ramirez, Maria Ramirez's Esposo and Victoria Ramirez's Papi lived for four excruciating days but eventually died as a result of his wound. Teto had always liked Celina's boyfriend, Rudy, and was certain one day Rudy would become his son-in-law so he told the young man if anything ever happened to him, Rudy could have the 1945 Knucklehead motorcycle. Teto's wife, Maria, knew this was her husband's wish so Rudy took possession of the dead biker's vintage Harley Davidson. Maria Ramirez was a former crack addict back then trying to stay sober for her two young daughters. After her husband of twenty some years was shot and eventually died, Maria fell off the wagon hard. She neglected her two daughters and nearly died from her addiction. Her sister Adriana, Victoria's aunt, got Maria into rehab. Now Maria was in her second half-way house struggling to stay sober, and she was worried about her baby daughter, Victoria, and her unborn grandchild. She had always seen the gangster in Flavio.

Jack was winning money left and right on the Blackjack table, but his ass and back were sore, and he needed a break and a smoke. He stepped outside the front entrance of the Highwater Hotel and Casino into the hot desert heat, and stood and watched as two motorcycles rumbled into the front circle drive. The two young women on the back of the bikes got off and stood as the men backed the bikes onto a patch of gravel next to each other. Jack loved motorcycles, to him they were works of art, especially the older ones. Not just Harley Davidsons, but the older Indians, Aces and Crockers, too. He knew these bikes were both Harleys. One of them was a late model Fat Bob from its distinctive low profile, large headlamp and its cast wheels. Probably about a 1999. The other was a very old, and rare Knucklehead, Jack guessed it was mid '40's. He knew this from the distinctive 45 degree "V" shaped engine with the large bolts at the top. Jack stepped closer to where they had parked. He shook a Marlboro out, tapped it on the side of the pack, put it between his lips and lit it never taking his eyes off the bikers and their bikes. He took a deep drag and as he blew the carbon monoxide, hydrogen cyanide, and nitrogen oxides out of his lungs he pondered "Now that I don't have a wife to tell me no, I should buy a vintage Harley." He stood and thought about it for a few seconds, "Naw, I'd probably kill myself." The four Harley riders stood and talked as Jack stood watching them. One of them, a big Hispanic looking guy with tattoos on his arms, hands and face and a jacket that said "Chucho" Vagos M.C. on it, was arguing with a small pregnant girl. She was also Hispanic and very petite despite her obvious baby bump. Chucho grabbed her, suddenly, and she jerked away and started towards the Casino. The angry Mexican followed her and within seconds had pushed her down to the gravel lot and was above her yelling at the top of his lungs. "I'll kill you bitch! Don't fuck this day up for me or I'll fucking kill you!" She was crying uncontrollably now.

Jack headed towards the biker. He wasn't sure what he was going to do, but it didn't matter, he was committed now. Security people from the Casino ran past him and two burley guys grabbed Chucho and drug him away from the young girl. Victoria Ramirez was helped up by Jack and another man in a Tennessee Titans hat and minutes later paramedics showed up and placed her in an ambulance to check her and her baby for injuries. Chucho was screaming obscenities and threatening, "You know who I am? I'll kill the whole fucking bunch of youse." He pointed at Jack and the other man who had helped Victoria, "You two honky fucks are dead!"

Jack raised his eyebrows and the guy with the Titans hat turned and went, immediately, into the Casino. The police showed up and Chucho was placed in handcuffs and put in the back seat of one of the police cruisers.

"Poor Chucho", Jack said to no one in particular, "Your day just got shittier didn't it?" He flicked his cigarette in the direction of the angry Mexican staring out the side window of the Police cruiser and headed back into the airconditioned Casino. Chucho spit on the inside of the police cruiser's window and watched Jack until he disappeared inside the door.

Karl Schulz had been with the Laughlin Police Department for seven years. He started as a patrol officer and rose, fairly, quickly through the ranks. The Police Chief was well aware of Karl's abilities and promoted him to Detective years earlier than he had ever promoted any other patrol officer. The guys who used to patrol the streets of Laughlin with Karl thought he deserved the promotion more than any of them, he was extremely good at his job and would make a great detective. Newly promoted Detective Schulz, in his Kenneth Cole suit, was patrolling the strip along the river when the call came in. A member of the Vagos Motorcycle Club was being questioned by local Police and Security guards from the Highwater Hotel and Casino. He had, allegedly, pushed his pregnant girlfriend to the ground and threatened her. Karl called dispatch and told them he was available to help. He made a U-turn on South Casino Drive and headed North to the Highwater. When he arrived at the front entrance, he pulled up next to a Laughlin Police Department cruiser. Standing next to the cruiser was his old partner Mike Briggs.

Karl leaned out the window, "Hey big guy, what's up?" he could see the Biker sitting in the back seat of Mike's cruiser and knew he had seen the man before.

"Damn, Karl! Are you slumming today?" Mike joked with his ex-partner.

"No", Karl answered him, "Just bored, thought I'd see how you boys were doing. Jimmy at the Doughnut Hole hasn't seen you in a few days and was wondering where you've been."

Mike faked as if he were hurt by the comment and responded, "Funny guy! You missed your calling. Instead of being a detective in Laughlin," Mike pointed back at the Highwater, "you should be in one of these Casinos doing a comedy act."

"Might pay better, "Karl kidded his friend. Getting more serious Karl asked, "Who you got in the back seat, there?"

Mike leaned in so no one could hear him as he told Karl, "Chucho Valdez, President of the Vagos Chino Chapter."

"Wow! President!" Karl exclaimed, "Big time bad guy!"

Mike looked around, "The prick, allegedly, pushed his pregnant girlfriend to the ground in front of all these people but, of course, after word got around it was Chucho Valdez, no one seems to have seen a thing. His girlfriend, Victoria Ramirez, refuses to press charges. If no one comes forward soon to say they witnessed the crime, we'll have to cut him loose."

"Let me talk to him, he and I know each other." Karl stated matter-of-factly.

Mike stepped back and swept both hands towards the biker in the back seat, "Go for it. Good luck!" Karl noticed the string of spit on the window, opened the door and leaned in close to Valdez, so close he could smell sweat on the Mexican biker. "How's it going today. Flavio?" Flavio ignored the detective. Karl asked, "Do you remember me?" Karl had arrested Flavio Valdez a few years ago, drunk, riding his Fat Bob doing nearly 100 mph.

The arrogant biker looked Karl in the eye and said, "Fuck you, Ese!"

Karl said, "Come on, Mr. President, are you beating up pregnant girls, now?"

"Like I said, Fuck you Ese! I ain't talkin' to you or no one else without my lawyer."

Karl knew Chucho was done. The detective let out a big sigh, "OK, you just sit tight, I'm going to go talk to your pregnant girlfriend." Putting emphasis on the word "pregnant." He closed the door hard and went to find her.

There were no shortage of witnesses in the Casino, but none were willing to talk to Karl about what had happened. They admitted they saw what happened, but they were not getting involved. Everyone knew the power this piece of shit wielded. You snitch on Chucho Valdez, you end up with a bullet in your head. The girlfriend, Victoria Ramirez, a petite Latina, was being guarded by two Security people from the Highwater Casino. One of them told Karl quietly, so the young girl couldn't hear, "She's not willing to co-operate, claims she fell or something. Her name is Victoria." Karl nodded, sat down and introduced himself to the teen. She ignored him and refused to look him in the eye. Chucho has this girl brainwashed, Karl thought to himself. Karl asked her flat out, "Did your boyfriend push you to the ground outside in the parking lot?" Without looking him the eye, she told the detective.

"Flavio's just tired and pissed from the long ride from Chino. He never pushed me, I slipped on the gravel and fell."

"How old are you?"

"16"

"How many months pregnant are you?"

She looked around as if looking for someone to help her get out of this situation, "I'm not sure how many months. I ain't been to no Doctor."

Karl raised an eyebrow to her. "Are you telling me a doctor has never checked you or your baby."

"No." She answered Karl so low he had to lean in to hear her.

Karl leaned back and tried to scare her a little and said, "You don't want to lie to the Police, young lady. If Flavio continues to push you or hit you or be abusive to you in any way, your unborn child is in danger of being injured also. Do you know what a miscarriage is?" Karl winced, he wished he wouldn't have asked the last question.

"I don't got anything else to say to you." Victoria told Karl. Obviously Chucho had trained her well. Karl stared at the young girl for half a minute, her gaze never changed. "Okay, well, thanks for nothing Victoria. I hope your baby is fine." He paused again, watching her for signs of cracking. Again, she just stared into space. "I hope your baby's fine." He repeated as he walked back out into the already stifling desert heat.

Mike let Chucho sweat in the back seat of the hot police cruiser for an additional half hour after Karl told him to release the biker. Flavio "Chucho" Valdez arrogantly jumped out and waited for Mike to uncuff him. He spit on the ground at Mike's feet and flipped him the bird. He was smart enough to not be packing a gun when he was arrested. He had handed his .38 pistol to Rudy when he saw the Hotel's Security guards come out the front door in his direction and Rudy had hidden it for him. He flipped the bird to every law enforcement officer he passed as he stomped into the Casino and, along with Rudy and two other gangster henchmen, took the elevator up to his room. There were other Vagos there in the room when the four gangsters entered it, about twelve, total and about as many women. Everyone in the room let out a cheer when their leader walked in. Rudy presented Chucho his .38 like a Knight would present a sword to his King in Medieval Times. Chucho accepted it and tucked it in his waistband. He was passed a huge Olive green and Forrest Green glass pipe loaded with the best OG-18 weed straight out of Compton. He torched it, took an enormous hit and held it a few seconds before blowing it towards the ceiling. Everyone in the room erupted yelling and cheering. The stocky, tattooed, bald man standing in front of them in a green and black vest was their hero no matter what he did to his lady. Chucho yelled out, "We give what we get!" And they all echoed the same words back to him.

Amber sat at the bar nursing a drink. Benjamin, the bartender walked over to her. He and she had gone on a couple dates and he really liked her. He could see the two of them as a couple someday. Benjamin played Bass guitar in a local Metal band called 'Season of the Dead'. He hoped someday to make that his main job but until then he had this bartender gig and the pay was good. "You ready for another drink 'A'?"

She smiled at him and shook her head. He asked,

"You hungry?"

"No thanks, I'm good."

"Okay, let me know if you need anything," he smiled slyly, and leaned closer, "And I mean, anything."

She grabbed his hand. "Look Benjamin, I really like you, and we had some fun, for a minute, but we'll never be an item. Okay Sweetie?"

He smiled a big, toothy, smile, she loved his smile. She ran her fingers through his thick dark hair. "Besides", Amber continued. "You deserve someone better than me. I'm trouble, ask my Ex."

Benjamin smiled at Amber and said, "You'll come around." He winked, "You will! They always do." He tossed the bar towel onto his shoulder, turned and walked to the other end of the bar.

She watched him walk away and when he was out of earshot, she said out loud. "Great ass!"

Jack was the only player at the Blackjack table and John, the dealer, was dealing. Jack looked down at his hand. "You pat"? John, the dealer, asked. Jack had a Queen and a three laying there, the house showed a five of hearts. Jack looked at his bet, $600, a healthy bet. "You think I should double down?" He asked John.

John leaned back, and let out his breath, "Phew!! I wouldn't, the odds are against you. In my opinion you should wait and let the house bust, safer move. But you've been so lucky the last few days…" he left it hanging in the air.

Jack smiled at him, He stacked another six black chips next to the original six and made the required motion with his hand, so the cameras caught it. "Hit me and be nice." Jack pleaded to the dealer in the white shirt and black vest.

John shook his head and turned over the seven of Clubs. "20! Nice hit, sir!" John said it loud enough for the Pit Boss to hear.

Carlos, the Pit Boss heard his cue and walked down and leaned against the table, watching. He liked Jack, he tipped well and not just the dealers, also the pit bosses.

John, the dealer turned over the house's hole card, an Ace, giving the house a 16. He flipped the next card, a King.

John announced, "Bust!"

Jack raised his fist in victory.

"Nice!" Carlos said, and patted Jack on the shoulder. John stacked two purple chips, and two black ones next to the original bet.

"Wow, dude you're on a heater, big time!" John said with a huge smile.

Jack also had a huge smile. He looked around and saw Amber Beever, with two 'E's, sitting at the bar talking to the bartender. Amber Beever, gotta love that name, Jack thought, stacking his winnings. She was more attractive than he remembered. He glanced back at her. Her hair was down and was a beautiful shade of red. She was wearing a white blouse with the top three buttons undone, a black vest, tight black leather pants and matching black leather boots. "Goodness!" Jack declared and turned to John, the dealer. "I think I'm gonna take a break, John. I see someone I need to talk to."

John looked over at Amber sitting at the bar and nodded.

"Can you take care of these chips for me?" Jack asked. He had two tall stacks of black $100 chips and now a few purple $500 chips sitting there. Jack grabbed two of the black chips and slid them to John.

"These are for you and Carlos to share."

"Thanks, Jack. Appreciate it. Your chips are fine right there, Carlos will rack them up and they'll be waiting for you when you return."

John gathered the two black chips Jack had slid to him and put one aside and slipped the other into his tip box.

Jack walked over to the bar and sat next to Amber, "I think I may owe you an apology." He shyly announced to her.

"Oh yeah?" she eyed him up and down and offered a solution, "Buy me a Bicardi and Coke and I'll accept that apology."

"Sounds like a plan."

"You're Jack from the other night."

"Yes, that's correct."

"Where's your handsome friend?"

"Oh, he had to get back to San Mateo, and back to work."

"That's a shame."

A few drinks later Jack was beginning to feel comfortable with the gorgeous red head. He asked Amber first about her name. "Beaver?" he asked. "Gotta be a joke."

"No, it's my real name, I got teased a lot in school."

"I would expect so," Jack grinned at her.

"I was married a few years back, He was a dealer. Cards, not drugs!" she quickly cleared that up.

Jack nodded and she continued, "Good looking guy, Gorgeous dark blue eyes with tiny gold specks" she sipped from her drink. "His name was Jack Tilly," she smiled and seemed to be remembering good times with her former beau. She snapped out of it and sighed, "Fucker broke my heart and ran off with a rich fifty-something blonde bombshell. They live in the Hollywood Hills, I think. If he hasn't dumped her by now for something better, or she hasn't dumped him for someone younger."

"So, I assume it's Amber Tilly now?" Jack asked.

"Oh, yeah of course, I wonder sometimes if I just married him for his surname." She smiled a little devilish smile thinking about Jack Tilly. "Oh my god, I loved that guy." she said almost whispering.

"Well, of course, any guy named Jack is a guy anyone could love." Jack said to her.

"Is that right, big guy?" she asked the Jack sitting next to her and put her hand on his leg. Her hand was nice and warm, he smiled but he ignored her flirtations.

"Tell me about working at the Highwater. "Good place to work?"

Amber took her hand off Jack's leg. This guy is no fun, she thought, and nodded her head, "Yeah, I like working here, the tips are great, and the more that the clients see of the girls, the better the tips."

Jack shook his head, "The girls?" He looked confused.

"You know the girls," She said as she shook her tits in front of him.

"Oh, right. The girls", he chuckled and felt himself blush a bit.

"Sometimes I make hundreds of dollars a night, just in tips."

"Wow!" Jack said, still a bit embarrassed. He took a big gulp of his drink.

Amber continued, "There are other perks. Management is very laid back here. Remember the set-up us dealers have out those doors?" She said pointing at the door clearly marked "Emergency Exit Only" in giant red letters. "You were out there a few nights ago with your friend. I'm pretty sure you were trashed."

She thought for a second, "Yeah, now I know why you bought me that drink. You got a little frisky with me." She got a sly smile and poked her finger into Jack's chest. Benjamin the bartender had been standing there with two more drinks for Amber and Jack. He had heard what Amber said and saw her poke Jack.

He set the drinks in front of them and told Jack, "Through that door is our private hiding spot. We've got chairs out there and a nice little fire pit. Basically, anything the casino throws in the dumpster that is still useable ends up in the little 'Lounge by the River.'"

Amber interrupted Benjamin, "Jack and his friend joined me the other night out there." She turned to Jack ignoring Benjamin, "The best part, there aren't any cameras back there so we can take our breaks outside, smoke a little weed, or whatever and nobody is the wiser."

"What do you mean, no cameras?" Jack asked. "I thought every square inch in and around a Casino had to have a camera. I thought it was some kind of a Gaming law."

Amber sipped her drink, "It is a law and definitely a gaming law but Management here let us take out one camera, the one straight out from that door," She pointed again, and Jack looked again.

Benjamin walked away to pour someone a Stella Artois.

Jack pulled a cigarette out and asked, "This bother you?" Amber shook her head and waved her hands, "Nah, you're good." She was a bit tipsy and was talking more than normal, "Our little area isn't monitored by anyone so we can sit out there and not be bothered by the 'Eye in the Sky"', she made quote marks with her fingers. "The head guy here, Brad, has no problem with it, and so far, the Gaming people have missed the fact there's no camera out there."

Jack leaned back, "I am truly enjoying your company Miss Beever, with two 'E's", they both laughed.

Amber decided to invite Jack that evening and said, "I'll be out there tonight about midnight, should be a few of us dealers. That's my dinner break, I get a full hour break. You should meet us there again. I've got a nice fat joint in my purse, it's some kind of 'Purple Nurple' or something like that." She squinted trying to remember the name of the weed she had rolled into a joint earlier.

"Purple Nurple? Okay, that sounds great. Midnight huh?"

Amber nodded her head and a lock of her hair covered one eye.

Jack was intrigued by this gorgeous young lady, he smiled at her and said, "I just may see you out there."

Amber looked at her watch, 7:50 pm. She finished her drink, said goodbye and walked towards the High Stakes Poker Room, where she would be working most of the night. Jack thought about it for a minute, what the hell, she's very attractive and I got nothing to do at Midnight.

I'll be there. Benjamin walked down with a new drink for Jack. Jack had said, "Keep 'em coming." and Benjamin was a good server and did his job well. Jack was one of only three customers at the bar, so Benjamin stood and talked to Jack for a while. He told Jack about his band and asked the older man what type of music he listened to.

Jack thought a minute and answered, "Oh, I like John Scofield, Patrick O'Hearn, Michael Franks." Benjamin raised his hand. "Dude stop please. I may spew right here. I need to hook you up. You've been brainwashed by that 'White Jazz' shit." Benjamin dug through his backpack behind the bar and handed Jack a stack of CD's.

Jack looked through them. He didn't recognize any of the bands and started reading the names out loud. "Disturbed, Papa Roach, must be a reference to smoking weed."

Benjamin said, "Actually it's a reference to one of the bandmember's Granddads."

Jack shook his head and continued reading the names, "Godsmack, Rage Against the Machine, Lamb of God." The last one reminded him of Dave Holloway. "Oh yeah. I've heard of these guys." He fibbed to the bartender and pointed to the Lamb of God CD.

Benjamin was impressed but a bit dubious. He said, "John Campbell is killer! Right?"

Jack repeated what Benjamin said. "Killer!"

Benjamin looked at Jack and said, "You don't know who that is do you?"

Jack immediately said "No, not at all. Is it the granddad?"

Benjamin burst out laughing. "You're a funny guy Jack!" He paused, smiled and said, "Look, you're going to be here a few more days. Take those with you and listen to them. They will broaden your musical knowledge, it's always good to do that. I'll get them from you before you leave."

"Okay, sounds good, thanks." Jack said looking at the CD's front and back. He said, "Good night." to Benjamin, threw a hundred-dollar bill on the bar to cover his and Amber's tab, and headed to the bathroom.

-Chapter 8-

The party in Chucho's room was winding down. Victoria had shown up about an hour ago. She was curled up on the bed with a pillow over her head. Only the four who rode in together and a few stragglers were left in the room, listening to Gangster Hip Hop blasting on the stereo. 'Straight Outta Compton' was pumping out, "When I'm called off, I got a sawed off. Squeeze the trigger and bodies are hauled off. You too boy, if you fuck with me. The police are gonna hafta come and get me." The skinny guy from the front desk got out of the elevator, stomped down to the noisy room and banged on the door. Rudy yanked the door open and startled the poor guy.

"What!" Rudy barked.

The kid said, "I'm sorry sir, but uh, your neighbors on this floor are complaining. The sign on the door clearly gives the um, the required quiet hours. They are 9:00 pm to 9:00 am and it's 9:20 right now."

Rudy pulled his vest aside and showed his Walther .45 to the kid. The kid bent down in a bow with his hands in front of him and walked backwards to the stairway. He turned and burst through the door and disappeared down the stairs. Rudy closed the door and he and Chucho and a few others roared with laughter. The skinny kid ran down four flights of stairs scared he was going to get shot in the back the whole time.

Rudy decided he should probably take Celina and head to the casino before the cops came back up, with the skinny kid leading them, and started arresting people. He had a few warrants and didn't feel like spending the night in the Laughlin jail. He had already done that another time here.

"Chuch, we gonna bug out man." Rudy waited for a response.

Chucho frowned and looked at Rudy, "Whatever Homey, I'm fuckin' starving anyway. Me and Victoria gonna go get us a steak or something. Right Vic?"

Victoria sat up on the bed and pleaded. "I'm tired Flavio. I just want to get some sleep."

Chucho raised his fist as if he were going to strike her. She flinched and put her hands over her head for protection. Rudy and Celina had seen enough and left the room to head downstairs.

Jack was drunk and staggered back over and sat down at "Third Base" on the same Blackjack table he had been on a few hours earlier. John, the dealer wasn't there anymore, and the new dealer asked if his name was Jack. Jack nodded and the new dealer put the trays of Jack's chips in front of him. Jack looked at the dealer's name tag, ***Paul Hasskamp, Traverse City Michigan***. "Well hello Paul Hasskamp from Michigan. We may be related. I have a cousin in Aitkin, Minnesota named Donald Hasskamp. Any relation to you by any chance?"

Paul thought for a few seconds. "I don't think so, my parents are both from Michigan. I don't remember them ever mentioning any relatives in Minnesota."

Jack asked drunkenly, "That's a little strange isn't it? Hasskamp is such a unique name. I can't believe there isn't some relationship there; second or third cousins, maybe?"

"Possibly," Paul gave in so the drunk would quit asking questions.

"Let's say we're third cousins." Jack suggested.

"OK," Paul agreed. Jack turned to the couple sitting to his right. "This is Paul, he's my third cousin from Michigan." He introduced the dealer.

"We're happy for you," the man said back to Jack and rolled his eyes at his wife. Jack spread $3000 on the felt.

"Changing three thousand," Paul announced to the Pit Boss.

"Three thousand", answered Carlos and waved to Jack.

"Let's make some money." Jack said to the couple.

"Let's do that." The woman replied. Her husband just scowled and shook his head. Jack had played about an hour and was up nearly a thousand dollars. Paul Hasskamp was starting to like Jack. Carlos had told Paul that Jack was a generous tipper and that was, certainly, the case.

Jack was starving and told Paul, "I think I'll go grab a steak or something to eat."

Paul put his hand up for Jack to stop and wait and called Carlos down and told the Pit Boss that Jack was a, long lost, cousin and asked him if he could, possibly, hook his kin up with some sort of food comp. The Pit Boss, Carlos, looked at Paul and then looked back at Jack. Speaking directly to Jack, he asked if he claimed Paul as his cousin.

"Of course, "Jack responded.

"Fair enough," Carlos smiled and wrote Jack a $50 comp for the Steak House on the second floor. Jack took the comp paper from Carlos, thanked him and got up from the table.

"Don't worry about your money." Paul said. "It'll be safe here."

Jack said, "You're a good man, Paul Hasskamp." He tossed his cousin a couple $100 black chips and pointed at Carlos, "Split that with my friend please," and headed off in search of grilled meat.

The restaurant wasn't busy, and Jack was cutting up a huge medium rare T-Bone within fifteen minutes of sitting down. He was happy to be eating something, he was definitely drunk and knew that eating would help him sober up a bit. He couldn't stop thinking about Amber, the red headed Poker dealer. I wonder how old she is he thought to himself. Can't be more than twenty-five, or so. Shit, he was in his forties now. What was that? He put down the utensils and started counting on his fingers. Out of the corner of his eye Jack saw the tattooed Mexican biker and his pregnant girlfriend enter the restaurant. She had been crying and clearly didn't want to be there. She was leaning away and her loudmouthed boyfriend, Chucho, was gripping her arm hard. He steered her toward a booth and started yelling for a waitress.

"Hello, hello, anybody here? We need food!" He saw a waitress pouring coffee for an older couple in the back and pointed at her, "You! Do you see us here? We're fuckin' hungry, Puta."

The waitress, clearly upset with the biker, excused herself from the older couple and grabbed a couple menus for the angry Mexican and his pregnant girlfriend. "Sorry sir, I didn't see you here." She said a little sarcastically. "What drinks can I start you two off with?"

"Bring me a Modelo Negra in a bottle with two limes. Two limes." He repeated and stuck two fingers in the waitress's face.

"Water for her, and we'll take two T-Bones medium rare, and hurry it up we got shit to do."

"I'll bring it to you as fast as the Chef gets it to me, sir." She coldly said to him.

Jack tried to mind his own business but there was something wrong with the young girl.

He was staring at her when Chucho saw him, "Hey Gringo! What the fuck you looking at? Mind your own business you honky Mother Fucker!"

Jack put his hands up as a sign of surrender and looked down at his plate. The older couple put down their utensils, threw some money on the table and got up and left. "Yeah, that's right, you old, gringo fuckers, get out of here. The less white people in here the better." The angry Mexican yelled as they exited the restaurant.

Jack noticed something about the young pregnant girl. There was blood matted in her hair. "What the hell?" Jack said under his breath. He continued to sneak looks at the girl, she didn't look right.

Chucho got up and announced to her he was going to go piss. "Stay here, bitch," he ordered and disappeared down the hall.

Jack thought for a second, I've got to get her some help. He stood up and walked over to her. "Are you alright?" he asked her anxiously looking down the hall for Chucho.

"I'm so tired' she moaned, "and Flavio won't let me go to sleep."

Jack looked at her head, there was a large gash under her bleached hair. Her left pupil was enormous but her right one was normal size. She was clearly concussed. She closed her eyes and looked as if she would soon slip into unconsciousness. Jack flagged down the waitress and asked her to sit with the young girl and he ran to the nearest employee with a 2-way radio, a slot tech sitting at the bar watching a Lakers game. "You gotta get an ambulance here, there's a girl in the restaurant who's very sick and is bleeding."

The slot tech could smell liquor on Jack's breath and leaned back, but he got on his radio and started calling for help. Within minutes two paramedics arrived with three burly Security guards. The EMT's ran to Victoria and started treating her right away as the Security guards stood watch. One of them held his hand over his ear and said, "Right away" and left in a hurry to go to the front entrance of the Casino to meet any cops that showed up. The Laughlin P.D. arrived and a few minutes later a guy in a suit arrived and took over the scene. He looked familiar to Jack. Where had he seen this guy? He finally figured it out, this was the same cop who had been talking to the Mexican biker in the back of the police cruiser. Jack decided his help was no longer needed and he left to return to the Blackjack table that he had left earlier.

Karl Schulz was heading home when the call came in.

"Possible 415, Highwater Resort,10-52, code 2, Karl you got a copy?"

He grabbed his mic. "I read you, Lilly."

"Are you 10-8?" she asked him. Karl sighed and let out his breath. Sandra was not going to be happy with him. Lilly had just asked him if he was available to take an assault call at the Highwater Casino. He was literally a block from there and couldn't refuse the call.

"Yes, I'm 10-8, what's up?" he asked the dispatcher.

"I think your biker friend assaulted a woman in the restaurant there. You're close to the end of your shift, want me to call Sandra for you?"

"Please do, she's not going to be happy with me, it's our 20th anniversary."

Lilly gushed into the mike, "Well, congratulations Loverboy!" She started making smooching sounds. Karl thanked her a little sarcastically.

Lilly said, "Sandra will understand, she's a great lady, I'll call her right away."

Karl turned into the Highwater parking lot, parked, jumped out and headed inside. A Security guard was waiting and directed the detective to the restaurant on the second floor. Karl saw that Victoria Ramirez was being attended to by two EMT's. He walked directly to her.

"Victoria, who did this to you?"

"I don't know."

"Well, I know who it was. Where's Flavio?"

"I don't know" she started crying, "But he didn't do this.

"Of course not," Karl muttered under his breath. He saw a familiar face among the first responders. "Chuck!" he called to the uniformed officer. "Get a few of your boys to search the grounds, we're looking for Chucho Valdez. Black and Green Vagos vest. I guarantee he's armed and dangerous. Find out what room is his and send someone up to his room and break down the door if you have to." He glanced at the pale sixteen-year-old, on the gurney. "We need to find this douchebag."

Chucho had seen the flashing lights and all the uniforms running around and decided he needed to get away, fast. He walked briskly out the South door of the Casino and up the Riverwalk to the Riverside Casino and went to the farthest corner from the door. He'd just hang out here, he told himself, and wait for things to quiet down. He grabbed the barmaid, ordered a Modelo with two limes and settled in for what may be a long evening.

Jack got up from the Blackjack table with three full racks of mostly black and green chips well over $6500. He decided he should go to his room and freshen up before meeting Amber and the other dealers in their little "Lounge by the River", so he headed upstairs. The red light on the phone was blinking so he set the chips on the desk and called the front desk. The man that answered said, "Yes, Mr. Martin, Detective Schulz from the Laughlin P.D. would like to talk to you about what happened earlier in our restaurant. Do you want his number?"

Jack looked around and grabbed the pen and paper on the nightstand, "Yeah, sure, go ahead." He scribbled the number down. He read the instructions on the phone for an outside line. He dialed all the numbers, cleared his throat and waited for someone to answer. Detective

Schulz's phone went right to his voicemail. Jack didn't leave a message. What could he help the Detective with anyway? He asked himself. Pretty clear cut he thought, Chucho beat up his pregnant girlfriend and hopefully he is behind bars right now. Jack wadded up the phone number and pitched it into the trash can.

At 11:45, Jack headed downstairs to the dealer's "Lounge by the River." He passed the Blackjack table and nodded at John, the dealer. John pointed at Jack and flashed him a big smile and everyone at the table turned and looked at Jack. Jack paused at the Exit door before opening it. He was a bit concerned alarms and flashing lights would go off if he opened it. He remembered Amber just bursting through the door. He looked around, "Oh well, here goes nothing," he said to no one and pushed on the bar to unlock the door. There were no alarms, no flashing lights or Security people running over to stop him. He quietly slipped through the door and headed down a dirty, carpeted ramp to another door that opened to the outside. Several chairs, of different types, were set up around a big fire pit. There was already a person sitting there smoking a short, fat cigar. Jack squinted hard and recognized him as Carlos the Pit Boss.

Carlos looked back, and his face lit up. "Jack! How the hell are you? What are you doing out here?"

Jack looked at the Colorado River just 100 feet away. It was high and moving fast. "Amber invited me to your little lounge here, I hope that's cool." He answered Carlos.

"Of course, my friend, you're always welcome. I'm almost done with my break but Amber and some of the others will be here shortly." Carlos looked at his watch and held his hand out towards a chair. "Sit, Jack."

Jack chose a slightly crooked leather recliner and dropped down into it. "This is awesome! Look how high the river is." He said to Carlos.

The Pit Boss took a big puff of his Cohiba and let the smoke out. Jack couldn't see Carlos's face but heard him say, "I think they're letting water out of one of the dams upstream, I've not seen the river this high in years."

Jack pulled out a cigarette and lit it. He blew the smoke up and watched it as it disappeared among the millions of stars.

Carlos stood up, stretched and said, "Gotta get back to work, have a good night." He stubbed his cigar out in an ashtray and tossed the butt into the fire pit. Jack watched the Pit Boss as he went through the door and up the carpeted ramp to the Casino floor.

Within minutes Amber showed up and sat next to Jack, "You made it!" She said and seemed genuinely pleased.

"Yes, yes I did." Jack answered her but felt a bit anxious sitting next to the very attractive woman. She smelled fantastic. They sat for a few minutes watching the river roll by.

Finally, Amber pulled out a hand rolled joint and lit it. "It's called 'Purple Urkle' not 'Purple Nurple'." Amber told Jack clearing up her confusion of the name earlier in the evening. She handed the joint and a red lighter to Jack.

Jack nodded. "Purple Urkle." He repeated and torched the joint. They passed it back and forth and had smoked over half of it by the time the other dealers showed up at which time Amber let the dealers finish what was left. Jack was very high and having a great time. He sat listening to the dealers talk and trade stories about the day's events. Amber was quieter than normal, but she finally spoke up and asked Jack, "Did you get a buzz, Jack?

He answered her. "Yah, I did, I appreciate it."

"No worries, we're here almost every night about this time, and you're always welcome to join us."

Jack checked his watch. It was ten minutes to 1:00 am. The dealers got up and started to disappear through the door and back to work. Amber and Jack were left alone and looked at each other.

They both burst out laughing at the same time. "Damn, Jack you look stoned!"

Jack looked through squinty eyes and said to her, "You should see how stoned you look!"

Amber stood so Jack did, too. She gave him a big hug, said "Later" to him, turned and disappeared through the door. Jack sat back down and looked at the stars in the sky. It was a nice, warm morning and he was happy. Last full day here he thought. It was March 16th. A smiling and very high Jack sat alone and watched the river. It suddenly hit him, "This is the same river that runs through Glenwood Springs, back in Colorado." He said it quietly to himself. He stood up and went through the door back into the casino. He had no idea how much he, and his life would change in less than twenty-four hours.

Chucho stood up and looked around him. He had been hiding behind the Riverside Casino near the river. He had seen some cops walking through the lobby of the Riverside earlier and had left the bar and come here to hide a while. He checked his Rolex watch, 12:50 am. He looked both ways on the concrete river walk before stepping out on it. He headed towards the Highwater Hotel, he needed to find Victoria, get his bike and haul ass out of here and back to Chino. As he approached the back of the Highwater, he heard muffled voices followed by laughing. He stopped and stood watching, a man and woman were sitting near the back of the casino. He watched them for a few minutes. The man took a big drag on his smoke and Chucho saw his face. It was the same guy that had been in the restaurant earlier. The same guy that had caused Chucho to sleep on the ground by the river instead of his comfortable bed in room 410. Chucho said, "Pinch Cabron!" and reached into his waistband at the small of his back and pulled out his silver Smith & Wesson .38 Special. This fucker's got to pay! He thought to himself. The girl stood up and hugged the man and disappeared through a door. Chucho started heading, slowly, towards Jack, pistol at the ready. Jack was staring into the sky, oblivious of the approaching gangster. Suddenly, Jack stood and went through the door and back into the casino. Chucho lowered the gun and stuck it back in his waistband. The Gringo piece of shit will have to be dealt with later, he needed to find Victoria.

Karl was lying awake in bed beside his wife, Sandra, who was snoring lightly. Luckily, Sandra wasn't mad when he finally came through the door two and a half hours before, around 10:45 pm. When her husband finally got home Sandra had taken his hand and led him out onto the patio behind the house where she had a table and two chairs set up with dinner, wine and flowers. The roof of the patio was strung with small, white lights that mimicked the real ones sparkling above them.

"The dinner's long cold but should still be delicious." She said to him.

Karl was blown away, Sandra had dozens of candles around the patio and on the table which she started to light for him. There were two big lobster tails sitting there.

He handed her a small wrapped present and an envelope and started apologizing, "I'm so sorry Sandra! I was this close to heading home when the call came in." Karl held his thumb and finger up with a small gap between them.

Sandra put her finger to his lips, "Shh! Let's not talk about your work tonight, I'm sure you're starving, I know I am."

They did talk later, in bed. Karl told her about the sixteen-year old victim, Virginia. He described the petite, very pregnant young girl laying on the gurney bleeding and concussed by her gangster biker boyfriend. He had followed the ambulance to the Western Arizona Med Center and had stayed until Virginia was assigned room 305 on the 3rd floor. Karl talked to Virginia, in her room, for a while. She was more willing to talk about her boyfriend, now. She told him how Flavio had gotten mad at her because she wouldn't have sex with him before they ate. She was not in the mood for sex or food. She just wanted to go to bed. He had hit her in the head with his pistol and stormed out of the room. She lay on the floor bleeding for several minutes, before he returned. She heard him come through the door and was deathly afraid. "I thought he was going to shoot me dead!" She started tearing up.

Karl handed her a box of tissues. Chucho, roughly, pulled her up and out the door. "I'm hungry bitch, and you are too." He spit at her angrily. They had gone to a restaurant on the second floor, but she didn't remember much else. Karl wanted to let Victoria rest and get home to his wife, but he had one more question for her. "Who helped you in the restaurant, who called the cops?" He asked her. She wasn't sure. He posted a deputy at the door to the room and left to go home to his wife.

Chucho hid behind a car and looked towards where his Fat Bob had been parked. It was nowhere to be found. Detective Schulz had had it towed to the impound lot as soon as they had determined which bike belonged to the gangster. Rudy's Knucklehead and a few others, owned by the Vagos, were parked there still. Chucho cursed under his breath and headed to the Hotel. He had removed his vest and stashed it near the river. He pulled a hat, he had bought at the Riverside, low on his head hoping no one would recognize him. The lobby was empty, and the casino only had, maybe twenty people in it, none of the poker tables were open. All twenty gamblers were focused on their slot machines. Chucho, carefully, walked through the casino towards the elevators. Everything was quiet. He headed to rooms 410 and 411, the rooms the four of them were staying in. Hopefully, Victoria was still there, and he could grab her and get Rudy's keys, take Rudy's bike, and head back to Chino. He had lots of places in Cali he could hide until this all blew over. Rudy and Celina could figure out some other way home. When he got to the door to room 410, he put his ear to the door and listened. Nothing, no sounds, until someone in the room, a male, coughed. Earlier the manager of the hotel had used a master key card to let the police into the room. They clearly saw drugs on the bedside and were able to get a judge to issue a warrant for Flavio "Chucho" Valdez. Karl had left two Laughlin Police Officers in the room in case Chucho happened to show up. Chucho leaned back, turned and quietly walked down the hall to the elevators. He rode down to the casino, walked out the front door and disappeared into the early morning.

-Chapter 9-

Jack woke early the next morning and decided he would rent a car and explore the desert around him. Despite the fact he simply could not lose at Blackjack, no matter how he played or how much he bet he was tired of gambling. He grabbed the wad of bills on the nightstand and counted it. Just over $9,000! He called the front desk and had the concierge arrange a rental car for him. He packed a small cooler with water and hopped in the shower. The car was waiting for him when he finally got down to the lobby, a bright red 2016 Toyota Camry with a dark grey leather interior. Jack signed the paperwork and looked up at the Concierge who was holding the car keys in front of him. "If for any reason you decide to keep the car longer than you intended, just give one of us a call and we'll adjust the paperwork for you." The smiling young man said to Jack. Jack thanked him and snatched the keys. He headed North on Casino Drive to Bullhead Parkway and out into the already hot and dry desert. He popped one of Benjamin's CD's into the dash and "The Sound of Silence" by Disturbed started playing. It was a remake of the old Simon and Garfunkle song done over fifty years ago. Jack liked it and sang along. He stopped in Searchlight, Nevada, and had a big breakfast at Terribles Casino. The waitress walked over, chewing gum and smacking her lips and asked "Coffee?" Jack said, "Please." She left and Jack watched her walk away. Oh my gosh, this woman is right out of a sitcom he thought to himself. She was wearing a pink work dress with a white collar and short white sleeves. There was a white apron tied around her waist, and her bright red hair was ratted as big as possible and piled high on her head. On the peak of her hair, balanced there, was a small white paper hat. She looked and acted like a waitress he had seen on TV. Jack searched his memory. He couldn't remember the sitcom. He and his brother, Joey used to watch it all the time. It finally came to him. Flo!

Jack shook his head and said under his breath, "Too funny!" Flo walked back and set a steaming cup of dark clear liquid in front of Jack. He could smell the wonderful aroma of it. Flo's nametag said Mildred.

"Thank you, Mildred." Jack said to her.

"Oh? Are we on a first name basis, here?" She asked incredulously, "'Cause if we are, I gotta know your name.

That's only fair." Jack smiled and told her, "My given name is Jack." She got a puzzled look and shook her head no.

"Nope. You're no Jack, no way no how. You look more like a 'Pete' to me. I'm calling you Pete." She announced to him.

Jack said back, "Just don't call me late for breakfast, Mildred." Mildred rolled her eyes and reached into her apron pocket and pulled out a dozen packs of pink sweetener, six tiny white plastic cups of cream and a pad of paper. There was a pencil stuck into her mass of hair and Flo pulled it out, licked the tip and said to Jack, "Okay Pete, what can I get for you?"

While Jack was paying the breakfast bill, he bought a map of Nevada and picked up several tourist brochures showing the things to do in the immediate area. He sat in the rented Camry and perused the brochures. There were a few that looked interesting, there was a ghost town just a few miles away that he thought he would definitely check out. Suddenly the air was filled with a thunderous roar, a guttural and crackling sound. Several big motorcycles were turning into Terribles' parking lot from the direction of Henderson. All the men wore the same green and black vests that Chucho and his entourage wore but they said, 'Sacramento Chapter'. These bikers were headed to Laughlin to party with Chucho, Jack was certain of that. He started the little red Camry and cranked the Lamb of God CD to cover the roar of the motorcycles. He put his right blinker on and pulled out of Terribles parking lot in the opposite direction the bikers were heading. The further he was from these gangsters the better he thought.

Karl and Sandra Schulz got in the bright elevator and headed to the 3rd floor and room 305. Karl recognized the officer sitting looking at his phone outside Victoria's room. Karl nodded, and said "Derrick." Derrick nodded back at Karl and went back to his phone. Victoria was eating oatmeal when they knocked on the door and stepped in. Karl introduced his wife to the young girl.

"Nice to meet you, Sweetie," Sandra said to her. Victoria shook Sandra's hand and said, "You too."

There was a small uncomfortable pause and Karl broke it by asking the teen. "How are you doing, young lady?"

"I guess I'm doing better, but, I was sitting here thinking, I'm homeless now."

Sandra frowned, "What about relatives?" She asked the girl, "Mom or Dad?"

Victoria looked out the window, "My Papi was murdered when I was little, and my Mommy is in a halfway house trying to get sober. I can't go back to Flavio he might hurt me or the baby." Victoria broke down and started sobbing. "I'm a orphan now." The uneducated teen said not realizing her grammatical error. Sandra handed a box of tissues to the teen. "Hector and I are going to have to live on the street."

"Hector?" Karl and Sandra asked in unison.

Victoria wiped her eyes with a tissue, "I decided today that Hector is what I'm naming my baby. I found out today it's gonna be a boy!" She put both hands on her protruding stomach as if she were holding the unborn child. She looked out the window at the light blue cloudless sky and continued, "My Papi's name was Hector. He would be happy to hear

I'm naming the baby after him." She sniffed, grabbed another tissue and blew her nose. Karl thought about that name a minute, Hector Ramirez? He recognized the name from somewhere. He searched his memory. Finally, it came to him, Hector "Teto" Ramirez was a Vagos member out of California. He was shot in the back supposedly by a rival gang member in a bar in Gardena, years ago, sometime around 2009. It took a few days for Victoria's dad to die. No one was ever charged with the murder, the people in the bar all claimed they hadn't seen a thing. Victoria was Teto Ramirez's daughter. Holy Shit!

An hour later Sandra told Karl she would like to stay with Victoria when Karl suggested they leave and let the young girl get some rest. "I'd like to stay" she quietly said to Karl, "She needs someone to be with her for a while. I'll call a cab to get home, don't worry, I won't be too late."

Karl agreed, kissed his wife, patted Victoria on her leg and left the hospital. He decided to go to the Highwater and the Riverside to interview a few more people and watch for any sign of Chucho Valdez. One of the barmaids at the Riverfront had seen the gangster biker in the bar, there, and had called the Laughlin P.D., this morning, to tell them. But by the time they got there, Chucho was long gone. Karl was certain the gangster biker was still in the area. He pulled into the parking lot and decided to drive around the three levels. Perhaps the fugitive biker was hiding among the cars. After searching for half an hour Karl parked the unmarked police car in the garage and deliberately walked past the Harley Davidsons parked side by side and across the drive to the Casino entrance. He entered and walked through the Highwater and out the back. The Riverwalk was crowded with people and Karl sat at a table and watched the crowd.

Chucho was hiding near the bank of the Colorado River. He had found a spot where some homeless people had a small camp and decided to join them. A few of them watched him closely. He was not one of them, he was definitely some sort of gangster or possibly a drug dealer. Chucho had face tattoos and was a scary looking guy. Chucho laid down on an abandoned blanket and pulled a hat over his face thinking he would blend in better if the cops came through. He still had his .38 and wasn't afraid to use it. He would have a shootout with the cops, right here, if that was the only alternative. The homeless people continued to watch him as they went about their normal business.

Sandra stayed with Victoria for over eight hours. It was starting to get dark when she climbed into an Uber to head home. She and Karl had a daughter, just a few years older than Victoria. "Kaitlyn" was in her first year of College at Dixie State University in Saint George, Utah. Sandra couldn't quit thinking about her daughter and what a wonderful life they had given her. Victoria was a few years younger than Kaitlyn and she had lived a horrible life. Victoria needed to get back into school and become a normal teen, again. Susan was certain she and Karl could help Victoria do just that. Karl was home when she arrived, cooking pork chops on the grill outside. Sandra grabbed a cold beer out of the fridge, walked out, handed it to her husband and gave him a huge hug. "Kaitlyn and I are so lucky to have you in our lives." She told Karl.

He kissed his wife and reflected on the day, "It's funny how we take everything for granted isn't it? That poor teen in the hospital is someone's daughter. She's never had a good life, just one full of drugs and guns and gangsters. I'm so lucky to have the two of you in my life, as well." He popped the top on the beer. The cold liquid felt good going down his throat. He thought back and remembered a poem he had read in College. The author escaped him. He recited part of it from memory out loud to Sandra. "God has a brown voice, as soft and full as a good beer." She smiled at her husband. She had heard him recite these same words over their years together. She loved him so much.

Jack drove into the parking garage of the Highwater Hotel and parked near the elevator. He had had an enjoyable day. He put a lot of miles on the rental car and saw a bunch of the desert. Early March had seen a lot of rain in the surrounding area and the desert flowers were incredible. Mildred had said it was called the "super bloom." "You hafta see it." She told him when he stood to pay his bill. She was right, the Ocatilla all had bright red flowers and the rest of the desert was covered with a sea of gold, purple, pink and white flowers. Everywhere you looked there was a carpet of multi colors. On the dark hills there were explosions of orange as if an airplane had dropped water balloons filled with orange paint. Jack knew these flowers were poppies. He had cranked the car's stereo and driven all over the surrounding areas listening to Benjamin's CD's. He liked some of them, not all of them, but the bartender was right. People needed to broaden their musical horizons. Around 2 pm, he had driven to the Ghost Town he saw in the flyer and, after paying a $15 admission, he had wandered around for hours looking through each building. He even bought a T-shirt in the gift shop, with a ghost on it that read, "I'm here for the Boos." He got out of the warm Camry, in the parking garage and grabbed the bag with the new t-shirt. The Camry's engine was cooling down and made a quiet ticking sound. Jack looked at his watch, quarter to nine. He had a while 'til Amber and the other dealers were at their outdoor "Lounge", so he went to his room and laid down to take a short nap, making sure to set his alarm for 11 pm.

Jack was sleeping hard when the alarm went off. He turned on his back and tried to remember the dream he had just been awakened from. Susan was here at the Highwater, with Mark and three toddlers. They were all standing by two big, heavily chromed, Harley Davidson motorcycles. He chuckled to himself, where the hell did the kids ride? "What a stupid dream", he said to the empty hotel room. He got up, showered and got dressed. He decided to wear his new tee shirt and put it on. He looked at his reflection in the mirror. Looks good, and is comical he thought, and headed out the door.

There was no money tray and no dealer at the Blackjack table, but Carlos, the Pit Boss, was standing leaning against it. Slow night Jack figured. Carlos nodded at Jack and Jack nodded back. He was going to miss all these people when he left in the morning. He walked over and pushed the bar on the "No Exit" door and walked down the dirty carpet and outside into the desert air. It was a beautiful evening, probably mid 70's and there were millions of stars in the sky. There was barely a sliver of a moon, so it was very dark, and he squinted to see if anyone was out here. He sat in the same leaning lounge chair he had sat in last night and glanced at the river. There was a small light at the edge of the river, and he could see the water was, even, higher than the previous night. Jack sat watching, when out of the shadows a stocky guy walked down the riverwalk and climbed onto the short concrete wall by the river. Jack focused harder on the dark male figure standing there. The guy seemed familiar. It hit him all at once. Chucho! The asshole biker who beat up the poor girl in the restaurant was standing on the wall unzipping his pants. Jack was thankful it was so dark he didn't want the bad guy to see him sitting there. Chucho pulled out his member and proceeded to urinate into the dark rolling river. Jack felt flushed, all sorts of things were running through his head. He was pissed at the Mexican biker for hitting his pregnant girlfriend earlier and for pushing her into the gravel a few days ago. He looked into the fire pit. Someone, probably one of the dealers, had built a huge wood teepee in anticipation of lighting it at a later time. There were, several, different diameter logs the length of a man's arm and shorter. One in particular seemed to call to Jack. Before he realized what he was doing, he grabbed the heavy piece of wood and started heading towards Chucho, standing on the concrete wall by the river. The biker never heard Jack walking towards him holding the wood above his head with both hands. Chucho shook his penis and tucked it back in his pants and stepped down off the short wall still facing the river. Jack brought the heavy log down fast and hard and hit the gangster square in the head. The force of the blow split the biker's head open like a ripe watermelon. Jack saw the biker's bloody, pink brains in the faint light. Chucho fell to his knees and stayed there a few seconds with his arms out, palms up, as if he were an Islamic man performing Salaat. He finally slumped over with his face planted against the concrete wall. Jack could see a silver pistol in Chucho's back waistband, and reached for it, but his hands were shaking so badly he could barely get it out. When he did maneuver it out, he tucked it into his own waistband. The biker had a big wallet in his pocket and Jack took that, also, and stuck it in his pocket. He wasn't sure why he had taken the wallet he thought a voice in his head may have suggested it. Jack was breathing heavily, too heavily he thought, and he tried to calm himself while he quickly looked all around for anyone else out there. There was no one in sight and if there was it was too dark for them to see him and the dead man slumped over on the concrete walk. Jack reached down and, with all he had in him, he shoved the biker up and partway over the short concrete wall, but he couldn't get the biker's body completely over it. Jack's face flushed and beads of sweat stood out on his forehead. He looked around, about fifty yards to the South a couple was walking towards Jack holding hands and swinging them as they walked. He crouched down and using his legs to help lift the deadweight he was able to push the dead biker over the short wall and into the black rolling Colorado River. The body made a splashing sound and floated facedown to the right, to the South, towards Mexico. Jack pitched the bloodstained log into the river as far as he could into the darkness. He watched the couple, crossed the Riverwalk just behind them as they passed and headed back to the makeshift river lounge. Jack was physically shaking, now, his chest was heaving. He glanced at his watch, 11:52. The dealers, as well as Amber, would be out in a matter of minutes! He had to settle down. He lit a cigarette and tried to calm himself. Minutes later John, the dealer, was the first to walk out of the door. Jack sucked the last of the Marlboro, flicked it towards the river and tried to be nonchalant. He had just killed someone! There was a dead body floating towards the Gulf of California and he, Jack Earl Martin, was responsible for that. He took a deep breath and closed his eyes.

"How's it hangin' Jack?" John asked as he lit his cigarette. Jack could see John's face for a few seconds in the light of the flame. He knew John couldn't see the terror in his face, he took another Marlboro out, lit it turning his head away and blew out the bluish white smoke, "Not bad John, just enjoying the evening."

"Dark one, isn't it? Must be a new moon."

"Yes."

The two of them sat in silence. A couple more dealers walked out and sat down with John and Jack. Jack recognized both. One of them was named Joe, Joe Moss, Jack recalled, and the other was named Kurt. They all exchanged pleasantries and the three dealers started going over their evening, thus far, with each other.

"I had a guy win over ten grand tonight, in about an hour. Left the table and gave me a Five-dollar tip. Cheap Fuck!" Kurt angrily told the other two dealers.

"I had the same guy at my table yesterday" Joe said, "He left my table without tipping me a penny! Guy's name is Robert Jolly. He made a fortune in the pot business and he can't afford a descent tip?"

Jack listened to them for a while, but all this talk was just noise to him, he couldn't stop thinking about the dead Mexican floating face down in the river with his brains exposed. Understandably, he wasn't feeling well. I have to get out of here, Jack thought seeing spots in front of his eyes. He stood up and announced he was tired and was going to call it a night. All three dealers nodded and went back to their conversations. Jack walked back into the Highwater Casino, found the nearest restroom and, standing at the sink, started splashing water on his face. The cool water helped quite a bit. Jack studied the horrible person in the mirror and looked down at his reflection. "Oh, shit!" He gasped. The front of his shirt had blood on it, blood from the dead biker. He looked around, there was someone in one of the stalls, but otherwise, the bathroom was empty. He quickly pulled the shirt over his head and began rinsing it in the sink. Crimson liquid swirled around the white porcelain and down the drain. Jack stood there, bare chested. He looked in the mirror towards the occupied stall, there on the stall door hung a black windbreaker. He quickly walked over and snatched the jacket. The guy in the stall was stunned someone was taking his coat, "Hey! That's my coat!" He yelled and started frantically unrolling paper from the roll. A loud buzzing started in Jack's ears and he quickly headed towards the door, he stuffed the wet tee shirt in the trash as he ran past it. He stood in the Casino for a second trying to decide what to do now, glancing back at the entrance to the Men's bathroom. He found the nearest exit and slipped out into the early morning, heading towards the Riverside Casino, next door. The same gift shop he had bought condoms in a few days ago was open. Jack snatched up a tee shirt he thought would fit and headed to the cashier. After paying the cashier he walked to the nearest Men's room, slipped the shirt on and hung the windbreaker on one of the stalls. Maybe someone will turn the black windbreaker in, and the owner will get it back. Oh my God! Jack thought, I just killed someone and I'm worried about returning a man's jacket! The bar at the Riverside was not busy so Jack grabbed a stool and sat down."Morning Sir, what can I get you?"

"How about a shot of Patron, and a slice of lime?" Jack asked, then changed his mind, "You know what, bring the whole bottle and an entire lime."

"Bad night, my friend?" Asked the man behind the bar opening the new bottle of Patron.

"Yah!" I've had better." He raised the glass to the bartender and said, "Skol Vikings!"

Rudy and Celina were concerned. Neither of them had seen Chucho or Victoria since early Tuesday. It was Thursday morning. "His bike ain't in the garage, they ain't here." Rudy told his wife.

Celina was beside herself with worry. She hugged Rudy, "Victoria would never leave without letting me know she was leaving." She sniffled, holding back tears. "I'm worried that fucker hurt my little sister. You saw him, he was going to hit her the other night in their room. He's out in the desert burying her right now!" Celina started bawling hard now.

Rudy shook his head and quietly shushed his wife, "Chucho ain't killed your little sis. They're out somewhere partying. They'll be back, I promise." But Rudy was very worried. Chucho very well, may have killed Victoria. Their leader wasn't happy about her being pregnant. She may be buried in the desert and Chucho could be hightailing it back to Chino right now. He kissed his wife on the head and slapped her ass. "Come on Baby. Let's go up to our room and go to bed, you'll see your sis when we wake up."

Jack woke in his hotel room with a huge hangover. He had stayed at the Riverside bar until around 4 am. How he got back to his room, God only knows, but here he was, all safe and warm in a king size, deluxe, bed. He got up and turned on the local news. Nothing was said about a dead biker being found floating face down in the Colorado River with his head bashed in. Jack flipped around all the channels. Nothing. He decided he needed to haul ass out of Laughlin, and quick. He glanced at the clock on the nightstand, 9:45 am. He quickly packed his bags. His flight was leaving at 11:35 and he needed to leave soon to catch it. He thought about the red Camry he had rented and remembered the guy at the front desk telling him all he had to do was call down and let them know if he wanted to keep the rental car for a longer period. Jack would have to cancel the Southwest tickets but that was probably the thing to do. Once the dead Mexican was discovered all the flights out would be scrutinized by the local authorities. He picked up the phone and a female voice answered on the second ring. "Front desk, how may I help you?"

After arranging to keep the rental car Jack dialed Southwest Airlines. Marjorie, with Southwest told Jack, in a monotone voice, that if he wanted to cancel his return flight to Denver, that was fine, they would just save his fare for him and he could use it at a later date, not to exceed one calendar year, for some other trip with Southwest Airlines. She sounded like a robot to Jack. "Thanks, so much Marjorie. You've been a big help." He said, not hiding his sarcasm, and hung up.

-Chapter 10-

Joseph, "Joey" Martin Macklin was going through some new inventory in his store when his cell phone rang. He answered it and Jack asked, "Hey Joey, how you been?"

Joey yelled into the phone, "Oh my God! Jack! How are you? We haven't talked for months. I was just thinking about you, wondering how you were doing after the, uh you know,"

"After the divorce." Jack finished his little brother's sentence.

Joey continued, "I'm sorry Jack, I always liked Susan, but not her snooty parents!" He waited for his brother's response.

"Aw, you know. Bygones!" Jack finally said. "It's all good. Look, Joey, I'm in Laughlin, it's a long story, but I've got a car. I'd like to come hang out with you and Aidan for a few days, if that's cool with the two of you."

"Of course!" Joey yelled into the phone, "Aidan and I would love you to come for a visit. But stay more than a few days, we never get to see each other."

"Maybe, we'll see."

"I'll put some nice Egyptian sheets on the bed for you and pick up some Grain Belt beer!"

"Don't worry about the beer, I've got a couple bottles of good whisky."

"When do you think you'll be here?"

"I'm on the road already. Probably four hours, or so."

"Can't wait to see you, big brother." Joey gushed.

Jack hung up the cell phone and cranked the Papa Roach CD. "Oh shit!" Jack blurted out. He had forgotten to return Benjamin's CD's. He would see if Joey could box them up and send them to the Highwater in Laughlin, in care of Benjamin the bartender. That should work.

Aidan Macklin, Joey's husband, was excited when Joey called him and said they were going to have a visitor, he liked Jack. Jack hadn't cared that his little brother had married another man, unlike the brother's parents who accepted it but would never be comfortable with it. Joey and Jack's folks, Fred and Gladys Martin loved both of their sons equally. They just didn't understand why, the youngest one, liked men over women. "Oh, you know, he's always been a little feminine, Gladys." Gladys agreed with her husband and said, "I pray for Joey every day hoping he'll become normal, again."

"God can do dat, you betcha!" Fred assured Gladys. "Remember how Jack was always moody, and how much he stayed in da bed, der?" Fred nodded towards Jack's old room.

Gladys shook her head yes.

Fred continued. "Well, you prayed for him and Pastor Jim prayed for him. Heck, we all prayed for him and he's fine now. It takes time, sometimes, but da Lord hears us and loves us."

Gladys nodded her head in agreement and said, "I still pray for Jack since his divorce."

"Dats why I love you so much." Fred said to his wife and kissed her on the top of her head.

Joey was studying his bruised and battered face in the mirror when Aidan walked into the consignment store. In his best "Serious" voice, Aidan said to Joey, "You need to tell Jack about the Dego extortioner who beat you up, yesterday."

"I can't", Joey, quietly answered, while still looking in the mirror. "I think I can hide it with just a little more foundation."

Aidan felt flushed from anger, but he kept his voice calm, "Joey, the police weren't any help, right? They know what Beneventi's doing but that beast is still on the street. You can't continue to give him extortion money. It has to stop." Vincent (Slugger) Beneventi was a former lieutenant in the Riccardo Toscani Mob family. All the various family members were either dead or behind bars in Federal lock ups around the country, but Beneventi had gotten off on every charge brought against him. He was the only one left. He was a two-bit hustler now, a nobody, but a lot of people were scared to death of him. He regularly visited several businesses along Palm Canyon Drive to muscle the owners into giving him protection money. He persuaded the business owners to give him a monthly fee by threatening them with a Louisville Slugger bat that he carried everywhere. Because of this he had gotten his nickname, "Slugger". Joey Macklin was one of the business owners that Vincent visited each month. Joey was extremely scared of the beefy Gangster in the cheap suit. Despite telling Aidan that this had only been going on for a few months, every month, for over a year now, Joey had given Vincent anywhere from Four hundred to Eight hundred dollars in a plain white envelope. Vincent would arrive, unannounced, with bat in hand demanding his money. Joey always had the envelope ready for the gangster, but business had been slow this past month, and he didn't have the money, yesterday, when Benventi walked through the shop's door. Vincent had knocked Joey to the floor and kicked him in the face. "I'll be back in a few days, you fucking fag! I suggest you find my money by then", he yelled at the thin man, lying bleeding, curled up on the floor. That's where Aidan had found his husband when he arrived about fifteen minutes later. Despite protests from Joey, Aidan had called the Palm Springs Police Department. Two uniformed officers had shown up and interviewed both Joey and Aidan, separately. They put out a call for anyone who might encounter Vincent Beneventi to hold him for questioning. The taller cop explained to them, "If we can contact Mr. Beneventi, we can charge him with assault, but until that time there's not a lot we can do. We heard he's been shaking down businesses in the area, we just can't seem to find him."

"He's like a ghost", the other cop added.

"Or the Devil." Aidan offered.

Jack pulled into a gas station, in Twenty-Nine Palms, California, and checked his phone for the address of his brother's store. Joey had named his store "Man Jose Consignment" because Aidan was from San Jose, California. The state of California had made it legal for same sex couples to marry in 2008 but it only lasted a few months when voters approved a ban. After the U.S. Supreme Court refused to acknowledge the ban same sex marriages were legalized again and marriages recommenced in late June of 2013. Joey and Aidan, fearing the law would change again got married on July 1st of 2013 at the San Bernardino County Courthouse. Jack had flown to California and attended the ceremony. Their parents chose to stay away. Joey took Aidan's last name, Macklin, and the happy couple packed up and moved to Palm Springs where there was a large L.G.B.T. community. They both felt Palm Springs was a perfect fit for them. They rented a two bed, two bath Bungalow with a pool, in Cathedral City, for $2000 a month with an option to buy. They decided they would rent for a year and then buy the small home if they were still comfortable there. Joey had found a small empty store front to lease on North Palm Canyon Drive and had invested all his savings redecorating it and putting a huge sign out front with his and Aidan's caricatures on it. The neon sign had cost him over twelve hundred dollars alone. Aidan found a job in a chic clothing store, a few blocks away from Man Jose, and they settled in to enjoy their new life together.

"1162 North Palm Canyon Drive, Palm Springs." Jack said the address out loud to help him remember. He typed the address into the Camry's GPS, texted his little brother ***Be there in about an hour*** and got back on the highway heading Southwest. The Papa Roach CD was still playing, and the singer was saying something about murder. Jack turned it up and listened to the words. "Somewhere beyond happiness and sadness, I need to calculate what creates my own madness, and I'm addicted to your punishment and you're the master and I am waiting for disaster. I feel irrational, so confrontational, to tell the truth I am getting away with murder. It isn't possible to never tell the truth, but the reality is I'm getting away with murder. Getting away, getting away, getting away with murder." Jack pulled the Camry over to the side of the road and replayed the song. It was appropriately called 'Getting Away with Murder'. Jack sat listening to the words thinking how befitting the song was of his recent indiscretion. The dead gangster biker with his brains hanging out filled Jack's thoughts. He could feel himself starting to lose it. His mind was racing, and he felt like he was being crushed and couldn't breathe. Jack flung the door open and a car zoomed by honking its horn. Jack stumbled out into the open desert and bent at the waist. He took deep breaths and finally after a few minutes he felt calmer. He stood and looked around, he was completely alone. There were no cars in sight. "Holy shit!" He yelled out loud, "I killed someone! I'm a killer!"

It had taken Jack about thirty minutes to feel normal again, standing, screaming in the hot dry desert. Ninety minutes later he walked through the door of "Man Jose Consignment." Joey ran from behind the counter and gave Jack a big bear hug.

"It's so great to see you, Jack!"

"Great to be seen. Your sign out front is fantastic!"

"Thanks. We love it." Joey gushed and smiled. Jack stared at his younger brother's face a few extra seconds. He knew Joey wore make up, but he had gone a bit overboard today.

Aidan came in the front door, he had left work early because Jack was coming to visit. He hugged Jack, leaned back studying his brother-in-law's face and claimed, "You're as handsome as ever." Joey and Jack could almost be twins they looked so much alike. Joey was a shorter version of Jack and was in better shape, though. Joey was so excited to see Jack that he closed the shop early and the three of them walked a few blocks to a nice little bar called 'The Alibi'. They ate, drank and talked for hours. It was dark when they left the bar. Aidan stopped at the Camry with Jack. He told Joey, "Go finish up and grab your car, I'm helping Jack find our little home.

Jack said, "I've got a GPS." But Aidan wouldn't hear of it. "Oh honey. It would be so much easier if I just showed you." Jack shrugged and Joey returned to the store to finish a few things and get his car.

Aidan and Jack had just turned onto East Palm Canyon Drive, heading to Cathedral City when Aidan asked, "Did you notice anything about your little brother, today?"

"You mean besides the excess amount of make up on his face, what's up with that?"

"Your brother was assaulted yesterday by a man named Vincent Beneventi. I found Joseph on the floor, beaten and bloody." Aidan told Jack. Jack pulled the Camry to the side of the road, switched off the ignition and turned to listen to Aidan. By the time they arrived at Joey and Aidan's house, Jack knew about everything. Aidan got Jack settled in the guest room and was making them all dirty martini's when Joey finally got there. Aidan confessed immediately, "I told Jack everything, hon."

Joey started to cry. Jack shushed his little brother, he had a plan, he asked Joey, "When did this mother fucker say he was coming back to your store?"

"He just said, in the next few days, Jack, don't get involved, he's an animal. His nickname is Slugger because he beats people with a bat if they don't pay him." Joey stared at the floor.

"Well", Jack searched for the right words, "I'm a different person since Susan divorced me. I don't want to go into details, but I know how to handle pricks like this guy."

Joey frowned and asked, "When did you start cursing?"

Jack just shrugged. Aidan grinned at Jack, "Are you going to run him over with your Camry?" He asked.

Jack flashed a big smile, "That car's a rental, I can't do that." Jack paused and took a deep breath, "Look, I'm tired. I'm gonna hop in your pool, grab a shower and go to bed. Let me think everything over and tomorrow we'll talk more." He started down the hall, stopped and said, "I almost forgot, do you think you could mail something for me tomorrow or the next day?" Joey nodded yes and Jack went into the guest room and got a box with Benjamin's CD's inside. Handing the box and an address to Joey he explained, "I borrowed these and forgot to return them. Joey looked at the address and Aidan and said, "My honest and upstanding brother."

Jack woke to the smell of bacon and fresh brewed Kona coffee. He got dressed, shaved and brushed his teeth and wandered out to the kitchen. Aidan had the table all set and was stacking pancakes on a plate.

"Morning Jack, sleep well?"

"Surprisingly well, actually."

Aidan turned and called out, "Joey, honey, hurry up and get in here, breakfast is getting cold!" The three men ate breakfast in silence, everything was delicious. Aidan missed his calling, Jack thought, he should cook for a living, and said the same to his brother and Aidan. Aidan lit up and put his hand on Jack's shoulder. "Keep that thought Jack. I've got to get ready for work." He excused himself and disappeared down the hall and into their bedroom. Joey got up, put some nitrile gloves on and started fixing soapy water to wash the dirty dishes.

Jack asked him, "How much is this fucker expecting from you?"

"Eight hundred dollars, it started as Four hundred," was Joeys answer. Jack asked his little brother to sit at the table with him, so Joey pulled off the gloves he was wearing and sat down. Jack looked his little brother in the eyes.

"You have to do what I ask you, okay? No questions,"

"Sure, Jack, of course."

"I need a dark sweatshirt and a dark baseball cap and grab me a couple pair of those gloves."

Joey jumped up and pulled two sets of gloves from beneath the sink and tossed them on the table as he hurried to the bedroom. After a few minutes Joey returned with a black baseball cap with a rainbow on it and a black sweatshirt with the same rainbow." Jack took them and shook his head but said "Great, these will work." Aidan walked out and announced he was going to work. Jack was happy, he needed to talk with Joey some more, alone. Aidan kissed Joey and put his hand on Jacks shoulder and left. Jack drank his coffee and waited a minute before continuing, "I'm going to come to work with you until Vincent shows up. You can say I'm your new employee. Everything needs to stay the same with this guy, okay?"

"Yes."

"How do you give him the money?"

"In a small, plain white envelope", Joey answered.

Jack pulled out his wallet and counted out eight crisp one hundred dollar bills. "Here, take these and put them in an envelope like you regularly do."

Joey took the money and stared at his brother. "Where did you...?" But Jack interrupted him, "When this fucker gets here do as you're told, and don't call the cops when he leaves. Okay?"

"Yes." Joey answered and pressed his hands together. He was scared and a bit confused.

Jack asked, "Can you gay me up for this?"

Joey burst out laughing at that question. "I would love to 'gay you up'!" Joey continued laughing. "My husband will love it! He's always had a little crush on you."

Jack scrunched up his face and shook his head. "I'm not joining your team, you bonehead, I just want Beneventi to think I'm not a threat, Okay?"

"Okay." Joey answered and jumped up to get his make-up case.

About thirty minutes later, Jack got up from the kitchen table and looked in the mirror, "Holy shit, Joseph, I'm a flamer!"

Joey rolled his eyes and said, "Fred and Gladys would have a cow if they could see you now."

Jack shook his head, walked over and stuck his finger in Joey's face. "If any of this ever gets back to Hoffman, I'll kick your ass!" He smiled so Joey understood his big brother was only kidding him.

The first day was very quiet, just a few customers and no sign of Vincent Beneventi. Aidan showed up around 5:00 pm. He noticed the makeup on Jack immediately. "Oh my." Aidan gasped.

Jack said, "Don't get excited, I'm wearing this for Vincent. I want him to think I'm a gay employee and not a threat."

The three of them went to the house in Cathedral City after they closed the shop and had another fantastic meal prepared by Aidan. The talk at dinner was all about Jack and his new look. Jack just sat and shook his head through most of the meal. At one point he said, "Enough, already." Aidan and Joey giggled but stopped talking about it. Jack liked being with Joey and Aidan, they were a wonderful, gentle couple. He may just stay with them longer than a few days, Joey had said something about him staying longer so it shouldn't be a problem.

The second day several hours went by. The shop had three times the customers than the previous day. "Man Jose Consignment" took in a lot of new inventory and made a lot of money. Joey started counting the bills in the cash register. Aidan showed up again around 5:00 pm and started helping shut down the store for the evening. Jack went in the back to look for a vacuum cleaner that was supposedly there. Aidan turned off the "Open" sign and was reaching to lock the front door when Vincent Beneventi burst in. Instead of his trademark bat, he carried a small pistol in his hand. He put it up to Aidan's head and yelled to Joey, "Your faggot friend is dead if you don't have my money!"

Jack heard the commotion and stayed out of sight in the back. He peeked through the crack of the door and put his hand on Chucho's silver .38. Joey pulled the white envelope out, started waving it and said loudly, "Don't hurt him, I've got your money right here!" Vincent snatched the envelope, tore it open and counted it. He looked at the cash register and asked Joey, "How much is in there?"

Joey quickly said, "I'm not certain, it's a lot."

Vincent released Aidan and told Joey, "I'll be taking it all with me, for my trouble." Joey scooped the money from the register and handed all of it to the mobster. Vincent sneered at the couple, "You two cock suckers have a gay old time, I'll see you next month." He turned and disappeared out the front door. Aidan ran to the door and turned the dead bolt. He rushed back to Joey and they embraced.

Joey was sobbing and Aidan was comforting him. "It's okay, he's gone. We're okay. Please don't cry." Joey suddenly yelled, "Jack, Jack, are you here?" His brother was not in the back of the store anymore. When Vincent exited out the front, Jack went out the back, fired up the red

Camry and was driving down Palm Canyon Drive, three cars behind Vincent Beneventi's Silver El Dorado.

Vincent made two more stops. Both times, he parked the car and sat for a few minutes to make sure no one was following him. He scoured the area for any vehicle that may be a police vehicle. Then he went into the business for a few minutes and each time returned to his car carrying a white envelope which he, casually, stuck in his inside coat pocket before driving off. Jack watched him from the rental car. He pulled out a few cars behind the mobster and followed him onto Date Palm Drive and eventually onto the freeway heading east. Jack was very careful to stay a safe distance behind so the mobster wouldn't suspect anything. He followed the silver Caddy for about an hour until it exited the highway at Desert Center. "Where, the fuck, are you going Vincent?" Jack asked out loud. Vincent drove a few more miles before entering a small community. The sign said Lake Tamarisk, "A lovely place to retire.", there was another smaller sign that said, "Please be respectful of your neighbors in Lovely Lake Tamarisk." Jack came around the corner just as the garage door of a small home opened and the mobster pulled his silver Cadillac in and shut it off. Jack stopped two houses down the street and turned off the car's headlights. Vincent walked out of the garage, looked up and down the street, returned to the garage, and a few seconds later the garage door closed. Jack sat in his rental car and waited. He took a wet wipe and cleaned the makeup his brother had put on him from his face. Lights came on and went off throughout Beneventi's house. Jack pulled out a smoke and lit it, he may be here a while. Finally, three cigarettes and nearly an hour later he climbed out of the Camry, put on the dark sweatshirt and the dark baseball hat, stuffed some things in his pocket, and started for the small house. The neighborhood was quiet. It looked as if the houses on either side of Vincent's house were vacant. They both had for sale signs in the overgrown front lawns, and they were both dark. No lights or movement to be seen in either house. Vincent has the perfect hiding place in this small retirement community, Jack thought to himself. No wonder the cops can't find him. He checked his watch, 9:25 pm. He felt for the silver pistol. It was still there and cold to the touch.

After watching Vincent's house for an additional half hour, Jack saw Vincent's house go completely dark. Being there for that length of time gave Jack time to map the layout of the house in his head. The master bedroom was in the front, East, corner. The kitchen was in the back as well as another bedroom. Jack had peeked through a few windows in the vacant homes to help him figure all this out, they were the exact same model home. He eventually was able to peek into the mobster's house a few times, also. If Vincent had a wife or if there was anyone else living there, they weren't at home. Jack was sure Vincent Beneventi was alone tonight. He slowly and deliberately made his way to the back of the house. No dogs in the back yard, that was good. He visually scoured the outside of the house. No security cameras another good thing, but Vincent had a motion sensing floodlight. Shit! No good! Jack eased into the back yard moving slowly, but the light came on and bathed the entire back yard in a bright white light. He stooped low and watched for lights to come on inside, but none did. Eventually the motion light extinguished. He moved another forty feet and the light came on again, again he stooped down and waited. One more move about the same distance and he would be at the back door. The motion light extinguished again. Jack raced to the back porch and the light came on before he got there. Jack pulled the pair of green nitrile gloves Joey had given him out of his pocket, slipped them on and tried the sliding glass door. It was locked. He glanced in Vincent's windows, the entire house was dark. Jack's heart was pounding trying to exit his chest, a rhythmic thump, thump, thump. He gave up on trying to wait out the motion light and worked on gaining entry while being bathed in the full white light. Jack checked the first window beside the door, same as the sliding door it was locked. The second window, a bigger one was unlocked. You gotta be kidding me, Jack thought to himself, Vincent must feel completely safe here if he leaves a window unlocked. He couldn't believe his luck. He slid it open without a sound and waited with his hand on Chucho's .38. There was no movement or lights from inside. If for some reason Vincent appeared in the window Jack would shoot him in his fat face. The noise from the weapon would arouse the neighbors but he was sure he could get to the Camry and get the fuck out of there before anyone saw him. Finally, Jack climbed through the window and found himself standing exactly where he thought, in the kitchen. He sat in a kitchen chair and placed the silver pistol on the table, waiting for the motion light to time out. He was a sitting duck until the light timed out. Jack listened for any sound. In a minute or so the light extinguished and he sat some more so his eyes could adjust to the dark. He listened and could make out soft snoring from the front bedroom. He got up and inched his way towards the sleeping mobster. The snoring was louder now. He was, literally, within feet of the beefy mobster. He held the .38 in front of him as he entered the bedroom. It was lighter in the bedroom and he could see Vincent soundly sleeping in his bed. Jack pointed the weapon at Vincent in case he woke up. If he did Jack would shoot him in the head, he had no qualms about that. If the fat fuck of a mobster woke up, he was a dead man, but the snoring continued. In the corner a small light illuminated the room. Jack looked closer, it was a Sponge Bob Square Pants nightlight. The irony of a tough mobster sleeping with a child's night light was not lost on Jack, He chuckled out loud. He held the pistol level, in front of him as he approached the bed. He stood for a few seconds watching Vincent sleep, before finally raising the silver weapon up and slamming it down, hard, on Vincent's head. It exploded and the noise was sickening. Droplets of bright red blood splattered the headboard and the clean white pillowcase as well as Joey's Black sweatshirt. The sheets around Vincent's head were starting to stain in crimson. The mobster groaned loudly and started pushing the covers down. Jack hit him again with the pistol. Vincent lay motionless, but still breathing, albeit shallowly. Jack pulled some plastic zip ties from his pocket and zip tied the mobster's hands together. He threw off the covers and zip tied the mobster's feet, also. Vincent was wearing striped boxer shorts and black dress socks. He pulled the socks off Vincent's feet and crammed them into the fat man's mouth. Jack walked around turning on lights and exploring each and every room. He was alone with the beast who had beaten his little brother. While looking through the garage he found a roll of duct tape and some rope. He, immediately, went back and tied Vincent's hands to his feet and tied both to the bed frame. Then he duct-taped Vincent's sock filled mouth. He thought about taping his eyes, also, but decided, if, and when the fat mobster woke up, he wanted him to look directly into the eyes of the person who broke in to kill him. The mobster's hair was saturated in bright scarlet blood and was matted to his face. Jack spoke to the still unconscious man, "You don't look so good big guy. Kinda puny. You should have that wound looked at." Jack lit a cigarette and waited for Vincent Beneventi, the gangster to wake up.

It was about ten minutes before Vincent Beneventi finally stirred, came to his senses and focused his eyes. Jack was sitting on the bed, still holding the gun while he sat counting money and smiling from ear to ear. A cigarette dangled precariously from his lips. He had found money in Vincent's coat pocket and in various other places around the house. He fanned over $7000 out and held it close to Vincent and said to him, "I'll be taking all this with me, for my trouble." Jack winked at him.

Vincent's eyes grew wide and he stared at Jack trying to figure out who his tormentor was. Jack pointed Chucho's .38 at Vincent's face. Fright gripped Vincent and he started thrashing around. Jack raised the pistol over his head like he was going to hit the mobster again and Vincent shook his head and settled down.

Jack stared at the piece of shit lying hogtied on the bed, and asked him, "How should I kill your fat ass, Vincent?" But Jack knew tonight's script, he had already thought it through in his head. He knew exactly how this cock sucker was going to die and it wasn't going to be pleasant. Jack was enjoying his little act. He put his finger to his lips as if he were pondering the matter. "What to do?" he asked out loud. He finally pressed the pistols barrel against the mobster's forehead. Vincent made a squealing noise and tried to turn away. Jack squeezed the trigger. The pistol just clicked. "Oh shit", Jack said, staring into the open end of the gun's barrel, a definite no no for anyone who has ever had gun training. "Did I forget to load any bullets in this thing?" He shoved it, hard, into Vincent's duct taped mouth, he heard some teeth break. Vincent scrunched his eyes and squealed again. Jack squeezed the trigger and, again, the gun just clicked. Sweat beads broke out all over the mobster's forehead, and he shook his head. Jack turned the pistol sideways like the gangsters in the movies and on TV. He pulled the trigger four more times in quick succession and still the pistol only clicked. Jack had emptied the six bullets from the gun while the mobster was out cold and had the ammo in his pants pocket. "I guess I did forget to load bullets." He taunted Vincent. A wet stain formed on Vincent's underwear and he started to cry. Big tears rolled down his cheeks and onto the bed. Jack stood up, and in a voice a parent would use for a toddler, he tilted his head and asked, "Did wittle Vinny pee his pants?" He threw the gun at the crying mobster and it hit him in the chest and bounced onto the carpeted floor. Jack bent down and grabbed a red, plastic gas can he had found in the garage. His nostrils flared a bit from the sweet, benzene smell of the amber liquid. He lifted the gas can and poured its entire contents onto Vincent and his bed. When it was empty, Jack threw that at Vincent as well. Vincent was choking from the gas fumes and struggling to get free. Jack had found a box of wooden matches on the kitchen stove, he pulled one out and struck it on the side of the box. He held the burning stick in the air, smiling a huge toothy grin at the tough guy mobster with the piss stained boxers. Vincent was making screeching noises now. Jack threw the match on the bed and ran for the back door. The sound of the gas igniting was overwhelming, the concussion hit Jack in the back, and he stumbled and fell to the kitchen floor. Vincent continued the screeching noise. Jack stood up, unlocked the sliding door, and ran to the Camry.

-Chapter 11-

Sandra Schulz got in her car and drove to the hospital to sit with the young girl, Victoria, again. She and Karl had talked for hours last night lying in bed together, about Victoria and her future. "We should just adopt her, Karl!" Susan blurted out at one point during their conversation.

Karl frowned and asked, "What?"

"Well, we have two extra bedrooms, now that Kaitlyn is in College, and even if she moves back home after College, we still have plenty of room."

"I don't think you can just adopt someone when they still have family, Sandra. She said she was an orphan, but she still has family, somewhere."

Sandra walked into the hospital lobby, stopped in the gift store and bought Victoria a small cuddly teddy bear and some daisies in a small vase and got on the elevator for the third floor.

Victoria was laying in the hospital bed watching 'Price is Right' when her sister and brother-in-law walked in. Celina ran to the bed and hugged her little sister. Rudy stayed by the door watching the hall, he looked at Victoria and nodded to her.

"How did you know where I was?" Victoria asked Celina.

"Some cops talked to us about Chucho and asked us if we knew where he was at. They said you was here." Celina told her sister.

Victoria cautiously looked at Rudy and told Celina, "I ain't going back to him when he shows up. He tried to kill me, he hit me with his gun. I thought I was gonna die. I don't know what I'm gonna do or where I'm going to live but he ain't gonna be in my life no more."

Celina leaned in close to Victoria and told her, "Rudy ain't gonna let you live with us so don't even go there. He's loyal to Chucho and won't have none of your bullshit in our place."

Victoria shook her head, "Some white people have been helping me. They've been really nice to me and can't wait for Hector to be born." Victoria saw the puzzled look on Celina's face. "Hector is what I'm naming my baby. Papi would be happy about that."

Sandra had just exited the elevator and saw the big Mexican biker leaning out of Victoria's room watching the hall. He stepped inside the room when it was obvious the white lady carrying a vase full of flowers, was here to visit Victoria. Sandra knocked on the open door and peeked in at Victoria. Victoria's face lit up and she motioned for Sandra to come in. Sandra set the flowers on a table and handed the teddy bear to Victoria who hugged it to her chest. Rudy stepped around Sandra and stepped out of the room anxiously looking around. Victoria addressed Sandra, "Thank you for the little bear, I love him." She pointed at Celina, "This is my big sister Celina, Sis this is Sandra. She's been helping me a lot."

Sandra held her hand out to Celina who just smiled and nodded but didn't take Sandra's hand. Rudy looked in the room and said, "Celina, let's roll."

Celina told her sister, "I love you baby." She kissed and hugged Victoria and swept past Sandra without acknowledging her.

Rudy grabbed Celina by her arm and the two of them went down the hall towards the elevators never looking back. Sandra turned to Victoria and apologized, "I hope they didn't leave because of me. They could have stayed, and I would have come back later."

Victoria shrugged her shoulders and said, "They don't like white people." Her face flushed and she quickly tried to fix what she had blurted out, "I'm sorry, that sounded bad, they don't know how much you've helped me. Rudy makes Celina act like that, he's a bad guy. I'm just happy Karl wasn't here, him and Rudy might get into it with each other." Sandra was happy about that, as well. Karl was a wonderful man but did not like gangsters.

Later that morning, at work, Karl went over the conversation he had had with Sandra the night before. Sandra was excited and dearly wanted to adopt Victoria Ramirez. Karl got online and checked the adoption laws in Nevada and California. He had talked with a few of the other guys at work, including his newly promoted, and once again, partner, Mike Briggs, and they all had said they thought anyone could adopt anybody for any reason, family or not. The fact that Victoria was only sixteen might make it harder, however. "Go talk to her Mother in California," Mike said to Karl, "Tell her how much better Victoria's life would be if she lived with you and Sandra. Make sure to bring up the baby."

So here he was, staring at a computer screen, sorting through all the legal jargon associated with adoption laws in both states. He realized that he was considering what Susan had suggested about adopting the young girl. He called an old friend, Brad, who happened to be a lawyer and told him all about Victoria, the pregnant teen with no home and the discussions he and Sandra had last night. Brad said, "Karl, sounds like you and Sandra are serious about this."

Karl downplayed it a bit. "Oh, we were just tossing some ideas around, we're just trying to help her out. She has a mother in California in some type of halfway house, cleaning herself up."

Brad said to Karl, "Stop by my office, I'll draw up some papers that you can take to the girl's mother. Explain to her that Victoria and her baby would be better off living with the two of you and try to get her to sign the teen over to you. Her parental rights, that is."

Karl hung up and called Sandra. He told her what Brad had told him. Sandra told him about meeting Celina and Rudy in Victoria's room and how they had acted towards her. Karl said, "They aren't good people. We need to get them out of Victoria's life."

Sandra agreed and said to him, "I'll meet you at the hospital, we can both talk to Victoria first and then maybe drive to California and talk to her mother. She may not want to live with us, let alone be adopted by us." Karl checked his watch and agreed to meet Sandra in about an hour.

There was a lot going on in Victoria's room when they arrived. There was a Doctor sitting with the teen going over some paperwork with her. Karl interrupted, "'Scuse me, what's going on?" He asked.

The Doctor turned and looked at Karl and Sandra standing there. "We are getting Victoria ready to be discharged, are you two family?"

Karl and Sandra both shook their heads in unison. "No".

Karl told the Doctor, "But she has nowhere to go if you discharge her."

The Doctor seemed puzzled, he turned to Victoria. "I was under the impression you had family picking you up and taking you home." He looked at the teen. Victoria looked sheepishly around the room and shook her head no. The Doctor asked the nurse, "Didn't you tell me she had family coming for her?"

The nurse shot a nasty look at Victoria, "She obviously lied to me."

The Doctor turned to Victoria, "Do you need us to contact Social Services to help you get placed somewhere?"

Karl stepped closer to the Doctor and said, "We'll take her to our home. We know her and she's welcome to stay with us."

Sandra stood by the bed and asked the young girl, "Victoria honey, would you like to come stay with us for a while?"

Karl added, "Until you get on your feet again?" He sat next to the teen, "You can't go back to Flavio, Victoria. He's looking at some time in prison once we find him."

Sandra took the girl's hand. "Come stay with us, you'll be safe with us."

Victoria liked Sandra she had been very nice to her the past few days. "I think I'd like that." She finally announced.

The Doctor said, "Well, that's that." He signed the paperwork and left to visit another patient.

Jack sat at the bar in the Spotlight 29 Casino nursing a very strong Bloody Mary. He was looking at the breakfast menu and keeping an eye on the news on the television above the bar. No dead bikers and no dead mobsters were mentioned. Jack started to wonder if Chucho was even dead. Maybe the biker had awakened in the river, swam to the bank and was somewhere, right now, looking for Jack. No, he shook his head, he's dead, I saw his brains when I pushed him into the river. The female bartender startled Jack, "Some breakfast, hon?" "Uh", Jack looked at her, "A couple eggs, over medium, hash browns and bacon, please." He answered. "And I'll have another of these." He lifted the half empty drink for her to see.

Rudy sat on the idling Harley Knucklehead and waited while Celina checked out. He couldn't figure where Chucho was. He must be back in Chino or somewhere close to there, hiding out. Rudy had made several phone calls to people back home, but no one had heard from their leader. Rudy was frustrated, Chucho always kept him in the loop, he was the leader's right hand, man. Celina ran out holding her purse and climbed on the back of the bike behind her husband. Rudy kicked the bike into 1st and slowly rolled through the parking lot. Celina asked, "Can we stop real quick at the hospital and check on Victoria?" Rudy groaned and said, "We ain't got time for that Celina." "Please Rudy, just a minute. I may never see her again." She knew Chucho would be pissed at Victoria and may harm her again or the white people may take her away from her family. Rudy reluctantly said, "Okay," and headed for the hospital. Within fifteen minutes they were pulling into the hospital parking lot. Rudy stopped suddenly and Celina asked him, "What's goin' on?"

He pointed and Celina saw her sister being helped into the white couple's SUV.

"Fuck, Rudy! Now what?"

Rudy said, "Sorry babe, you ain't seeing your little sis today." And he twisted the throttle, let out the clutch and hauled ass out of there towards Chino, California.

Karl helped Sandra get the pregnant girl to their SUV. He gave his wife a kiss and waved to Victoria, "See you both tonight." A loud motorcycle revved and sped out of the hospital's parking lot, the noise of it was overwhelming. Karl stood and watched it roar down the street. He said, "Where's a cop when you need one?" And chuckled at his own joke. He settled into the police cruiser and was buckling his seat belt when Lilly's voice crackled over the radio.

"Karl, you got a copy?"

He scooped up the microphone, "I'm here Lilly."

"Karl, Needles P.D. found a 419 in the Colorado River and are asking if we have any missing persons." Lilly waited for the detective's response. 419 was code for a dead body.

"Who is the contact in Needles?" Karl asked the dispatcher.

"Detective Bryant." She answered him.

"Bill Bryant? I know Bill, I'll give him a call." Karl had Detective Bryant's phone number in his cell phone, he dialed it and a voice answered. "Detective Bryant, how can I help you?"

"Billy, it's Karl from Laughlin."

"Hey Karl, are you calling about the dead guy we pulled out of the Colorado?"

"Yep", Karl answered him and continued, "We aren't missing anyone, as far as I know. Is it a homeless guy from one of the River camps?"

"I don't think so, Karl. This guy has a bunch of gold jewelry and is wearing a Rolex Daytona. The body's in bad shape but it's a Hispanic guy."

"No I.D., I assume?"

"None, we're checking dental records and fingerprints, as we speak. Just thought you might be missing someone."

"Nope."

"Okay, well, I've got to go. I'm checking other jurisdictions upriver. Take care Karl."

"You too."

Jack pulled into Joey and Aidan's driveway and knocked on the door. A sleepy Joey in a silk robe answered it and excitedly said, "Jack!

Oh my God! I couldn't sleep worrying that crazy mobster had hurt, or maybe killed you." He pulled his big brother into the small house. "Aidan!" he called out, "Aidan, get out here, Jack is safe!" Aidan ran out and the two of them hugged Jack.

An hour later, Jack had filled them in on what had happened the previous night. Jack left out the fact he had hogtied the gangster and set his house on fire and he changed some of the details. "Tell me again", Aidan asked Jack, "You threatened him and he's going to leave us alone now?"

Jack was careful with his words, "I followed him to a house in Indio," He lied, "When he parked in his garage, I jumped out and pointed a gun at him and told him he was a dead man if he ever came to your shop again."

"And he pissed his pants?"

"Yep, he pissed his pants, right there in his garage. I took his gun and all his money."

Jack pulled an envelope stuffed with seven thousand dollars, out of his pocket and set it on the table. "This money is compliments of Vincent Beneventi." He told them both while patting the fat envelope. Jack continued his tall tale, "I threw the gun into a dumpster at a Wendy's in Indio." Part of that was true, Jack had stopped at a Wendy's and dropped the bullets from Chucho's gun into the dumpster. This lying stuff was starting to come easy to Jack Martin. "You sure he won't be back, again?" Joey asked. "Guarantee it!" Jack answered and thought of the burnt, lifeless body the authorities had, most likely, found by now.

-Chapter 12-

Karl had been at the office for an hour or so. No one had seen, nor heard from, Chucho Valdez, he had simply vanished from the face of the earth. "He's probably back in Chino by now." He said to Mike who was going through his emails and not paying attention to Karl, but nodded in response. "I'm sure he has a bunch of rat holes there to hide in. He's gonna be very hard to find." Mike still wasn't listening but nodded again. Karl announced to Mike, "I'm going to Safeway across the river. They have a Starbuck's there. You want something?" This time Mike was paying attention, He asked Karl, "Can you grab me a Caramel Macchiato?" Mike started digging for his wallet. Karl waved him off and stood. He said to his old partner who was now his new partner, "You look better in a suit and tie, big guy."

Mike looked down and straightened his tie and said, "Thanks, I think."

As soon as Karl left the parking lot at Safeway heading back to the office his cell phone rang, and he answered it. He was holding a tall paper cup of hot coffee and the phone and trying to steer so he tucked the phone under his chin and said "Hello, this is Schulz."

Bill Bryant was on the other end, "Karl, the dentals and fingerprints came back. The dead guy is Flavio Valdez, you know him?"

Karl dropped the phone on the floor. He reached down and fumbled around trying to retrieve it. The coffee cup spilled on the cruiser's front seat. The police car drifted into the other lane and the guy in the car beside him honked and flipped Karl the bird. Karl swung the car to the shoulder and braked. He could hear the gravel crunching under the cruiser's tires. He put the phone to his ear and was probably way too loud when he spit out, "Holy Crap, Bill!" He calmed himself and told

Bill, "Sandra and I have Valdez's girlfriend at our home right now, she's living with us. Chucho beat her up four or five days ago." Karl counted the days in his head. He sat and looked out the windshield watching cars zoom past him. "Holy Crap!" He repeated as Bill gave him more details.

Jack decided under the circumstances he needed to leave the area. He called the Southwest Airlines 1-800 number and asked about flights to Denver from Palm Springs, leaving today or tomorrow. A woman with a Southern accent said, "No Sir, I checked all the flights out of Palm Springs to Denver in the next two days. Everything is full and right now I have people on standby for every flight to Denver. I am so sorry."

Jack asked her, "What do you suggest?"

She answered him, "Well sir, if you can travel in four days, I can get you out of Palm Springs and to Denver leaving at..."

Jack interrupted her, "No ma'am, it has to be today or tomorrow. Money is not an issue." "I'm sorry sir. Please hold." He heard her typing on a keyboard.

"The only other thing I could suggest would be flying out of Ontario, California. There is a direct flight out of Ontario to Denver this evening leaving at 7:25 pm getting into Denver at 10:48 pm."

"How far is Ontario from Palm Springs, do you have any idea?"

"I think it's about a seventy mile, or so, drive. Ya'll should be able to drive it in just over an hour, depending on traffic. I'd allow an extra twenty minutes if I was you."

That would have to do, he thought, it was a small detour, no big deal. He went ahead and booked the flight. He packed his belongings, said goodbye to his brother and brother-in-law. They hugged Jack and thanked him for helping rid them of Vincent Beneventi. Jack thought if they only knew what really happened to Vincent. They walked Jack to the red Camry and waved as he drove down the street. Jack stopped and fueled up before heading West, through the desert, to the Ontario Airport. He got to the Airport Terminal about four hours early, so he found the nearest bar. The place was packed for March Madness. #4 Villanova was playing #2 North Carolina and they were tied with 3:12 left in the game. Jack was lucky, he had walked into the bar just as a man and his wife were putting on their jackets to leave. Jack stood behind them and slid into one of the open chairs when they left. He was staring in the mirror behind the bar at the crowd behind him when a cute young lady yelled to him, "What'll you have, sir?" He thought for several seconds and finally said. "I'll have a Jack straight up and a water, no ice." It was so noisy in the bar she had to lean in very close to Jack. Jack realized she hadn't heard him, and he repeated his order. "Jack straight up and water." He yelled it this time. The female bartender nodded and headed off. He couldn't get the two dead men out of his head. Chucho laying on the concrete wall with his brains hanging out of his open head, and Vincent hog tied and choking, his eyes wide with fear staring at the match that would burn him to a crisp. He held his hand out in front of him, it was shaking, uncontrollably. He quickly put it down and looked around to see if anyone had noticed. A man in a black leather coat was staring at Jack. Jack turned back to his drink. Who was the guy and why was he watching him? Jack shifted a bit in his seat, he could see the man in the mirror. The man shifted also and was still looking at Jack. "Fuck." Jack said under his breath so only he could hear it. He wondered if this guy was a cop or maybe F.B.I. Everything that had happened in the last few days was starting to sink in. Jack surveyed the bar. It was getting even more crowded now. Everyone outside the bar wanted to see what was so exciting on the televisions so they crammed in to watch too. The waitstaff had all but given up trying to maneuver through the crowd. Four or five people who couldn't find seats together were crowded in tight behind Jack and one of the women had a big leather purse that kept hitting him in the back. Jack did not like being this close to other people. Jack started feeling claustrophobic and he still couldn't figure out why the guy in the black leather coat was staring at him. He felt like he wasn't breathing enough, he couldn't get enough air. His ears started to ring lightly, and his vision narrowed to a tunnel. Jack knew what was happening, he was starting to have a full-blown panic attack.

The guy behind Jack in the black leather coat was watching the basketball game on the TV just above Jack's head. He couldn't figure out why the guy below the TV kept looking back at him, and every time he shifted to see the TV better the guy under it did the same and blocked his view. Finally, the guy under the TV jumped up and quickly headed out of the bar. The guy in the black leather coat watched Jack as he tried to work his way through the crowded bar. He doesn't look good he thought to himself and went back to watching the game. He had a grand on North Carolina.

Jack suddenly felt like he had to leave and get outside. He left his drink and tried to work his way through the crowded bar. The feeling of claustrophobia was over whelming and he needed to be outside where he could find more air. Jack finally made it through the crowd and into the terminal. His breathing was labored, and it felt like he was about to pass out, so he sat down, next to a recycle bin, on the dirty worn carpet. He looked around and people were watching him with concern, he tried to say something, but nothing came out of his mouth. People came over and were asking him questions, but he couldn't hear them. Jack's vision narrowed and his ears were buzzing, he slumped over and lost consciousness. A minute later, Jack opened his eyes and looked around. Several people were around him in a circle talking to him, but he still couldn't hear them. He threw up on the floor beside the recycle bin. Within seconds the buzzing in his ears was replaced by several people asking him if he was okay, to which he replied "Yes, I'm fine. I just need to lay here for a few minutes." Paramedics arrived, while Jack was laying on the floor, and immediately started a saline drip. An oxygen mask was placed on his face and a young woman in uniform applied a cool compress to his forehead. She smiled and told Jack, "Just lay there and relax a few minutes, we're giving you some fluid and you should begin to feel better soon." Jack did as he was told and, just as promised, he started to feel less sick but more embarrassed. A Hispanic woman showed up with a mop and smeared the vomit around but got the majority of it out of the carpet. Jack struggled to his feet, with some help, and stood there answering questions.

"Are you still dizzy?"

"No."

"What is your name?"

"Jack Martin."

"What's the date?"

"March 19th."

"Who's the President?"

"Barack Obama."

When the paramedics were satisfied that Jack was okay, they removed the I.V., had Jack sign a few release forms, packed up their gear and left. Jack gingerly walked out the terminal's doors, a young man about eighteen years old was beside him holding his arm the whole way. Jack thanked the nice young man and sat on a bench outside the Airport terminal and watched the people coming and going. After about ten minutes he got up and returned to the bar. The bar was about half as full as before. His drink was gone. He still owed the bartender for the drink. He waved at her and asked, "What do I owe you?" She answered, "Nine fifty." Jack put a Twenty Dollar bill on the bar and headed to the gate for his flight to Denver. He looked at his watch, he still had over two and a half hours before they would start boarding his flight to Denver International Airport.

Karl had seen a few dead bodies in his short career, and it had not bothered him, but standing in the Coroner's cooler looking down at the bloated and bruised dark colored body of Flavio Valdez was completely different. The dead biker's head was split, nearly, in two. The red and pink goo that was once his brain had big chunks missing from it. Karl assumed that fish had been feeding on the contents of the Mexican's head as he floated downriver. One of Flavio's eyes, the left one, was wide open and staring straight ahead. The other eye was swollen shut and bruised a dark black and blue. Both of the biker's hands were curled by rigamortis and were black. He had been wearing shoes, Karl assumed, but they were gone. He had one sock on and one bare foot, and the bare foot was black, also, up to his ankle. "This is definitely Flavio Chucho Valdez." He told the Coroner. The Coroner handed Karl a clip board with papers on it and a pen. Karl signed his name and handed the clip board back. Now, Karl thought, how do I tell Victoria that her former boyfriend is laying in a drawer in the Needles Morgue?

Jack found a section of the airport terminal that was under construction. The workers were gone, and it was very quiet. He set the alarm on his watch for an hour and fifteen minutes later. That should give him plenty of time to freshen up and return to the gate where his flight was leaving for Denver. He laid between two seats and shifted around until he found a comfortable spot. The vacant terminal was completely quiet, and Jack started to doze. He was just about to enter R.E.M. when an extremely heavy, noisy woman and her friend walked in laughing. They plopped down into a couple chairs just twenty feet from Jack. "Oh shit!" The heavy woman squealed to her friend, "Did you see the look on the T.S.A. guy's face when I told him off?" They both started laughing very loudly. Jack sat up and looked at the two women sitting there. "Oh man, Allie, you crack me up!" The smaller woman said to the heavy one.

Jack was not happy and pleaded, "Ladies, can you be a bit quieter, please?"

The heavy woman looked directly at him and yelled, "Can you shut the fuck up, please?" The two women roared with laughter, they were obviously very drunk. Jack thought of a line from the movie Animal House and he said it to the heavier of the two women, the one that had yelled at him. Jack quoted the movie line, "Fat, drunk and stupid is no way to go through life young lady!"

The heavy woman's smile disappeared, and she hurried over to Jack and started pummeling him with her fists. The smaller woman yelled, "Kick his ass, Allie!"

Jack stepped away from the large woman, held up his hands and said, "Look, Allie, please don't make me hit you." He thought if he used the name the smaller woman was calling her friend she may come to her senses and leave him alone. Allie snarled at Jack, "You don't know me, don't say my fucking name!" Jack tried to get away from the insane woman, but she grabbed him and swung him around. Jack lost his footing and fell to the carpeted floor. The crazy woman tried to kick him while he was down, but he swung his leg around and knocked her off her feet. She fell to the floor with a huge thud. She laid there stunned, Jack stood up and ran towards the busy terminal and safety. The smaller woman swung at him as he ran past her. He grabbed her arm and pushed her away from him, she knocked a trash can down while falling to the floor. Jack ran towards the terminal, never looking back.

Karl and Sandra were at home sitting across the dining room table from Victoria. He had just told her about Flavio. He intentionally left out the part about him floating in the river, with his brains hanging out. She stuck her lower lip out, but never cried and finally said, "He was not a good person. I saw him do terrible things to people. To me, too. My baby and I are better off without him."

Karl and Sandra both nodded yes. Victoria had called Social Services and they had set her up in a shelter for unwed mothers. She could move in Wednesday of next week. Sandra desperately wanted the young girl to stay with them, but Victoria wanted to live in the shelter, where she wouldn't be a burden to anyone and she could be around others like her. Karl told her he and Sandra would both drive her to the shelter and stay until she was settled in and comfortable, and they would visit every day. The phone on the kitchen wall rang and startled all three of them.

Karl jumped up and answered it. "Hello? This is he. Oh yeah! How are you Todd?" He listened for a few minutes while Todd talked. Finally, Karl asked Todd, "What does that have to do with me?" He paused, listening. "Wow! Are you sure?" Another pause. "Wow! Thanks, I'll be there in the morning." And Karl hung up.

"What happened?" Sandra was curious and wanted to know.

"Excuse us Victoria." Karl said to the girl, walking down the hall pulling Sandra behind him and into the bedroom, closing the door. Sandra was confused and started to ask something, but Karl started talking excitedly, "That was Todd Paulson, a detective in Riverside County. Some mobster, I think he said the guy's name was Benefetti, or something like that, was tied up, beaten and his house set on fire somewhere between Blythe and Indio in the Mojave Desert. I asked him what that had to do with me. Todd said he had heard about Chucho Valdez being found dead floating in the Colorado River and Bill Bryant told Todd I was in charge of the investigation."

Susan was still confused, "I don't understand." She said shaking her head as if she were trying to clear it.

Karl continued, "They were digging through the ashes today and found a silver .38 pistol. They sent it to ballistics, and it came back registered to Flavio Valdez, Chino, California."

"Wow!" Sandra exclaimed.

"That's what I said!" Karl replied. The two of them stood and took it all in.

Jack was in the "A" group, he had paid extra money for that, so he was one of the first to board the plane. He headed to the very back of the long plane and sat in the window seat on the left. 36A. He buckled up and leaned his head against the window. His breathing got slower and within minutes he was fast asleep. He dreamed that Allie and Vincent Beneventi were stalking him in an empty office building. He was hiding in some type of closet and he could see the couple through the crack between the door and frame. They were holding baseball bats, checking every room looking for him. Just as they were ready to open the door to the closet where he was hiding, he heard a loud bell ding once. It startled him out of his sleep, and he opened his eyes and looked around. The guy next to him smiled at him. Jack was confused, he looked out the window, they were flying over snow covered foothills and he could see Denver's skyline off in the distance.

The bell dinged again, and a voice came over the speakers, "Uh, hello ladies and gentlemen. This is First Officer Golden. We are beginning our descent to D.I.A. and expect to be on the ground in about twenty minutes. The weather in Denver is a balmy 49 degrees, so you might want to get a jacket out of your carryon, once we're at the gate of course. Please, if you haven't done so already, return your seatbacks and tray tables to their original position and make sure your seatbelts are fastened. Flight attendants prepare for landing." Jack leaned against the window and dozed lightly. The thump of the plane's tires contacting the runway woke him again and he cleared his throat and sat up. Somewhere, in front of him, he heard Allie, the woman who had been trying to kill him. She was laughing at a high volume. He peeked through the seats and tried to locate her. She was three rows ahead of him. She would get off before him and he decided to hang back a little, so he didn't have to face her again.

Nearly everyone was off the plane and the cleaning crew was starting to pick up trash and wipe things down, when Jack decided it was probably safe to leave. He got up, exited the plane and walked up the ramp to 'C' Terminal. He sat down to give Allie more time to get ahead of him. He did not, ever, want to see that crazy bitch, again. After about ten full minutes he headed towards the escalators and down to the trains.

He exited the train and checked the arrival board to see where his luggage would be waiting. ***Southwest, Flight 362 from Ontario, Arrived, Baggage Claim 7, East Side***. His bag was the only one on baggage carousel 7. He scooped it up, pulled the handle out and headed out door 513 to the parking lot buses parked on row 3. He found the red bus with stop signs all over it and "The Parking Stop" printed on the side. He started up the steps of the bus just as a tall thin Middle Eastern man reached down and grabbed Jack's suitcase from him and stacked it in the rack beside several others. Jack thanked him and walked to the back of the bus and plopped into a seat. He was exhausted. The driver said something into the microphone, closed the door and pulled away from the curb. A loud voice yelled, "Stop that bus!" and the driver put on the brakes and opened the door. None other, than Allie, entered the bus and looked around for a seat. Jack slumped down behind the seat in front of him. He did not want the loud mouthed bitch to see him. In a loud voice she told a young man, "Scoot your ass over!" Which he did, and she dropped hard into the aisle seat next to the young man. The bus made several stops, and after ten minutes or so, Jack checked, there were five people left on the bus including Allie. Suddenly she yelled out, "Right here! Let me off! My car is right here!" The driver slammed on the brakes and the woman waddled down the steps. The driver set her suitcase on the gravel and stood waiting for the usual dollar tip, but Allie ignored him. He turned and climbed back onto the bus and into his seat and drove off. Jack stood and watched the heavy lady out the window. She seemed to be having trouble opening her trunk. Jack looked around and his truck was just a few rows over. Jack yelled to the driver, "I'll get off here!" Again, the driver slammed on the brakes. Jack grabbed his bag and was out the door before the driver had a chance to help him. Jack stood watching Allie while the bus drove off. She had the trunk open and was struggling to get her suitcase into it. Jack looked around and saw his truck a few aisles away and made a beeline for it. He opened the back door and put his suitcase on the back seat, locked the doors and headed back towards the obnoxious lady.

Allie Simmons was still struggling with her suitcase when he walked up behind her, she was cursing like a sailor. "God damn, fucking piece of shit." Her cheeks were bright red and beads of sweat formed all over her face as she stood there struggling with her bag. Jack could smell the pungent sweat on the woman, he grabbed her around the throat and neck and squeezed as tightly as he could. She tried to fight him off but was tired from the struggle with her suitcase. Jack kicked her foot out from under her and forced her to the gravel. He sat on her, pinning her arms to her chest, she kicked her feet and tried to scream but it came out as a gurgling sound. Jack was sweating and breathing heavily but was still squeezing her throat, now putting his entire weight into it. Allie was barely struggling now, her eyes bugged out and her face went from a bright red to a purplish color and when she finally went limp her face turned an ashen gray. She laid in the gravel staring into the starlit sky. Jack stood and looked around, there was no one in sight. The Parking Stop bus was several rows away. Too far away for anyone on it to see him or the dead woman. He was heaving now, he bent down and checked her for a pulse. The heavy lady named Allie was dead. Jack's pulse was racing. He emptied her purse in the gravel and took her wallet and put it in his pocket. Jack hurried back to his truck, huffing and puffing, and climbed in behind the steering wheel. He felt himself starting to panic again. He took several deep breaths and tried to figure out how he was going to get out of this mess. Jack looked at himself in the rearview mirror, he looked like a killer. His face was drenched in sweat and his hair was plastered down on his forehead. He felt as if he couldn't get enough air. He concentrated on his breathing, in through the nose and out through the mouth. In through the nose and out through the mouth. Several minutes passed and his panic attack subsided enough that he knew he wasn't in danger of passing out. The windows of the truck were fogged over and the condensation started dripping down. He wiped his face on his shirt and sat thinking.

Jack had been sitting in the dark cab of his truck, for about forty minutes. In that time, he had looked in the dead woman's wallet, there was over $2500 dollars in it. He took all but $50 and, after wiping the wallet off, he walked back a row and threw it back towards where Allie lay dead. He didn't want to leave the parking lot yet. When the authorities found the dead woman, the first thing they would do would be to check all the people in every vehicle that had left the lot this night. He needed to figure out how to stay here, at least until tomorrow morning, without being seen, but he couldn't be here if someone saw the dead lady and the cops showed up. How would he explain that? He decided to hide her body under her vehicle. No one would see it until it started to smell which may be days. No, that was a bad idea, she was way too heavy to move in the state he was in, also he had no gloves and he didn't need to leave DNA all around. He might have already left some on her throat as far as he knew. He said out loud, "Think Jack, think." He heard a voice in his head. It said, 'Look around, the answer is right outside the fence.' Jack had started hearing voices in the last few days. He glanced around and saw the Omni Hotel sign right away. The Hotel was less than a hundred yards away from the Parking Stop's perimeter fence, and the parking lot for the hotel butted up to the same perimeter fence. He would hop the fence and walk to the nearby hotel, check in and stay there a few days before retrieving his truck and driving home to safety. The problem with that plan would be showing his I.D. to the desk clerk. Every hotel required some form of I.D. to rent a room. He thought about this for a few minutes, going over it in his head. I need someone else's driver's license. He sat deep in thought and finally he jumped out, opened the back door of the truck, and started rifling through his suitcase. He remembered grabbing Chucho Valdez's wallet before he pushed the dead biker into the rolling river. The wallet was in his suitcase. He grabbed it and returned to the front seat of the truck. He emptied the wallet into his lap and started digging through everything.

There was over seven hundred dollars in the wallet, along with six I.D.s and seven credit cards. None of them with the name Flavio Valdez on them. He picked up the I.D.s and looked for one that may resemble his particulars. The very last one he looked at was a white man, Glenn Freeman, from Rancho Cucamonga, California, Fifty-Two years old, 5' 11", 195 lbs., with green eyes and grey hair. He was certain he could pass for this guy. Jack was six years younger and had blue eyes but, the rest was fairly accurate. He put the I.D. in his pocket along with the seven hundred dollars. He gathered everything in his lap and stuck it all under the front seat on the floor. He put his own wallet in the glove box and locked the glove box. Never can be too safe, there are a lot of dishonest people out there. Jack grabbed his suitcase, locked his truck and headed for the fence surrounding the parking lot.

The front entrance to the Omni Hotel sat just eighty yards from the fence surrounding the parking lot. Jack crossed the parking lot and then the manicured lawn and walked in the front entrance. He was greeted by a young blonde girl he estimated to be in her early twenties. He checked her name tag, it read, ***Hailey, Denver, Colorado***.

"Good evening sir, how may I help you?"

"Evening young lady, do you have any rooms?'

"Yes sir, we have a few available for tonight. Did you want to stay longer than just the one night?"

"Tonight, and tomorrow night, if I may."

"Of course, sir. Let me check." Hailey typed for several seconds and finally said, "I have a standard room, Two Queen beds, on the third floor available for both nights, umm, let's see, $198 per night. Will that work for you?" She asked.

"Yes", Jack answered her, "That will be fine."

"I'll need a credit card and driver's license, please." She smiled at Jack.

Jack fumbled around in his pocket and handed her Glenn Freeman's driver's license. "I lost my credit card this morning," Jack said with a sigh.

"Oh no, I'm so sorry." She commiserated.

Jack continued, "Can I just pay in cash?"

Hailey looked at the driver's license and looked back at Jack. There was a split second, where he thought about fleeing out the front door, but that would be a dead giveaway and Hailey would most likely call the authorities. She smiled at him and said, "Of course Mr. Freeman, I think under the circumstances we can forego the credit card." Well, that was certainly close, Jack thought and paid for the two nights plus a hundred dollars for a deposit. He got his key card and headed to the elevator. While he waited, he kept one eye on Hailey, she was busy typing on the computer and wasn't paying attention to him. That was good, he thought. The green light came on above the elevator and Jack stepped in and pushed 3. The room was nice, he walked to the window and looked out, he had a clear view of his truck and Allie's car and the dead body. "This will definitely work." He said out loud. He turned the room lights off and pulled the desk chair close to the window.

Jack had been watching the parking lot for over an hour, in the dark, and decided it was safe for him to shower and go to bed, he was spent. Off to the North he saw a small silver car drive close to the fence and stop in the Omni's back lot. Three teens got out and peeked over the fence into the parking lot. Jack looked at his watch, 11:42 pm. He watched the teens as they removed part of the fence and crawled through the resulting hole one after the other. They obviously had done this before. They went to the first car, a white four door sedan. Two of them tried all the doors first, while the third one siphoned gas from the cars tank into a red and silver can. Jack watched as one of them trying the doors pulled out some tools from a canvas bag. Within a minute one door was open and seconds later all the doors were open. They rifled through every nook and cranny, tossing everything they found of value into a cloth duffle bag. Within minutes the threesome finished and went on to the next car. Jack couldn't believe his luck they were just thirty yards away from the dead woman. He left the room and rode the elevator down one floor. He wandered around until he found a house phone by the service elevator. He picked up the receiver and waited. A cheery voice announced, "This is Hailey, how may I help you?"

"May I have an outside line to make a local call, please?"

"Absolutely," She answered him. He heard a few clicks and then a dial tone. He quickly dialed 911. "911, what is your emergency?" The female operator asked. Jack tried to disguise his voice, he made up some ridiculous accent on the spot,

"Hello, I'm staying in the Omni Hotel at D.I.A. and I just saw three teens breaking into cars at the parking lot next door. The 'Parking Stop.'"

"And what is your name, sir?"

"Oh my God!" Jack raised his voice a little, "I just heard a woman scream! Please hurry!" and he hung up the phone.

Within fifteen minutes three Denver Police Department cruisers came flying into the parking lot with lights flashing. A golf cart with a yellow light flashing came from the Parking Stop's office and followed the police cruisers. The officers immediately saw the three teens and apprehended them. Within minutes the teens were all standing with their hands cuffed behind their back and their heads down on the hood of one of the cruisers. The heavy man with a day glow vest on stood next to the teens talking to the Denver cop. Jack was sitting in the dark watching everything as it unfolded. The other two cruisers slowly drove around shining a spotlight on every car. Jack watched and waited. One of them finally turned down the aisle where Allie lay dead. The spotlight on the cruiser shined on every car, including the dead woman's car, but the cruiser never stopped. The cop or cops inside had missed the dead woman lying in the cold gravel beside her car. Jack was upset, he decided he may have to make another anonymous call, to tell them to check row 36 more closely, but the cruiser stopped. Two cops jumped out and walked back shining flashlights. Jack watched the two bright lights crossing each other the entire way to Allie's car. The lights finally came to rest on Allie's dead body. One of them bent his head and spoke into the microphone on his lapel. The other police cruiser was several rows away, it stopped and turned around, and joined the other one on row 36. The four officers bent down and examined the dead woman with their flashlights.

The eastern sky was just starting to get a little lighter and Jack was still watching the activity on row 36. More Denver police cars showed up and joined the others. The teens were put into the back seat of three different police cruisers and taken away in a small convoy. A gas generator and lights were brought in and set up. The generator fired up and the whole, ghastly scene, was illuminated in a bright white glow. The officers cast long shadows all over the crime scene and the area around the dead woman's car was taped off with yellow crime scene tape. Four uniformed officers stood around while two gloved detectives carrying plastic bags walked around gathering evidence. Allie's body was covered with a blue tarp, her left foot stuck out from underneath it and Jack could clearly see her untied yellow sneaker. He closed the curtains, stripped and hopped in the shower.

Karl finished his coffee, kissed his wife and headed East in his unmarked police cruiser. Sixty minutes later he rounded the corner in Lake Tamarisk and saw the burned remains of Vincent Beneventi's home. Not much was left, the fireplace and chimney were still standing and part of the garage. The house reminded Karl of pictures he had seen of bombed out London during World War Two. Riverside County Detective Todd Paulson was standing with a few other officers enjoying a cup of coffee. He shook Karl's hand and made the required introductions. Todd started,

"Vincent Beneventi, ever heard of him?"

"Doesn't ring a bell."

"Small time hood." Todd told Karl, pulling a photo of Beneventi out and handing it to the other Detective. Karl studied the man in the photo. Todd started talking again, "Vincent's nickname was "Slugger", because he conducted business while holding a baseball bat." Karl shifted his feet, "What was the cause of death?" He asked Todd. "Smoke inhalation. Coroner says his lungs were charred, so he was burned alive while breathing all the smoke and flames in. He was hog tied and gagged, also. The body was badly charred. I've never seen anything like it and hope I never do again. We're checking for prints but there isn't much left of the place, as you can see." Karl looked again at the carnage caused by the huge, extremely hot fire. "The killer was probably wearing gloves. Our CSI says gasoline was found all over the bedroom and on the victim." Todd said and shook his head clearly disturbed by the whole thing. He had white rubber gloves on and pulled a plastic bag out of a brown bag and showed it to Karl. Inside were three Marlboro cigarette butts. Karl reached for the bag, but Todd cautioned, "These haven't been processed yet. We'll do DNA tomorrow."

"What about the gun?" Karl inquired.

Todd walked over to his car and pulled out a plastic bag and handed it to Karl. "Silver .38 registered to Flavio Valdez. No bullets in it, you can pull it out of the bag if you'd like, our boys have already processed it." Karl opened the bag and pulled out the silver pistol, it left black smudges on his hands.

"Seems odd there are no bullets in it."

"What's odd is Flavio was murdered, what? A week ago? And his gun shows up here, in the middle of the Mojave Desert. What's the connection?"

"I'm as confused as you are Todd." Karl said and pulled out a small pad and wrote down. *Names of check outs Highwater past week.*

Check outbound flights from Bullhead.

Check rental car companies Laughlin and surrounding areas.

Check Cab Companies and Ubers from Laughlin Casinos.

Why no bullets in gun?

When Karl got back to the office, he pulled out the note he had written in Lake Tamarisk. He walked into his partner's office and gave it to Mike Briggs. Mike looked it over nodding his head yes. Karl also had a list of witnesses from the Highwater who had been there in the restaurant when Virginia was beaten and her assailant Flavio Valdez had disappeared.

"Look at this list, please Mike. Have we talked to all of these witnesses?"

"Let's see…yes, yes, yes. We were never able to contact two of them. Petey Townsend, the slot tech that got on his radio and called Security and Jack Martin, the guy who reported everything to Townsend and was with the girl when you arrived."

"Please, try contacting them again, Mike." Karl turned and went back into his office.

-Chapter 13-

The do not disturb sign he had hung on the door the night he checked in was still there, so the maid never bothered him. Earlier, he had watched a tow truck load Allie's car and leave with it, another tow truck had done the same with the teen's small silver car. The police were gone now, and all traces of a crime scene went with them, except one small piece of bright yellow tape. Jack watched as the piece of tape started blowing in the wind. It circled a few of the vacant, parked cars before finally getting stuck under one of the tires. After that Jack had crawled in bed, fully clothed, and that's where he had stayed with the TV on not really watching, but just staring at it. He was anxious and very depressed. He didn't feel bad about the dead biker or the dead mobster, they were scum and the world was a better place without them, but what had the heavy, loudmouthed woman done? A voice in his head said, fuck her, she deserved it. Again, with the voices, Jack thought. He knew in the back of his head this was an early sign of madness. The nightmares he had started to have were more violent, more graphic and more frequent now, another sign of madness. Last night he had dreamed that three teenagers in white lab coats showed up at his hotel room and two of them sawed his legs off. Jack had looked down and saw both of his bloody stumps pumping gallons of crimson liquid on the hotels brightly colored carpet his amputated limbs piled in the corner. The other teen, also in a white coat, was busily sawing Jack's shoulder joint so his arm could be removed. The pain of it all was excruciating and Jack could hear himself screeching. Most of the hotel room was covered with blood. Jack looked up and watched blood dripping from the ceiling. It was hitting him on his face. He could taste it and started to choke as a result of it. He woke up and rushed to the toilet gagging and heaving. He vomited for nearly an hour. Towards the end he was just dry heaving because he had completely emptied the contents of his stomach. He was sweating profusely and had a raging temperature. He laid on the bathroom floor, dozed off, and the nightmares came back. In his nightmare a, tall, thin figure was standing, watching him lying there. The figure was completely dark red, from head to toe. He had hooved feet and a long bi-furcated tail. He was holding a large forked trident. It smiled a big toothy smile and in a deep voice said, "You belong to your father, the Devil, and you must carry out your father's desires." Two bony hands slid underneath Jack and raised him high in the air. He gave in to the Demon.

Karl sat looking through the files on both murders, he couldn't find any connection between them, other than the silver .38 pistol. "What am I missing here?" He asked out loud. Either, Vincent Beneventi had murdered Chucho Valdez taking his pistol and then someone murdered the mobster, leaving the gun, or whoever murdered Chucho in Laughlin had taken the bikers gun and gone to Lake Tamarisk with it and killed the mobster leaving the empty gun behind. Karl believed the latter was the most likely, but still was confused about the empty gun. Mike knocked on the door frame and entered,

"I was able to talk to Petey Townsend, he said Jack Martin came to him and asked for help with Victoria Ramirez so he called the Casino's Security guards on his two way and dialed 911 on his cell, but he didn't know anything else. His shift ended before the cops got there to interview him. He had to catch a plane to Kentucky for a family reunion. No priors, nothing. He's as clean as a whistle."

"What about Jack Martin?"

"He's clean. Absolutely no record anywhere. None. I still can't get ahold of him, he seems to have disappeared from the face of the earth. I called his home in Colorado, his voicemail is full so I couldn't leave a message. I talked to his ex-wife and she said she had divorced him because he had started to act strange."

"What did she mean by strange?" Karl asked Mike and was suddenly very interested.

Mike looked through his notes, "Let's see, she said he has bad anxiety and depression issues and is obsessed with watching his neighbors, but she said he wouldn't hurt a flea. Not violent at all. She had no idea why he would be in Laughlin."

Karl thought for a few seconds, "Okay Mike, thanks. Keep trying to contact him by phone but, I think he's just sowing his oats since getting divorced, and it's looking like he had nothing to do with either of these cases other than being in the wrong place at the wrong time."

Jack felt someone shake his leg and say, "Get your ass up!" He woke up startled. He flipped on the light and looked around the room. There was no one in the room with him. He was in bed but couldn't remember how he got there. The last thing he remembered was lying on the bathroom floor too sick to move. The sheets were soaked with sweat as were his clothes. He cautiously stood up, stripped off his clothes and got in the shower. He stuck his head under the hot water and stayed like that for a few minutes. He heard the bathroom door close hard, it startled him, and he turned the water off. He stood there listening to the drip, drip of the water from the faucet. The hair on the back of his neck stood on end. He wrapped a towel around his waist, opened the bathroom door and walked out into the hotel room. There was no one there. He checked the door to the room, it was bolted, and the gold swing bar lock was engaged. No one had come in or left this way. Despite knowing this he unlocked and unbolted the door and looked up and down the hall. It was completely empty. He knew that was ridiculous. He locked the door again and walked to the window and checked it. It was a solid piece of glass. There was no way to open it. He stood there for a few seconds looking around the room. He must have heard the door to some other room and it just sounded like his bathroom door. Jack grabbed the chair from the desk, pulled it into the bathroom, shut and locked the door behind him and leaned the chair under the door handle so there was no way anyone would be able to enter. He opened the shower door and got back under the soothing water.

Around three a.m., there was a loud thump, Jack woke up, again, with a start, and glanced around the dark room. The room was quiet with no movement. The light from the hall filtered in under the door and illuminated most of the room. He definitely felt better, his fever had broken. The TV remote was laying on his chest, so he picked it up and held it so he could see it, "Odd!" He said. He didn't remember watching TV in bed after his shower. He shrugged and turned the TV on and started flipping through the channels. He had only flipped through a few channels when he saw Allie's face on the screen. He turned up the volume, "The victim's name is Allie Simmons, Thirty-One years old. Police report she was strangled and possibly robbed. Three teens were taken into custody as "persons of interest." The teens, all Seventeen years old, are being held in the Denver Juvenile Center, Downtown. All three of the teens have records varying from burglary to assault. A spokesperson for the Parking Stop said they are cooperating with authorities and are planning on adding an additional Security Guard to patrol the parking lot. That person will be hired and start patrolling as soon as possible." The camera switched to a tall nice looking, woman in a red dress standing in front of a map. She smiled and said, "We'll be back to tell you what to expect weather wise today." A commercial for a law firm came on and Jack turned the TV off, stood up and went to the window. It was dark out, but he could see that the parking lot was quiet. He decided it was time to get his truck and head home.

Jack checked out saying he was catching a Red Eye, the man at the desk took his cardkeys, returned his security deposit and printed out a receipt. Jack quietly slipped through the Hotel parking lot, occasionally looking behind him to make sure no one was watching and stopped at the fence. The portion that the teens had removed was repaired by two guys in a service van. Jack had watched them earlier so he knew beforehand he would have to climb the fence. Jack pitched his suitcase over the fence and climbed over to retrieve it. He stooped low and watched for any movement. The bus for the lot was dropping someone off at their car about twelve rows away. There was no way they could see him, he decided it was safe. He walked quickly to his truck, unlocked it, threw his bag in the back seat, and climbed behind the wheel. He paid the attendant cash so there would be less of a trail for the authorities to follow, and headed West towards home.

The sky was starting to lighten when he turned left onto Everett Street, heading south. He continued a few blocks and turned left into his circular driveway. Everything outside looked fine. Dave had been watching Jack's house, and it looked like Dave had recently mown the lawn. He parked his truck, entered the house through the garage and turned on the kitchen light. Dave had stacked Jack's mail on the kitchen counter. "Thanks Dave." Jack said to the empty house. He decided he would buy his neighbor something for taking such good care of his house while he was gone. Maybe a case of Rolling Rock beer, he thought, or better yet a case of Grain Belt beer. Jack smiled. The light on his answering machine was flashing so Jack hit the button and the first message started to play. He listened to half a dozen of the messages, two political messages, three hang ups and one from someone he didn't know. He pushed the button that was marked stop. He would continue going through them some other time. He was tired and wanted to get to bed. He looked out the kitchen window, there were no lights on in any of his neighbor's homes. The entire neighborhood was dark.

It was straight up noon when he woke. He stretched, yawned and got up to pee. He realized that he hadn't had a nightmare last night, he had slept like a baby. There's something about being home in your own bed, he thought. The doorbell rang and Jack groaned. He quickly dressed and went upstairs. He checked the peep hole and saw Dave standing there holding a plate of food, with a big smile on his face. Jack opened the door for his friend. "Come on in, buddy." Jack said to Dave.

Dave handed the plate to Jack and said, "Jen made enchiladas last night. She figured you wouldn't have any food in the fridge."

Jack took the plate from Dave, he was starving. "Tell Jen thanks a bunch, I'm going to warm this up right away." Jack put the plate in the microwave and turned it on. Jack and Dave sat talking while Jack ate the Mexican food that Jen had made. They each polished off a couple beers before Dave stood up and said he needed to get home. Jack thanked his neighbor for taking such good care of his house, "You're a good friend, Dave. I appreciate everything. Tell Jen thank you for the delicious food."

"I will," Dave answered and went out the door. Jack locked it and went into the kitchen, sat at the counter and started to go through the mail. This is going to take most of the day he thought. The phone rang and Jack checked the caller I.D., it was a number out of Laughlin, Nevada. Jack stood up and stared at the phone. This can't be good, he thought. After three rings the machine answered the call and the person on the other end said, "Hello, this is Detective Mike Briggs from the Laughlin, Nevada Police Department. I'm trying to contact Jack Martin. I've left several messages. We need Jack to call either myself or Detective Karl Schulz as soon as possible at 1, 702, 496, 2232." Jack looked around the room, he started to panic. He went to the front window and surveyed the street. Just the normal cars parked out there he told himself, trying to calm down. "Fuck!" He yelled and slammed his hand on the counter. He ran downstairs into the Spy versus Spy room and turned on the monitors. He rewound the recording to the beginning and focused on the front door cam. He put it on the slowest fast forward and watched the screen. Nothing, no one had been on his porch. His head was spinning, there is no way the cops in Laughlin knew what he had done there. "No fucking way!" He said out loud and heard a voice say, "Don't worry." He jumped up and surveyed the basement, there was no one there, he must have imagined the phantom voice. He felt like he couldn't breathe, like he was being crushed by a heavy weight. He climbed the stairs two at a time and burst out into the back yard. He couldn't catch his breath. He bent over and tried to control his breathing. Someone yelled "Pussy!" and Jack stood and looked around. "Who's there?" He asked out loud. There was no response. Jack walked to the back corner of his yard, a place, he knew, that wasn't viewable by any of Dave's cameras. He slumped to the ground and started to cry. "I'm fucked," He said out loud. The tunnel vision started, and Jack passed out.

Karl asked Mike if he had gotten in touch with Jack Martin yet. "I literally just got off the phone with his answering machine, again." Was Mike's answer. "His machine wasn't full like it has been the last several times I called. Someone has listened to the machine full of messages. Jack Martin might be at home now." Mike said to his partner.

Karl shook his head, "You can call and get your messages from anywhere on the planet. He may be home or someone watching his house may have finally listened to the messages and wrote them down for him."

Mike nodded, "That is true. I'll just continue calling his number three times a day." Mike was being flippant.

"That's all we can do, Mike. I'm still not sure Jack Martin is involved in any of this. Did you interview the other couple that Victoria said came to Laughlin with her and Chucho?"

Mike nodded his head yes. "Rudy Cabrera and Victoria's sister Celina, Yes. They were shocked after I told them about Chucho. They have no idea who killed him. I believe them but I've got all their info if you'd like me to get them in here so you can talk to them."

"No," Karl said, "Not necessary, Victoria said the same thing." He suddenly thought of Todd and him standing in Lake Tamarisk and asked Mike if he would call Todd Paulson with the Riverside Sheriff's Department and ask him if he had DNA results from the cigarette butts found on the street the night Beneventi was murdered.

Someone in the neighborhood started up a noisy lawnmower and Jack sat up. His breathing had calmed and he took a deep breath, let it out, and gingerly got up. He stood on his toes and gazed over the wooden 6-foot fence. A small Latino man was riding around on a big, flat mower running it over Bradley White's lawn. Another Latino man was following the first, with a weed whacker. The noise was overwhelming and Jack went into the house to escape it. His laptop was sitting on the kitchen counter, so he opened it and typed in 'Laughlin Murder Chucho' and clicked enter. Several sites popped up. Each one was about the dead biker, and each one said that the Police had no suspects, yet. The last one he read, from yesterday, however, said the police were getting closer to naming a suspect. Jack yelled, "Fuck!" He glanced around the kitchen, went to the liquor cabinet, cracked open a new bottle of Knob Creek Bourbon and poured himself a large glass.

Mike Briggs knocked and then walked into Karl's office. Karl was talking to someone on the phone, "Maria Ramirez, R.A.M.I.R.E.Z.", He said into the receiver. "Yes ma'am, I'll wait." He looked at Mike and asked, "What's up, Mike?" Mike walked closer to Karl's desk,

"Couple things, Karl, no DNA results from the cigarette butts yet and I still haven't been able to contact Jack Martin. The guy is nowhere to be found, but the car he rented in Laughlin from Jiffy Rent-a-Car was turned back in at the Ontario, California Airport."

"How far is that from Lake Tamarisk?"

"About 2 ½ hour's drive."

"Interesting," Karl said.

Maria Ramirez spoke into the phone next to Karl's ear and he held his finger up to Mike, as if to say, hang on a minute. Mike nodded and left Karl's office for his own. Karl started talking into the receiver, "Hello Ms. Ramirez, my name is Karl Schulz. I'm a Detective with the Laughlin Police Department,"

"Oh my God!" Maria Ramirez cried into the phone, "Is Victoria alright?"

"Yes, yes," Karl assured her, "I'm sorry, I didn't mean to scare you. Your daughter is fine." Maria Ramirez was skeptical, and she asked the Detective,

"Did that estu'pido Chucho Valdez hurt her?"

"No, ma'am, she is safe and sound, my wife and I have been helping her. Your daughter is in a safe house for unwed mothers, here in Laughlin. Chucho Valdez is dead. He was found floating in the Colorado River near Needles, Arizona."

"Gracias a dios!" Maria said, and started to cry. Karl gave her a minute to calm down and asked her,

"May I come visit you tomorrow afternoon? I can bring Victoria."

"Yes, of course."

She repeated, "Gracias a dios! Thank you, God!"

Karl was excited and said, "Great. We should be there about noonish, will that work?" "Of course, yes." Maria said and hung up before Karl could say goodbye. Karl and Sandra picked up Victoria at 7:00 am, at the Unwed Mothers home, and they headed towards the Saving Angel Halfway House, in Riverside, California. Maria Ramirez had been living there for the past two years. It was about a 4-hour drive from

Laughlin. Karl looked over at Victoria, "How are you doing?" He asked her. "I'm doing really good." She replied. He asked her, "Can you think of anyone who may have wanted Flavio dead?" Oh my God, Karl! Please quit being a cop for a few minutes! Sandra thought to herself and gave him a dirty look. Karl looked back at his wife and mouthed, ***What?*** Victoria answered Karl, "Lots of people wanted him dead, he pissed a lot of people off, but I don't want to talk about him. Is that okay?"

"Of course." Karl felt bad that he had mentioned her dead boyfriend right out of the gate. He looked at his wife, she was still frowning at him, she shook her head and whispered, "Let me talk to her, please." Karl nodded, yes, to his wife.

Sandra looked at Victoria and said, "Karl and I are taking you to see your Mom, but we have something serious to talk to her about, too. We think that you should come live with us, I know you don't want to be a burden on anyone, but we have plenty of room, and we truly want you to live with us. Victoria, honey, we want to ask your Mom if we can adopt you." Sandra watched the young girl to see her reaction, before continuing. The young girl was frowning now. Sandra continued, "Your Mom will still be your Mom, nothing will ever change that, but we would be your parents, too." Sandra stared into Victoria's eyes. She could see she was confused. Sandra went on, "You've had a hard life. You've had to grow up too fast. If you come live with us you can be a 16-year old, again. We'll get you into school, and help you get into college or a trade school, if you'd like. We'll be there to help you when Hector is born." Victoria finally spoke, "I have my Mommy. When she gets out of the halfway house, I can move in with her, and she can help me with Hector."

Karl butted in, "You'll always have your Mom, Victoria. That will never change."

Victoria said, "My Mommy ain't going to like any of this."

Sandra took Victoria's hand, "Listen to me sweetheart, if your Mom doesn't want us to adopt you, or you don't want us to adopt you, we'll drop the whole thing. We just want you to be happy."

Karl was nodding in agreement with his wife.

Victoria's eyes started to tear up. She asked the two of them, "Why do you want to help me so much? I just don't understand." Sandra started to say something, but Karl interrupted her by grabbing her hand. He had rehearsed what he would say to the teen if she asked this very question.

He got a serious tone and started what he had been rehearsing, "Victoria, we have a daughter just a few years older than you. Her name is Kaitlyn. She played sports at Laughlin High School, basketball and volleyball. She has friends who are her age who spend the night once in a while. She loves to wear her pajamas while she's watching a movie and eating popcorn. Sandra and I taught her how to drive when she was about your age and then we bought her a used car that she still has. She went to her High School prom with a pimply teenage boy who bought her a corsage, and he rented them a limousine for the night. She helped publish her High School yearbook and was in the Glee Club. Now she's in a College in Utah studying to be a nurse. She lives on campus there. She's had a good life. She's a happy young lady. No one has ever threatened her with violence or beat her or hurt her in any way. We truly love her with all our hearts. You're still a teenager. You deserve a life like that. No one should ever hurt you again for the rest of your life. Sandra and I just want that for you."

Now Sandra had tears in her eyes. She took Karl's hand and raised it to her mouth and kissed it.

Karl continued. "If nothing else comes from this trip, other than you getting to visit your Mother, we'll be happy." Karl's lip was quivering now and he decided even though he wasn't done, he should stop talking. The three of them sat silently with tears in their eyes.

Bradley White had spent $28,000 to have a professional gym built in his basement. It was a, smaller version of the other gyms he owned, but was filled with the same quality equipment as the other gyms. He never spared any expenses, especially when it came to his business or his home. Nothing but the best. He also had a few extra things installed, like a rock climbing wall, a juice bar, and four Sony 72" LED TV's. The last piece of equipment had arrived, just, this morning, and Bradley was anxious to try it out. He was so happy his gym was finally fully equipped that he tipped each of the guys, who hauled it downstairs, a crisp Hundred Dollar bill. It was probably as much as they made in a day, he thought. Bradley turned one of his four televisions to ESPN, hopped on the brand new Sole E42 Elliptical machine, and, fired it up. After about ten minutes, Bradley heard the garage door open. Kami, his girlfriend was there. He had installed a small dance studio, specifically for her, next to his gym. It had a stripper's pole in it attached to the ceiling. It was a surprise for her, and he was anxious for her to see it. She was a professional dancer at a Men's club called Dandy Dave's, in Denver. Kami came down the stairs carrying two bags of groceries. "Hi Baby, I have a surprise for you." Bradley told her and stepped down from the machine. He rushed over, held his hands over her eyes and led her to the small dance studio. She squealed with delight when he dropped his hands. "Oh Baby, I love it!" She ran to the pole and showed Bradley some of her famous spin moves. Bradley was grinning from ear to ear, his bare chest was glistening with sweat and he looked really good to Kami. "Go get a shower," She told him, "I'm going to show you, just, how much I love my surprise." Bradley took the stairs two at a time. He could feel himself getting hard and couldn't wait to get his girlfriend in bed.

An hour later Kami got out of bed and jumped in the shower. Bradley lit a joint and laid there, a satisfied and very happy man. He watched her, through the showers glass. She had a perfectly sculpted, tone body and was incredible in bed, very willing to try anything he suggested. She wasn't the sharpest tool in the shed, though. He lay there watching her soap her breasts and stomach, and felt himself starting to get hard again. Someday, I may just propose to her, he thought to himself, taking a big hit of the burning weed and holding it in. He thought about it a few more seconds, and said out loud, letting the pot smoke out in a big cloud. "Yeah, that ain't happening" He was still chuckling at his thought when Kami got out and wrapped a towel around her glistening body.

What's so funny?" She asked Bradley.

"Just your face!" He said and burst out laughing.

"You're such an Ass!" She yelled at him.

Jack was still sitting at the kitchen table drinking the Bourbon. The bottle was about half empty. Jack had discovered the more he drank, the less he was concerned about who he had become in the last few weeks. His anxiety didn't show up as much either. He gathered the half empty bottle and his glass and headed downstairs to the Spy versus Spy room. Mike Briggs, the cop from Laughlin had called again, this morning. Jack wondered if the Laughlin Detective who kept badgering him had called the local authorities. For all he knew, they may be outside watching his house right now. He turned on the TV monitors and scanned the screens for any cars that didn't belong on Everett Court. Just the normal cars he decided.

Sandra suggested the three of them stop for a quick bite and to go to the bathroom before they visited Maria Ramirez. They were just a few blocks from the halfway house, and they had all been crying. Karl went in and ordered three big Jim's burger combos and paid with a card. Sandra and Victoria went to the Ladies room to fix their makeup and freshen up.

When the two girls finally came out Karl was sitting with all the food separated and ready for them to eat. The burgers were excellent and the three of them wolfed them down as if they hadn't eaten for days. Karl glanced at his watch, just after 11:30 am. Karl had told Maria they should be there around noon giving them some leeway in case they ran into traffic. He asked Victoria if he should get her Mom something to eat. "My mommy doesn't eat much, she's very skinny because she barely eats. She does like ice cream though."

Karl and Victoria stood up and went to the counter, looking at the board above the cash registers. Small, medium and large ice cream sundaes, at least ten different flavors.

"What do you think?" Karl asked the teen.

Victoria said, "Hot fudge for my mommy and me."

Karl knew Sandra loved strawberry, so he ordered two medium strawberry sundaes and two medium hot fudge sundaes to go.

Jack checked the clock. It was 4:00 in the afternoon, the bottle sat next to him, nearly empty. He was feeling no pain. There was an ashtray on the table where he sat, it had at least ten butts in it. He had been watching the monitors for nearly 6 hours. Nothing unusual had happened in that time. Jen Holloway left the house with Chipper on a leash and came back home about forty minutes later. Dave Holloway mowed his lawn, fertilized it and swept his sidewalk and driveway. A truck backed into Bradley's driveway and two big guys unloaded a large piece of exercise equipment and carried it into the house. Thirty minutes later they closed the back of the truck, high fived each other for some reason and drove off. About fifteen minutes later Bradley's hot girlfriend pulled into the garage and unloaded a few bags of groceries from her Porsche. She looked incredible in her work out clothes, a tight top with no bra and tight workout pants. Her erect nipples poked out under her top. "Damn, she is so fucking hot!" Jack said out loud, feeling himself getting hard. He remembered when he was embarrassed by how she dressed and thought she should wear more appropriate clothes. Now here he was leering at her and wishing she wore less clothes. He had really changed in the last few months.

Kami sat on the couch with Bradley. He was watching some corny live Cop show on TV. Kami had driven over a curb and heard the bottom of her new Porsche Macan scrape and grind. Now the car sounded louder and was making a clanking sound and she mentioned it all to Bradley. "Take it to the dealer", he told her, "They'll fix it for you."

Kami cuddled up to him and said, "It's Sunday, the dealership isn't open. Can you look at it for me, please?" She reached down and stroked his penis.

Bradley moaned and said, "Shit! Alright, I'll look at it later, today." He grabbed her by her hair and pushed her face into his crotch. "But first, you need to take care of this for me."

Jack stepped out of the shower and toweled off. He had masturbated in the shower, picturing Kami, in her work out clothes, on her knees sucking his cock. He wiped the steam from the mirror and looked at his reflection. He looked horrible and was visibly trashed. He needed to get something in his stomach. He made a bologna sandwich with ketchup and threw an orange on the plate. "Won't get scurvy at least." He said and headed downstairs to the Spy versus Spy room. There wasn't anything happening on Everett Court. He sat there watching the monitors while he ate. He was just getting done with the pungent smelling orange when Bradley's garage door opened. Bradley's, tricked out, Black Ford F-250 backed out with Patten and Autie in the bed.

Kami was alone behind the wheel and she slowly went down the driveway into the street and left the development. A few minutes later, the muscle man pulled her Porsche out, got out of the car, laid on the driveway, and tried to crawl under it. This piqued Jack's interest and he zoomed in closer to watch. Bradley was having trouble squeezing his body under the low car. He got up, cussed and spit, and went into his garage. A few minutes later, Bradley was jacking the Porsche up. He raised it high enough to crawl under it and did so. Jack sat watching and wishing the wind would come up, blow the car off the jack, and crush his asshole neighbor to death. No such luck. Bradley lowered the car, removed the jack, jumped into the Porsche and left down the street.

-Chapter 14-

Karl, Sandra and Victoria sat with Maria Ramirez in the living room of the Saving Angel Halfway House. They had eaten their ice cream sundaes. Maria barely touched hers and it sat melting on the table where the four of them were sitting. Victoria was hugging her mom with tears in her eyes. Karl started the conversation. "Ms. Ramirez."

"Call me Maria," Maria told him.

Karl started again, "Maria, Sandra and I would like to help your daughter go back to High School and continue on to College or some sort of trade school. We'd also like to help her with baby Hector when he's born."

Maria was nodding the whole time he was talking to her. "Thank you, so much, my little mija can use all the help she can get." Maria told Karl.

Victoria spoke up. "Mommy, they want me to live with them. They want to adopt me."

Maria frowned and looked at the White couple. "I'm Victoria's Madre. I'm not sure what this all means."

Sandra sat forward and addressed the other woman, "Maria, if Victoria decides to live with us, she would have her own room. We would help her get enrolled at the high school in Laughlin, and once she graduates, we would help her, as much as we can, to get into College. Mojave Community College is right across the river from us in Bullhead City, Arizona. Karl is a Detective in Laughlin, Nevada and I'm a stay at home wife, so Victoria would be very safe with us."

Maria took Victorias hands, "¿Es eso lo que usted quiere, Mija?" (Is this what you want, daughter?) She asked Victoria.

"Ser no Seguro Mami, tengo meido!" (I don't know, Mommy. I'm scared!) Victoria answered her mother.

Karl spoke to Maria, "We want to adopt Victoria, but you will always be her mother. That will never change, but, if we adopt her, my insurance will cover the hospital expenses when Hector is born. When you leave here and move into a home, if you'd rather have Victoria live with you, we'll move her to wherever you are living. We just want to be a part of her life."

Maria thought about everything. This was a lot to take in. Who were these people, and why were they so willing to help her daughter? "I need to think about this for a while." Maria told the couple.

"Of course," Sandra replied.

Maria looked again at Victoria and asked her daughter, "Ser estos bueno gente?" (Are these good people?)

Victoria answered quickly, "Si Mami, ellos ayudar me una el lote!" (Yes mommy, they've helped me a lot!) Maria repeated to the couple, "I need to think before I give you my answer."

Jack saw Dave come out of his house and head his way. The doorbell rang. Jack remembered the intercom and the electric lock. He pushed a button and said, "Come on in Dave." He pushed another button and the door unlocked. Dave came in the front door and went down the stairs. When Jack saw this, he pushed the same button and the door locked. "Dave, what's up?" Jack asked him when Dave stepped into the basement.

Dave studied the TV monitors. "Watching our shithole neighbor?"

Jack answered him by nodding yes.

Dave took a deep breath and started talking, again. "Jen and I need to head to Steamboat Springs. Jen's Mom is in the hospital. The Doctors think she may have had a stroke."

Jack's look changed to one of concern and he shook his head, "Oh my gosh Dave, I'm so sorry."

Dave thanked Jack, "Jen and I are leaving right away. I know it's short notice but is there any way you could watch Chipper 'til we get back?"

Jack was already nodding yes.

Dave said, "No big deal if you can't, we'll just pack him up and take him with us."

Jack said, "Yes, of course, leave Chipper and head out. I owe you for taking such good care of my house while I was in Laughlin. Just make sure you bring over his bed and food bowls. Susan took all the dog stuff with her."

Dave thanked his friend and told Jack he would bring Chipper and all his things over right away. Jack nodded again, "Please, tell Jen I'm very sorry to hear about her Mom, and I hope she makes a full recovery."

Dave thanked Jack again and started up the stairs, "Keep an eye on that prick, Brad, for me. Okay?" "You know I will." Jack told him. He waited a few seconds and unlocked the front door to let Dave out, and when Dave closed the front door behind him Jack pushed the button to lock it. He leaned back, shook a cigarette out of the pack, put it to his lips and lit up.

Karl and Sandra sat with Victoria and Maria. They talked about other things besides them adopting the young girl. They talked about the weather and the halfway house. Karl had said it was one of the nicest he had ever been in. It was a cordial visit, but Karl was not optimistic about what the outcome of their visit would be. Maria seemed a bit stubborn and was leery of the white couple wondering why they were so interested in her daughter. She knew she would never be able to care for Victoria because she was a horrible mother. She also knew keeping Victoria away from her other daughter Celina and her husband Rudy was a good thing, but Victoria needed to be with her own kind, she needed to be adopted by a Latino family, not these two white people. Victoria liked the Schulz's they acted like family, but she also thought a nice Latino family would be a better fit. Sandra felt the same as Karl. It just didn't go as they thought it would. The ride home was, pretty, quiet. When they got close to Barstow, Karl suggested they stop to eat. They pulled into a Chili's Restaurant parking lot, parked and went in. They slipped into the most private booth they could find and ordered. While they were waiting for their food Victoria told the couple what she and her mother were saying in Spanish back at the halfway house. Sandra and Karl were both fluent in Spanish but let the girl tell them what was said anyway. When Victoria was done Karl said to the girl, "You understand the reasoning behind us adopting you, don't you?"

Victoria nodded yes.

Karl went on, "My insurance will help pay the hospital bills when Hector arrives. If you are still living in the Unwed Mother's place, you'll be responsible for the hospital bill. We will help you pay it if that's what you choose to do."

Sandra interrupted, "There's more to it than that. Karl and I have talked, a lot, about you recently. We both feel very close to you, we love you Victoria. We want to take care of you. We want you to be our daughter. Your mother will always be your mother, but honey, she may not be able to take care of you when she gets released from where she is now."

Victoria looked at Karl and asked him, "What happens when my Mommy gets out?"

Karl took a deep breath, let it out slowly and said, "When your Mom gets out, she'll be placed in low income housing. The state will help her pay for the apartment. Probably a studio apartment if she lives by herself. If she is put with a roommate or roommates the apartment will be bigger, of course, and could possibly be a house. She'll have to find a job, that's a requirement, and she'll have to attend drug or alcohol classes, that's also a requirement. She can't drink or do drugs while she's there. They'll give her random drug tests and if she fails the test she'll have to move out. I don't know the specifics about your Mom. A lot of times, if someone goes back to drinking or drugging, they can be put back in jail. Was your Mom in jail before the halfway house?"

"Yes, she was in a women's jail somewhere by San Jose, for three years. I don't know the name of it, I never went to see her it was too far."

"Valley State Prison?"

"Yes."

"If your Mom starts doing drugs again, she will go back to jail or a prison and serve more time. He paused to see Victoria's reaction, then asked the teen, "You know your Mom, better than we do, do you think she may go back to her old ways?" Victoria asked, "You mean doing drugs again?" Karl nodded. Victoria said matter-of-factly, "Probably. She is, definitely, a drug addict. She was always high when I was little. My Aunt told me my Mommy left me alone in our house for two days, one time, when I was about two. Someone called the cops and they busted the door down to get to me, I had been eating the dog's food and I had pulled my diaper off and was going to the bathroom on the floor."

Sandra got up, walked around the table and hugged the young girl. She stayed hugging her until finally, she leaned back and asked Victoria, "You have an Aunt?"

Victoria said no, her Aunt had died of Cancer a few years ago. "I don't have no one." She thought a second and corrected herself, "Well, I have an older sister, but Rudy, her husband wouldn't never let me live with them. He ain't much better than Flavio. Rudy's good to my sister though. He loves her. But he's a bad guy too. I seen him beat a man for bumping into Celina in a bar. The man didn't wake up and we got on the bikes and hauled ass."

Sandra said to the young girl, "Oh Honey, we need to get you away from those people."

Karl was leaning on the table holding his head in his hands and shaking his head. He couldn't believe the life this poor girl had been forced to live. The waitress arrived with their food stacked up her arm and set the meals in front of them. They were all somber now and it was quiet for a long time as they ate.

After their dinner, as they walked out of the restaurant, Sandra saw a Kohl's in the same parking lot and asked Karl if she and Victoria could shop. "Of course, yes. I'll wait in the car, take your time." He watched them walk to Kohl's and go in the front door. Karl got in the car and made some phone calls. He called his lawyer friend and said he didn't think it had gone well with Maria. The lawyer said, "We can claim the mother unfit and who knows? A judge may make her give Victoria up to you and Sandra."

Karl said no, that was not an option he didn't want to alienate Victoria, and besides Sandra wouldn't want that either. They talked a bit more and Karl hung up more discouraged than he had been before the call. He called Mike to see how things were going in Laughlin.

Mike was happy to hear from Karl, he said, "A couple things, I had two rookie cops scour the area along the Colorado for any kind of evidence to help us. They found some homeless people that were in one of the camps along the river and they said a guy that looked like Chucho was hiding in their camp. The people said they were afraid of him. They knew he was a bad guy. They mentioned face tattoos. That made me think it was Chucho, for sure."

"Of course," Karl said, "That explains where he was and why we couldn't find him for so long. Hiding out in the river camps."

Mike asked, "Do you think any of the camp people killed Chucho?"

Karl thought and said, "No, I doubt it. Those people aren't violent people. What else Mike?" Mike didn't answer Karl. Karl asked, "Mike you there?"

Mike came back on the line and said, "Hang on a second Karl," Karl could tell Mike was covering the phone and talking to someone else. Mike got back on the phone.

"Karl, when are you coming back?"

"We should be in Laughlin in about two and a half hours, three tops. Why?"

"We just got a call from a Riverside Sheriff's Department Deputy. Lilly was showing me the phone message when you called. There's a woman there named Rose Swanson who lives down the street from Beneventi's house. She says she saw someone the night of the fire. They were driving very fast out of the area. She saw the car, it was red, she's sure of that."

"Wow!" Karl said and thought about it. "Look, it's Friday. It will be late by the time we get back there. Get the woman's info and set something up for Monday early with her. Call Riverside and have the deputy meet us there, as well. Go home to the wife and enjoy the weekend. I'll talk with you on Monday." Karl sat and thought about everything that had gone on today. It was too much to think about. He picked up a suspense novel of Sandra's and started reading it. He was starting to doze off when Sandra and Virginia walked out of the store and ambled over to the car. They were each loaded down with big bags. "Well, we found Victoria all kinds of new clothes and some other things." Sandra said dropping the bags in the back seat and climbing in beside Karl.

"I guess." Karl said looking at the bags on the back seat. He looked in the mirror and asked Victoria, "What all did you get?"

Victoria was like a child on Christmas morning. She gushed over all the things Sandra had bought for her. "Three pairs of new jeans, some blouses and underwear. Oh man, Sandra helped me pick out two dresses. I never owned a dress before."

Sandra was as excited as Virginia, "Karl, you should see this young lady in a dress. She's beautiful. She's never owned a dress!"

Karl's stress evaporated. He thought of Victoria looking like a lady in a dress. Everything that happened today went right out the window at that moment. He got a huge smile on his face and he smiled the entire three hours back to Laughlin listening to his wife and the girl talking and giggling the whole way.

Kami got to Bradley's house about 8:00 am, she walked in with the two dogs on her heels. Bradley was watching porn in the living room. "Really, Brad?!" She asked him when she figured out what he was doing. He never took his eyes off the TV screen and asked her, "Are you jealous?"

"No. But, you have the real thing, right here. Why would you need to watch porn?"

Brad jumped up and slapped her in the ass, "You're starting to get a fat ass, I'm thinking of trading you in for a skinnier model."

She left the room to let the dogs out. "You're a fucker!" She yelled back at him.

He jumped up and followed her. "I figured out what was making the noise on your car, the exhaust came loose and was rattling. There's a coupling that attaches the exhaust to the tail pipe. I went to Auto Zone and bought the coupling this morning."

"Is it fixed?" She asked him.

"No, but I'll fix it tomorrow. You know what you have to do for that to happen, don't you?" He reached into his pants and pulled out his semi hard penis and tried to push her down on her knees. Kami was pissed, she started hitting Bradley and then backed away from him.

She stood and started screaming, "You fucking asshole! You need to learn how to treat me, I'm not just someone to fuck and suck you! You're a, uh, uh…" She was so pissed she couldn't find the words. She grabbed Bradley's truck keys off the counter and ran out and got in it.

Bradley followed her yelling, "I don't know why you're so mad!"

Jack woke up at 7:50 am, poured a bowl of cereal, and fed and watered Chipper. He saw his reflection in the kitchen window. "Holy shit! My hair is getting long." Jack said out loud and ran his fingers through it. When was the last time he had it cut? It's been over three months he figured. He hadn't had any nightmares last night, he had slept well. He started eating the soggy cereal while he watched the scraggly white dog eating. Chipper was a good dog, very easy to take care of. He carried his half empty cereal bowl with him as he walked down the stairs and glanced at the TV monitors. Bradley was talking to Kami in the driveway, she was in Bradley's truck and she was pissed. She was shaking her finger in Brad's face. She put the truck in reverse and squealed backwards down the driveway, and across Jack's lawn, into the street. "God damnit!" Jack yelled at the screen. Kami put the truck in drive and laid rubber halfway down Everett Court. Bradley stood there with both middle fingers in the air. "Trouble in paradise, asshole?" Jack asked aloud to the TV monitor as he sat watching Bradley walk back into his garage. He looked down and Chipper was as close to Jack's feet as he could possibly be. The little white dog was scared. He had anxiety problems like Jack. The poor little pup was shaking right now, so Jack reached down and stroked his hair. "It's okay, big guy, you're gonna be okay. I'm sorry I yelled." Jack settled in for another day of spying on the neighbor. The neighborhood was extremely quiet. Nothing going on. Most of the neighbors worked or if they were home, they kept to themselves. Jack was sure he and Bradley were all alone on Everett Court. Only two people in two homes he decided. Jack put his slippered feet up on the desk and sat back in the chair with his hands behind his head. He hadn't called his boss and hadn't gone to work since he got home, he wasn't even sure if he had used all of his vacation days yet. Fuck it, he told himself, if I get fired I can always find another job, but frankly he thought to himself, I'm doing alright in the killing business. There were several wads of money stashed in his sock drawer. He hadn't counted all of it but was sure it exceeded $13,000, about a third of what he made in a year at Champs. He looked at the TV monitors, Bradley had the Porsche out in the driveway and was jacking it up. Jack pulled some rubber gloves out of the bathroom cabinet and put them on. He grabbed a baseball bat out of the bedroom closet and headed upstairs, Chipper on his heels.

Bradley pulled Kami's Porsche out of the garage. He went back in the garage and came back holding a jack that he used to jack the car in the air. He laid on the driveway and scooted completely under the Porsche with a hand full of tools. He had bought a coupling that attached the muffler to the exhaust pipe, and because it was a Porsche part Auto Zone had charged him a fortune for it. That bitch owes me a month of blow jobs for this, he thought to himself. He was in the middle of the repair when he heard approaching footsteps. Bradley twisted under the car to see who was there. All he saw was a pair of brown slippers and a small white scraggly dog. Bradley started to say something, but there was a loud thump and the car fell on him, pinning him to the driveway. He tried with all his might to push the car off, but one of his arms was pinned to his chest. He was having trouble breathing and feared he would black out at any second. "This is for killing my dog, you, fucking, piece of shit." A voice yelled to the huge man trapped under the car. Bradley was starting to panic. Who the fuck was out there and why weren't they helping him? His head felt like it would explode, and blood was running down his face and into his mouth. He could smell the metal like scent of the blood and could taste its saltiness. His I-phone started ringing and he struggled to reach it but there was no way to get it out of his left pants pocket with his free right hand. Bradley kicked his feet but nothing he did helped in any way. Black spots started to form in front of his eyes, and he called out, as loud as he could, "Help me, please!" It came out as a whisper only. The person beside the car said, "I'm sorry, I couldn't hear you." Bradley felt the car door open and then felt the car sag under the weight of someone standing on the rocker panel. Jack grabbed the roof of the car and jumped up and down. Bradley grunted three times, blacked out and never woke up again.

Jack looked around before going back into his front door, everything was still quiet. No one in sight. He went right downstairs, with Chipper at his heals. Jack sat in front of the TV monitors. He watched for any movement in the neighborhood. He zoomed a camera in on the dead body under the Porsche. There was blood trickling down the driveway. The phone rang and Jack nearly shit his pants. He looked at the caller I.D. and saw the same number from Laughlin, Nevada that he had seen several times in the last few days. "What does this fucker need?!" He yelled and Chipper cowered at Jack's feet. Jack patted the small white dog on the head and opened another bottle of Knob Creek and poured a big glass.

Bradley White lay, dead, under the Porsche all that day, through the night and part of the next day. Nearly thirty hours.

The next day, just after 3 pm, a U.P.S. truck pulled in front of Bradley's house and parked in the street. A young man in a brown shirt and brown shorts grabbed a large envelope and headed up the driveway. He was listening to his I-Pod. Brian Johnson of AC / DC was screaming through his headphones. ***Dirty deeds, done dirt cheap!*** The putrid smell hit him as he approached the car. He covered his nose with the envelope. He noticed the dark stain on the driveway coming from under the Porsche sitting there. "Phew!" He exhaled. Whoever parked the car there must have hit a cat or racoon or some other animal. That explained the stain and the smell. ***Concrete shoes, cyanide, TNT, done dirt cheap!*** He rang the doorbell still covering his nose. He stared at the car as he waited for someone to come to the door. ***Dirty deeds, do anything you wanna do, done dirt cheap!*** There was something big and dark under the car. The driver bent down so he could see better, the dark thing under the car was human. ***Dirty deeds, done dirt cheap.*** The driver dropped the envelope and ran to the Porsche. There was a huge dead man under the car, and he was coal black. He ran to his truck and threw up by the open door.

Jack watched the U.P.S. driver on the monitor. The driver never noticed the dead muscleman under the Porsche when he walked to the front porch. But Bradley had been there so long the smell must be bad because the driver made a sour face and covered his nose. Eventually the driver realized there was a dead body under the car. He dropped the envelope he was carrying and ran back to his truck, after quickly glancing under the car. He was bent over heaving. A huge puddle had formed at his feet splattering his shoes with the remnants of a Santiago's burrito he had eaten earlier. The driver got on his cell phone and put his free hand on his head, obviously freaked out. Within ten minutes two Wheat Ridge Police cars showed up with an ambulance. They stretched crime tape up and down the driveway and interviewed the frazzled driver before allowing him to drive off. About forty minutes later a Mercedes van showed up . Jack grabbed Chipper and joined an older, grey haired couple on the street watching everything. Jack recognized the older couple as two of his neighbors from the house across the street. He had heard Dave say their names one time, he thought their names were Mario and Julianna. He was certain he and Bradley were alone in the neighborhood, but apparently, he was wrong. He studied the older couple to see if they gave any indication that they had seen him kill Bradley. They never looked his way, he walked over and introduced himself. Julianna nodded and tried to smile.

Mario asked, "Do you live in the neighborhood?"

"Yes." Jack pointed at his house.

Mario apologized to Jack, "I'm so sorry, we don't know the neighbors well. I'm embarrassed to say that. We just got home from the store a few minutes ago and saw all the commotion." Mario had a thick Italian accent and had his arm around his wife. Jack had his answer, the nice older couple hadn't seen a thing, they were at the store when Bradley's life was snuffed out. He was relieved not only for himself but also for the older couple. The Porsche was lifted, and Bradley's body was pulled out and with great difficulty zippered into a black bag. Julianna covered her mouth and turned her head. Mario said, "Come Julianna, let's go home." He led his visibly upset wife across the street towards the open garage of their home. Jack watched them walking away, he could see groceries in the open trunk of their car. Two men slipped a stretcher under the body and called for two of the policemen to help. The four of them struggled from the weight but, eventually, put the stretcher in back of the plain, white van. Jack turned and went into his home and locked the door. The Porsche's doors were taped shut to preserve any evidence there might be in the car and a tow truck loaded the car onto its bed and drove away, the Mercedes van following right behind it. The only thing left was a big dark skid mark where the police had drug the body out from under the car, a thin line of dried blood down the driveway and the huge puddle of puke in the street.

The doorbell rang and Jack looked at the front door monitor. A uniformed Policeman stood there for a few minutes, gave up and walked across the street to the Italian couple's house and rang the doorbell. Mario opened the door and stood to the side as the Policeman entered and the door closed behind the two men. The phone rang, and startled Jack, again. His pulse started to race, and he felt like the small room was closing in on him. He looked around and saw Chipper looking back at him, with his head cocked to the side. Jack started to see black spots and stood up. That was a mistake, he felt dizzy and sat back down. Before he passed out, he heard this, "We are each the Devil, and the world is our Hell."

When he woke up, he started vomiting, and did so for about twenty minutes. Chipper was there beside Jack licking up the vomit from the carpet. Jack felt paralyzed. He tried to get up, but his legs felt like rubber. The lights, suddenly, went out and Jack laid there unable to do anything. In front of him, just outside the door a dark figure stood staring at Jack. He could see the figure's eyes shining in the dark and saw the bifurcated tail swinging from side to side. He lay there and felt boney hands reach under him and lift him up. The room began to spin, and he heard the voice, again. "Be alert and of sober mind. Your master, the Devil, prowls around like a roaring lion looking for someone to devour." Chipper had backed into the corner of the room and was growling and barking.

-Chapter 15-

Mike Briggs and Karl Schulz turned into the entrance to Lake Tamarisk. They were meeting a Riverside County Sheriff's deputy at a house down the street from the burnt remains of Vincent Beneventi's house. According to the deputy who called Lilly from Riverside County, the owner of the house, an older woman named Rose Swanson, claimed she saw a red car leaving the area in a big hurry the night of the fire. Karl and Mike pulled up in front of Miss Swanson's house. Deputy Edgar Puga, a huge man was standing by his cruiser waiting for them. The three of them shook hands and talked a few minutes before walking to the porch and ringing the bell. Rose Swanson, a very tiny woman, in her mid-80's, answered the door in an apron and holding a hot pad in her hand. She invited the law men in. The house smelled like cookies, and Mike said to her, "Ma'am this is probably the best smelling home I've ever been in." She smiled and said to him, "I made you boys some chocolate chip cookies. It's a long drive from Laughlin to here and I knew you would need a snack, so sit down and make yourselves comfortable", she pointed to the round dining room table covered in a frilly crocheted tablecloth with flowers and fine china plates with gold edges, cloth napkins, tiny spoons and three cups of steaming coffee sitting next to a tiny tea pot and one little tea cup and saucer. The three men settled down at the table. Karl was 6' 1" and about 200 lbs., Deputy Puga was 6' 4" and about 255 lbs. and Mike was just over 6' and about 280 lbs. The large men sitting there in the frilly setting made for a comical sight. Karl was reminded of the many times he had sat with a much younger Kaitlyn at the small plastic table in her bedroom having pretend tea with her. Tiny little Rose walked up with a cookie sheet full of warm, gooey cookies and sat down next to the huge men. Karl had to cover his mouth so he wouldn't laugh out loud at the whole scene. He wished he had a photo to show Sandra, she would laugh out loud also. Mike frowned at Karl but was also eyeing the warm cookies Rose was offering them. Mike's wife had him on a sugar free diet and would not approve. The four big men and the tiny lady sat without talking for several minutes, the men drinking their coffee, Rose sipping tea, her pinky pointing straight out and all four of them eating the warm cookies. Finally, after a few minutes, Karl spoke up, "Miss Swanson, how well did you know your neighbor, Vincent Beneventi?"

Rose frowned a bit, "Who?" She asked the Detective.

"Vincent Beneventi, the man who lived in the house down the street. The house that burned down."

Rose answered him, "I didn't know the man, in fact, Joaney and I always thought that house was vacant. Nobody ever seemed to be there. There are a lot of empty houses in our little community here, nearly half of them. Some men in a truck, with a trailer, show up at that house once a week and mow the lawn, but we've never seen anyone go in or out of it."

Mike asked her, "Ma'am who is Joaney?"

Rose Swanson blushed, "Joaney is my lover, she lives here with me. She's in Blythe, visiting her sister." She was embarrassed and added, "I hope that doesn't shock the three of you. Two old lesbians in their 80's living together."

"No ma'am." Mike and Karl said in unison, and Deputy Puga shook his head no. Karl cleared his throat and asked the older woman, "Miss Swanson, can you describe the car you saw the night Mr. Beneventi's home burned down."

"Well, like I told the nice woman on the phone, it was just a regular looking red car."

"Did you happen to get a look at the license plate or maybe see who was driving. Was the driver white, Hispanic, Black?" Mike had asked too many questions. Rose, a bit overwhelmed, closed her eyes as if she were deep in thought.

She finally spoke, "The car had doors in the front and doors in the back. It was a fairly new car and as I told you, it was a bright red. The license plate started with JR. I remember that because that's our initials, J.R. for Joaney and Rose. It was too dark to see the driver, but he was speeding when he drove past here, he had a dark baseball cap on. We saw the fire shortly after that."

Karl asked rose, "Ma'am did you or Joaney call 911 about the fire?"

Rose answered the detective, "Joaney called but the fire had already been reported by another neighbor." Mike was busy scribbling on a notepad, in between shoving cookies into his mouth. Karl pulled a book out of his case and set it in front of Rose Swanson. The book was full of pictures of different cars from 2010 through 2015. Karl opened the book and said to the small woman. "Take your time and go through this book, please. It has all kinds of different cars in it. If you happen to see one that is shaped like the one you saw that night, point it out to Detective Briggs. I know this is a bit daunting to you. We're going to enjoy our coffee and your wonderful cookies while you look at the book." Karl poured another cup of coffee and sat back. Rose opened the book and sat staring at the cars.

Jack's nightmare was intense. He remembered it vividly. He was dressed in a dark red dress suit standing on a stage with a big curved Scimitar sword. People were lined up for what seemed like two full blocks in front of him. Susan was completely naked except for a red bandana covering her pony tailed hair and was splattered by dark red blood on her ivory skin. She was standing with Jack on the stage. She would take a ticket from the first person in line and then Jack would swing the sword and lop the person's head off. A man with a pointed goatee and a handlebar mustache would gather the head and throw it in a huge canvas bag stained with blood while another man in a top coat and top hat pushed the headless body off the stage with a big broom. The stage was slippery with a thick crimson liquid and Jack slid, and nearly fell, every time he swung the sword. A large slimy snake leaned in close to Jack. There was blood dripping from under its body near the throat and its long forked tongue was flicking in and out of its mouth. It whispered to Jack, "Death is what they need, so they may transition." The snake's breath smelled of death and Jack leaned back to avoid the horrid smell. The snake continued, "Death feeds the Devil and the forces of Evil."

Jack woke up and shivered from the memory of the horrific nightmare. He stood and went into the bathroom to relieve himself. He looked at himself in the mirror, he looked like shit. He had dark bags under his eyes and his gray hair had grown even longer and shaggier. He tried to run his hands through it, but couldn't, it was dirty, greasy. A light came on in the other room and it caught Jack's eye, he glanced out the open bathroom door and over at his laptop sitting on the couch, it was on. That's odd, he thought. He walked over to look at it. He didn't remember turning the computer on, last time he saw it, it was on the kitchen counter. There was a Cabela's website on the screen. Jack studied the page and saw that there were two items in the shopping cart. Jack clicked on the shopping cart. There on the screen was a picture of a Smith & Wesson M & P semi-automatic .45 caliber pistol and alongside of the gun was a box of Winchester USA 230 grain, full metal jacket bullets. Jack was puzzled but said out loud, "Can't have a gun without ammo." He vaguely remembered deciding a few days ago he should have some type of weapon, a pistol of some sort, for protection only of course. I must have been shopping in my sleep, Jack thought, but wasn't convinced of that. He read all the details about the weapon. It was on sale for $399. Jack liked that. He sat looking at the screen, all his pertinent information for the background checks was already filled out, as was his credit card information. Very strange, he thought to himself. He ran the mouse all over the page. Looks good to me he thought. He added another box of Winchester .45 ammo and clicked the purchase button. He immediately got an email stating, that depending on the outcome of the background checks, his new pistol would be waiting for him at his local Cabela's store within a day or possibly two. Jack leaned back in the chair, "Well, that was certainly easy." Chipper was laying on the floor across the room. Jack asked the scraggly white dog if he was hungry and Chipper turned his head trying to decipher what Jack was asking him. Suddenly there was a huge boom outside. Chipper ran under the couch. Jack looked at the ceiling, "What the fuck?" He said out loud. Then there was a sound like dozens of small rodents running across the roof, a rhythmic tapping becoming louder and faster by the minute. Jack ran upstairs, Chipper stayed hidden. As soon as Jack got to the top of the stairs he knew what was happening, it was raining hard. Jack ran to the front window, streaks of pure white crackled against the silver and gray billowy blanket of clouds and it lit up the whole room so Jack covered his ears. A few seconds later there was another jarring boom. The quick pitter patter turned to a pounding. Jack looked out the window, the yard was a swamp and the path a stream. There was a strange amber tint to everything outside but the sky was dark grey. Jack walked back downstairs into his bedroom, Chipper came out from under the couch and ran into the bedroom just before Jack closed the door. He picked the white dog up and put him on the bed. Jack kicked off his slippers, pulled off his pants and tee shirt and crawled under the covers. Chipper nosed his way under the covers, shivering. Jack reached under the covers and rubbed the white mutt on the head trying to soothe him. "It's okay little guy. It's just rain. We're okay." Jack laid back and listened to the faint, percussive noise of the falling rain. He loved the sound, it was very soothing. In less than twenty minutes the rain was done, and the house was quiet again. Chipper was buried under the covers. Jack could hear the little dog snoring lightly. Soon Jack was snoring also.

It took her almost forty minutes, but Rose Swanson finished and closed the book. She had pointed to four cars that she may have seen the night Vincent Beneventi was killed. They were a 2014 Nissan Sentra SV, a 2015 Ford Fusion, a 2015 Chevy Cruz and a 2015 Hyundai Elantra. Karl stayed with Rose and Deputy Puga while Mike went outside and started making phone calls. He was still making phone calls as Karl drove them back towards Laughlin.

The next morning, Karl and Mike, both, arrived to work early. The two detectives were excited, they had a few leads and wanted to continue with them. Mike had found out that there were only three red cars with the letters J and R, on the license plates, rented during the week of Chuchos murder. All three cars were rented at Jiffy Rent-a-Car in Bullhead City. Mike and Karl waited by the fax machine for the list of cars to be sent by Trisha at Jiffy. "Sweet old lady, wasn't she?" Mike asked, thinking about sweet, little Rose Swanson in her apron.

Karl smiled and said, "Yes, very sweet but I believe you would say the same thing about the Devil, himself, if he was holding a tray of warm cookies."

Mike thought a few seconds and nodded in agreement. The fax machine turned on and spit a sheet of paper out. Mike grabbed it and read aloud. "Let's see, looks like a 2016 Nissan Sentra, license 7AJR164, registered in California, rented to Michael Rudolph, Chicago. Next a 2015 Nissan Sentra, license JRZ1990, registered in Arizona, rented to Blanca Alvarez, Bullhead City, Arizona and finally a 2016 Toyota Camry, license JRO6531, also, registered in Arizona, rented to, Holy Shit! Rented to Jack Martin, Wheat Ridge, Colorado."

Karl raised his eyebrows. He was pleased, "I think one of these cars was rented by our killer." He told Mike and Mike agreed.

Dave Holloway returned home to a mess. The water heater's bottom had rusted out and dumped 50+ gallons in his basement. Luckily there was a drain within feet of the water heater and most of the water went there. Dave used his wet vac to suck the remaining water out of the surrounding carpet and then set up a fan to dry everything out. He searched around the basement and found a short garden hose that he screwed onto the spigot at the bottom of the water heater. He opened the spigot to empty what little water was remaining in it, which wasn't much. While it was emptying into the drain, he turned the gas valve off and started disconnecting the gas line and water lines. With that done Dave decided to look at the security recording from the last few days. He sat in the darkened room and watched the replay, on a faster speed so he could get through it all quickly. He saw Bradley pull the Porsche out, crawl under it, and then saw Jack and Chipper walk over. He slowed the replay back down to its normal speed. Jack was holding a baseball bat in his hand. He watched as Jack took the bat, and like Miguel Cabrera swinging for the fence, he swung the bat and knocked the jack out from under the car. The Porsche fell about 8" and was now on top of Bradley. Dave saw Bradley's feet moving around. Jack leaned down and said something else and then opened the driver's door and stood jumping up and down on the running board. Bradley's feet quit moving and Jack got out, closed the car door and looked around before heading back to his house with little Chipper bouncing along at his heels. Half an hour later Dave had seen everything, the UPS driver who discovered the body, the cops, everything. He even saw the coroner and an assistant place the huge man in a black heavy plastic bag and, with difficulty, zip it closed. Bradley was dead! Dave sat there in the glow of the monitors, in shock. Jack had killed that asshole, Bradley White, and hadn't said a word about any of it. Dave immediately went to Jack's and rang the doorbell. He waited but no one answered. Maybe Jack had fled. No, he thought, he would have seen Jack leave. Dave walked back over to his house, never taking his eyes off Bradley's driveway. He got into his truck and headed to Lowe's to buy a new water heater. He would try Jack's door, again, later.

Jack woke up, Chipper was lying next to him, still lightly snoring. He had heard the doorbell ring but was too tired to get up and see who was at his door, so he pulled the covers over his head and fell back asleep. About an hour later Jack got out of bed, walked to the small room and checked the TV monitors. Dave was in the garage struggling to get a big rectangular box out of the bed of his truck. Jack went upstairs and grabbed Chipper's bed and food bowls. Chipper ran home as soon as Jack opened his front door. Dave waved at Jack and leaned down to gather Chipper in his arms. The dog was licking Dave's face when Jack walked up to him with the dog bed.

"Hey, Jack. I came by about an hour ago and no one answered the door." Dave said to his friend.

Jack looked at his watch, 12:35 pm. "Wow!" I must have really been sleeping hard."

"I guess! How was Chipper for you?"

"Chipper's a good boy, he's never been a problem." Jack answered Dave and rubbed Chipper's head.

Dave commented on Jack's hair, "What's going on with the hair?"

Jack just shrugged. He pulled a cigarette out of the pack, put it in his mouth and lit it. Jack took a deep drag.

Dave told Jack "Jen's Mom is not doing well. She stayed in Steamboat to be with her."

Jack exhaled the smoke from the cigarette. "I'm sorry to hear that."

Dave smiled at Jack and suggested, "Maybe you could come over tonight for pizza and beers. I'm buying." Dave waited for his friend to give him an answer. Jack glanced at Bradley White's house. You would never guess there had been a dead body lying in the driveway, just a few days ago. The rain last night had washed all the gory evidence from the driveway and the street where the UPS driver puked his guts out.

Jack scratched his head and said to Dave, "What the hell, sounds good to me. What time?"

"Around 5:30?"

"Works for me." Jack answered and pointed at the large box sitting in the garage. "What's up with that?"

Dave told Jack about coming home, discovering a flooded basement and figuring out the water heater had dumped all the water in it on the floor. Dave said, "I was, just, getting ready to haul the new one downstairs and start installing it."

"I've got nothing to do right now. I'm no handyman by any stretch of the imagination, but let me, at least, help you get the new one downstairs."

"That would be fantastic!"

They carried the big box down the stairs and set it down, next to several tools scattered across the floor. Dave had drained and disconnected the old water heater, the two of them carried the old one upstairs into the garage.

Dave was out of breath and said, "Whew! Thanks Jack, I appreciate it."

"No problem, I'll see you tonight." Jack turned and walked home. When Jack got to his house, he punched a code on the garage and the door opened. He pulled a Marlboro out, tapped in on the pack, stuck it in his mouth and lit it. He stood and thought about his conversation with Dave. His friend and neighbor obviously hadn't heard about Bradley's unfortunate accident. Jack would have to think hard about what to say to Dave about Bradley's demise when he went over tonight. Jack took a big drag of the cigarette and flicked the butt into the river rocks by the garage. He turned and went in the house closing the garage door behind him. He went downstairs and laid down for a short nap.

At about 5:25 Jack headed over to Dave's carrying a new bottle of Cutty Sark. He had thought about it and decided he would find a time to sneak downstairs and destroy the recording from the last few days. Dave hadn't mentioned anything about Bradley being crushed, plus, Dave had been so busy with the water heater issue, he certainly hadn't had time to watch the recording yet. Dave met him at the door and invited him in. Jack could smell the pizza in the oven, he was starving. He thought about it and couldn't remember the last time he had eaten. Dave asked, "Hungry?" He offered Jack a beer. Jack nodded and took the beer from Dave as he held up the bottle of Cutty Sark for Dave to see. "Wow, Cutty!" Dave said excitedly, "What's the occasion?"

Jack just shrugged, "Just brought my buddy some good booze."

Dave thanked Jack and poured them each a stiff glass of the amber Whiskey. They sat for a while not talking and Dave finally broke the silence. "Anything interesting happen while I was gone?"

Jack was prepared for the question and said to Dave, "Yeah! Holy cow I almost forgot! A few days ago, I came home, and the cops were at Bradley's, I think he got injured, or something."

Dave faked being surprised, "Really! What happened?"

Jack had rehearsed what he would say to Dave, so he was ready. "I'm not too sure, there was an ambulance in the driveway, and I think they took Bradley to the hospital." That was it, that was all Jack had rehearsed.

Dave asked, "Were you home at the time?"

Now Jack was trying to think, on the spot, of an excuse as to where he was at the time. Not sounding sure of himself he volunteered, "I was up in Black Hawk, at the Lodge Casino, playing Blackjack all day."

Dave stood there smiling at Jack, "I've known you for years, Jack. What happened at Bradley's?" He asked Jack again.

Jack started to say something, but, stopped and stood there silently. Dave was smiling and said "I saw the recording. I saw you kill Bradley White."

Jack took a deep breath and let it out. "Hoo! What are you going to do about it, Dave?"

Dave winked at his friend, "It looks like you may have committed the perfect crime. I think this can be our little secret. Whadda you say?"

Jack looked at his friend, this is not the response he thought Dave would have. Dave was a different person when his wife wasn't around. Jack said, "Let's have some pizza and get plastered."

"That's my boy, Jack! Screw Bradley White!"

"Yeah, screw Bradley White!" Jack said back. They both raised their glasses of Cutty Sark Whiskey and clinked them in a toast.

They finished the pizza in short order, "Delicious!" Jack declared and poured the two of them a double shot of the Whiskey. The drinking went on for hours, until just past 9:00 pm, the Cutty Sark bottle was about 1/3 gone. Dave was feeling no pain. Jack drank, also, but when Dave wasn't looking, he would dump his beer or his shot of Cutty down the sink so Dave would think Jack had drunk as much alcohol as he had, and nothing was amiss. Dave sat, slumped in the kitchen chair, he put his head down on the table and began to fall asleep. Jack said, "Well, my friend. I'm tired. I'm heading home to bed. I'll let myself out." Jack headed for the front door.

"Sounds good," Dave said and stood up. "Come on, Chipper, let's go potty and go to bed." Chipper ran to the back door and started jumping against it. Jack paused and watched as Dave opened the door and went outside with the little white dog. Jack turned around and headed down the stairs. He went into Dave's basement and stood listening while staring at the ceiling. He heard Dave and Chipper come back in. Dave went to the front door and locked it. "Come on Chipper, little guy. Let's go to bed." Dave said to the pooch and stumbled up the stairs. Jack went to Dave's security room and searched for the DVR so he could erase everything on it. It was gone, there was a clean spot on the dusty desk where the DVR had once been. Jack looked through all the drawers and in the closet for the hidden DVR. Maybe, Dave stashed it in his bedroom. Jack had to devise a new plan on the spot. He looked around where Dave had been working on the water heater. He dug around in a few toolboxes and found a hacksaw. He turned the gas to the new water heater off at the valve, took the hacksaw and cut a small slice in the gas line. He turned the gas back on and ran up two sets of stairs to Dave and Jen's bedroom. He paused, at the door, Dave was quietly snoring. Jack went into the bedroom and looked around to see if the DVR was anywhere, but didn't see it so he scooped Chipper up, ran back down to the main floor and pulled the heavy door open. Suddenly, Chipper barked, and Jack panicked and grabbed the little dog's mouth to muzzle him. He backed out the door and closed it behind him.

Dave heard Chipper bark and then he thought he heard the front door close. Jen must be home he thought, and panicked, she wouldn't be happy that he was drunk. He tried to get out of bed but had a hard time. He slid off the bed onto the floor on his hands and knees. He felt flush and knew he was going to puke, he tried to stand but couldn't, he walked on his hands and knees towards the bathroom, the hardwood hurting his knees, but it was too late. Dave put a hand over his mouth, the vomit squirted out both sides and all over the bedroom wall and hardwood floor. He searched around the room and found a small trash can and fell to the floor puking into it. He was so sick, he called for Chipper. "Here boy!" Uhrruhhh! He puked more missing the trash and hitting the floor. Dave laid there feeling like he was dying. Little did he know. He saw a dark figure in the room with him and got goose bumps. The dark figure hissed, "You're not strong enough to weather the storm!" Dave was obviously hallucinating. He vomited again, tried to get up and slipped and fell on the slippery wood. He hit his head on a small table and fell unconscious. He wasn't coherent when the gas eventually was ignited by the pilot light of the furnace and the house exploded.

Jack and Chipper went down to the basement of Jack's home. Jack knew a huge explosion was forthcoming and tried to determine whether the blast would reach his house, but he thought to be safe he had better prepare for it. He pulled the sheets off the bed in his bedroom and dragged the mattress into the Spy versus Spy room. He closed the door and leaned the mattress against it, and he and the little white dog waited. It took almost forty-five minutes for the explosion. Jack felt the concussion and heard glass shatter. The ensuing fire destroyed Dave and Jen's entire home. The fire department spent most of their energy trying to save the outlying buildings on Dave and Jen's property by pouring thousands of gallons of water on them. Jack put the mattress back on the bed and cautiously walked upstairs, the living room was lit up from the conflagration down the street. The front window was shattered but still intact. He would have to call his insurance agent and get it replaced before it fell out on the floor but until then he decided he shouldn't use the front door. He scooped up Chipper and went out the back door and around the house to stand in the street with the other neighbors watching the horrible scene. The neighbor's faces were illuminated by the huge fire.

"Oh my!" said a woman that Jack recognized as Julianna, from the other night.

Her husband Mario was next to her and asked, "What more can happen in our lovely little neighborhood?" Julianna put her hand on the side of her face and Mario put his arm around her. Jack shook his head and said, "It's horrible, absolutely horrible."

Mike Briggs and Karl were looking through the faxes they had been receiving. Karl looked at one particular fax and read it aloud. It was from Jiffy Rent-a-Car in Los Angeles. "Michael Rudolph turned his red Nissan in at LAX Airport and was in Chicago the night Flavio was murdered."

"One down, two to go." Karl responded. They continued going through the faxes. Mike found the next pertinent fax from the Bullhead City Police Department and read it aloud. Blanca Alvarez had a long list of arrests and two convictions, one for assault and another for drug possession. She was, presently, married to a member of the Bandidos Motorcycle Club. Karl said to Mike, "Bingo! I think we can forget about Jack Martin. Either Blanca or her husband killed Chucho, and, put him in the river. Put an All-Points Bulletin out for both of them, Mike." Karl went out to his car and headed home. Victoria was still living at the Unwed Mothers Shelter. Sandra had picked the girl up, earlier, and the three of them were going to have a nice dinner together to celebrate Victoria's first day back at High School. Sandra had gone with Victoria to the High School and explained her situation to the principal. He immediately enrolled the teen and she started classes the same day. Karl was very happy, driving home, not only for Victoria but also for himself and Mike. He couldn't wait to end this case and focus his energy on Sandra, Victoria and her unborn son, Hector.

-Chapter 16-

Susan pulled up in front of her friend Jane's home in her Jeep. Jane was waiting inside the garage for the younger woman. Susan stepped out of the Jeep and helped her friend into the tall vehicle and the two of them headed towards Black Hawk, the small gambling town in the foothills West of them.

Jane told Susan, "I've got to look in my bum bag and see what coupons I have."

Susan looked at Jane and smiled, "Bum bag?"

Jane laughed and explained. "Back home in Ireland, what you call a fanny pack, in America, is called a Bum bag." She unzipped the small pack and continued, "Now let me check." Jane pulled out a flyer from the Casino and read aloud. "One free buffet at King's Restaurant and $35 in free play. The coupon expires today."

"Wow. I think I only have $5 in free play, but I have a free buffet also, so that's perfect."

"Thank you for driving, John doesn't like to drive me here he's not much of a gambler. I haven't been gambling since you and I went about a month ago. Back when I was married to Sean, we went nearly every weekend."

"Sean was a gambler?"

"Oh, heavens no. He just liked the free food. He usually sat at the bar and drank a pint or two while I fed the machines."

Susan said, "Jack and I never came up here gambling." And then corrected herself, "Actually, I take that back, one time, Jack's work rented a big bus and we rode up with his co-workers from Champs, but Jack lost over $50 and was never interested in coming again." The two sat in silence enjoying the scenic ride up highway 6. Susan turned the radio on, and a country song was playing. She spotted a few mountain sheep standing on the side of the rocky hill and pointed them out to Jane.

Jane said, "Sean and I drove up here early one Sunday morning and about a dozen of those sheep nearly ran us off the road."

"What happened?"

"Well the little buggers ran onto the road in front of us and Sean had to swerve to avoid hitting them and he nearly put us into the river. We had a small car back then, it was scary."

"Oh my," Susan looked at the high drop off to the river and thought about how scary that would have been. The two women sat listening to the radio. They pulled into the Casino's parking garage and a valet opened Jane's door and helped her out. Susan was given a valet ticket which she stuck in her purse and the two women walked into the noisy Casino and rode the escalator to King's Restaurant.

Jen parked on Everett Court in front of what was left of her home. She paused and finally got out of her car and was overcome by emotion. She was meeting some Insurance adjusters to survey the damage. A man and a woman stepped out of their rental car, the woman with a briefcase and the man with a camera. They walked towards the distraught woman. Jen shook hands with them, and introductions were made. Jen had tears in her eyes and the female adjuster put her arm around her. "Are you going to be okay for this? I promise it won't take too long."

Jen wiped her eyes with a tissue and nodded yes to the woman. The man was already taking pictures of the destroyed house. Dave and Jen's beautiful home was completely gone, nothing but a pile of black rubble. Just the outlying buildings were still standing. They had been saved by the Fire Department pouring ungodly amounts of water on them. Dave Holloway's remains, what was left of them, had been removed and taken to the morgue, mostly just bones and teeth. The coroner had been able to fit what was left of Dave into a small thirty-gallon plastic tub with a locking lid. After walking the property for about half an hour the three of them returned to the street. "That's about it." The female adjuster said to Jen. She put her hand on Jen's shoulder and asked, "Are you okay?"

Jen nodded, "I need to get my dog from the neighbor, and I need to thank him for watching the dog, are we done?" "Yes of course." The woman said to Jen and the two adjusters got in their rental car. Jen waved goodbye and then she walked over to Jack's home.

Jack was in the kitchen when the doorbell rang, it scared the bejesus out of him. He looked out the peephole in the door and saw Dave's widow standing there and relaxed, he opened it and invited Jen in. Chipper was beside himself after seeing Jen. He ran around the house barking and wagging his tail. He jumped into Jen's arms and she hugged and kissed the little dog. She and Jack sat in his living room and talked for hours. Jack told her about Dave coming home with the new water heater and how he had decided he would continue watching the dog until the next day because he figured Dave was busy with the new installation. Jen started crying and then Jack followed suit. Jack told her, "I've never had a better friend than Dave, and I never will. I loved him as if he were my own brother.

"And he felt the same way about you, Jack. We both felt so bad for you when Susan left."

Jack smiled at Jen and changed the subject.

"You had insurance, right?"

"Of course. That's who I was with this morning."

The insurance would rebuild their home, she told Jack, but she didn't think she could ever live there again, too many memories. She had found a small apartment in Steamboat Springs where she would stay temporarily. She wanted to be near her mom, who was told by her Oncologist that she probably only had a few months left on this earth.

"As soon as Mom passes, I'll probably move back to my birthplace."

"Which is?"

"Little Alcova, Wyoming. I have a lot of family there. Aunts and Uncles and several cousins." Jack nodded and Jen continued, "I'll have to sell the business here, of course, I've had offers and it should sell, I can't work there."

Poor Jen, Jack truly felt sorry for her. Jen decided it was time to leave and head back to Steamboat. It was a three-hour drive, and she didn't want to be driving after it got dark. Jack gathered Chipper up, put him in a brand new kennel he had bought a few days ago, and gathered a doggy bed and some bowls he bought at the same time. Jack had just been feeding Chipper people food for the time being, mostly bologna, until Jen came for the little dog. He carried the kennel with chipper inside to Jen's car. She had picked up the bed and everything else Jack had bought and followed Jack to her car. Jen said to him, "Jack, you are such a good friend. Thank you for taking such good care of our little Chipper. I'm so lucky Dave hadn't picked him up before..." She left the sentence hanging and started choking up. Tears were rolling down her cheeks. Jack nodded and gave her a big bear hug. They promised each other to keep in touch. She kissed Jack on the cheek and got in her car. He watched her drive away, until she was out of sight. Jack was beside himself with remorse. How could he kill his friend Dave? The guy was a saint. Jack wondered what kind of beast he had become. He stood in the street thinking and finally turned and went back in his house. He picked up the phone receiver and dialed the Wheat Ridge Police Department. He was done, he needed all the killing to stop. He was going to confess everything to whoever answered the phone. He let it ring a few times, but a voice ordered him to hang up, so he did. He stood there, thinking he needed to write down his thoughts right then before he lost his mind and descended into the total madness he knew would soon take over him. He looked around and finally in a drawer he found a blank journal of Susan's and started scribbling words in it. It started:

> ***I'm writing this in the event of my descent into total madness:***

Jack read what he had written aloud. It sounded good and he continued,

> ***I remember when I first became a killer. A disciple of Satan, the Dark Lord. I remember all the specifics about that night. I was sitting by the Colorado River in Laughlin, Nevada, looking up at all the millions of stars twinkling in the dark sky."***

Jack wrote for about an hour before he stopped and put the journal down. He was extremely tired, so he headed to his bedroom and laid down on the bed, fully clothed. Within minutes he was asleep, and a nightmare started playing in his mind. Jack was standing next to Dave in front of Dave and Jen's burning house. They both held a garden hose and were spraying water on the house with no effect. He could hear Jen screaming from inside the burning house. Jack looked closely at Dave, the skin on his face had been blown off in the explosion. In its place was a wet red and pink mass of bloody muscle. You could see part of Dave's skull near his hairline. Dave smiled at Jack and, nearly, all his teeth were missing. Dave said to Jack, "When someone is in Hell, only the Devil can point the way out." There was dark red spittle dripping from Dave's mouth. Jack stared at his friend. Suddenly Dave turned into the Prince of Darkness. The Devil was standing there before Jack, completely naked. His entire body was a dark red color, including his penis, which was completely exposed, along with his testicles, which hung nearly to the ground. His bifurcated tail whipped from side to side. Jack dropped the hose and began running. He could hear the Devil laughing uncontrollably as he ran towards a stand of trees behind Dave and Jen's home. Several different Evil entities chased him through a thick forest. Jack crawled into a hole he had found and covered himself with some brush. He lay there, holding his breath, trying to be quiet. He could hear the breathing of things walking around searching for him. Eventually, a large hairy beast snuck up and, with large sharp teeth, grabbed Jack by the scruff of his neck and started shaking him all around. He could hear his flesh tearing and tried to scream, but, when he opened his mouth there was no sound.

Jack sat straight up in his bed and screamed like a woman. He looked around. He was entirely alone in his bed in the basement. The room was starting to get dark. He checked the clock, he had been asleep for hours. He laid back down and tried to control his breathing. He was starting to have a full blown, anxiety attack. His bed was soaked from his sweaty body. He raised his hand to his face. It was covered in blood. He jumped out of bed and looked back down at the mattress. It was wet with blood, not sweat. He ran to the bathroom and stared into the mirror. He held his hand to his face, again. No blood. He returned to the bedroom, flipped the light switch on and stared at the bed. No blood. A voice in another room said, "Insanity will lead you to the place you belong." "What did you say?" He asked. Someone started laughing and he could feel the presence of someone in the basement with him. Jack ran up the stairs. He stood in the kitchen bent at the waist gasping for air. He looked outside into the darkening back yard and a dark figure with glowing eyes was standing in the far corner, the place that Dave's camera could never see, grinning at him. Jack lost consciousness and collapsed to the kitchen floor cutting his head.

Detective Briggs had found Blanca Alvarez. She was locked up in the Perryville Prison in Goodyear, Arizona and had been there for about a week. She had a rock solid, alibi. She had been pulled over by a Pima County Deputy for going over the speed limit, near Tucson, at about the same time Chucho was killed. Because of her outstanding warrants she was arrested, put in handcuffs and taken to the Pima County Jail and then to Perryville. Tucson was over three hundred miles and nearly six hours away from Laughlin, so she was out as a suspect. Mike had also found Blanca's husband, Enrique (Rico) Alvarez. He had been behind bars in Canon City, Colorado for more than three years on an attempted murder charge out of Scottsdale, Arizona. Mike walked into Karl's office and told his partner what he had discovered. "Damn" Karl said to Mike, "I really thought Blanca Alvarez, or her husband was our perp." It was 6:25 pm and the office was nearly empty except for him, his partner and two other detectives. Karl was disappointed, every time it looked like they were making headway in this case, something came up and they had to start from square one. He told Mike to head home. They had both been putting in long hours. Mike should be home with his wife. This was becoming a habit for the two detectives. Long hours chasing leads, then all the leads falling through. Mike picked up his jacket and left. Karl sat there going over the files for the Beneventi murder. He came across the interview with Rose Swanson and read through Mike's notes. Miss Swanson had said the license plate of the car that sped away had a J and an R on it. He looked at a poster Mike had pinned up on the wall showing the license plates of all fifty states. California's plates that year were white and had the word California, in red cursive writing, across the top. Arizona's plate that year featured a desert sunset and a saguaro cactus on the left side. They were different looking plates of different colors. He picked up the phone and dialed Rose Swanson's phone number in Lake Tamarisk.

Rose answered the phone right away and Karl said "Miss Swanson, this is detective Schulz from the Laughlin Police Department."

She said, "Yes Detective, are you calling for more cookies for your partner?"

Karl laughed out loud and looked around. The few others in his office stopped what they were doing and stared at him. Karl cleared his throat and said, "No ma'am, but I'm sure my partner would love some more of those cookies. They were yummy."

"How may I help you, then?"

She was thrilled to be talking to the nice Detective, again.

"Well, ma'am, you said the license plate on the car you saw had a J and an R on it?"

"Yes, that's correct." She told him. Karl glanced at the poster again,

"Do you remember the color of the license plate you saw that night?"

"Yes, I do." She replied, "It had the colors of a beautiful sunset on it, and it had a cactus on the left side." Karl glanced at the poster, "Arizona," He said more to himself than to Rose Swanson.

Rose said, "That's right, I lived in Arizona for a few years. It was definitely an Arizona license plate." Karl thanked her and hung up. He dialed his partner's cell phone.

Mike saw the name on his phone, he was just pulling into his driveway. "Karl, what's up?" he asked.

Karl said, "I think Jack Martin may be involved after all. Call his Ex again, and ask her if there is any reason Jack Martin would be in the Lake Tamarisk area."

Mike said, "You got it."

Susan began her Saturday writing class on time, there were eight older people in her class today, three men and five women. Her class usually lasted a couple hours depending on how many students showed up. Susan would set a timer and each person would read something they had written or sometimes something a professional author had written. The rest of the class would then critique what was read. Susan looked forward to her Saturday class every week. Because there were eight students, she set the timer for fifteen minutes and said, "Let's begin with Miss Weathersby. Carla is this something you wrote?"

Carla Weathersby timidly said, "Yes, I wrote it." The petite 85-year old widow cleared her throat and held her story close to her face so she could see it better, her frail hands shook as she started, "The warm gulf air swept in over the large manicured lawn and enveloped the small open veranda where Pierre and Monica sat staring at the starry sky. Monica sat and Pierre wrapped his arms around her. He slowly leaned in and kissed the blushing Monica on her ruby red lips. At first, she was taken aback but eventually she gave in to the handsome Frenchman with the thick, dark mustache, he was a gentle lover. His hand explored her body and settled on her heaving bosom. He could feel her erect nipple beneath her blouse. He tore the blouse open and smothered her bare breasts with kisses. Monica was breathing heavily and undid his trousers and reached for his erect penis. Pierre sat up and tore his silky shirt off and tossed it aside. Within minutes they were both completely naked and the sky opened up and warm rain started falling. Their naked bodies glistened from the rain as they explored each other and eventually made wild, passionate love, their bodies grinding against each other." Carla stopped and explained, "I don't quite care for some of it." She looked around at her wide-eyed fellow students. Susan was just as wide-eyed as the rest and said, "Wow! Okay. That was very descriptive and not quite what I expected from you Carla. Oh my!" Susan put her hand on her chest and asked, "Would anyone care to comment on what Carla wrote for us?" Seven hands shot into the air.

Jack sat in the kitchen holding a compress to the cut on his head, he started going through the caller I.D.'s on the phone. The call from Mike Briggs showed up and Jack took a tablet out of the kitchen drawer and wrote the number down and also wrote ***Detective Briggs*** next to the number. He decided instead of confessing to the local authorities he should confess to the Laughlin Police Department. After all, Chucho's killing started all this ugliness in motion. He picked up the receiver and paused, "What should I say to this guy?" He asked himself. "Should I just blurt out that I killed the gangster biker to help the young girl named Victoria?" Chucho's murder and Vincent's murder were justified, weren't they? Certainly, a jury of his peers would at least ponder letting him get off the murder conviction of these two seriously bad people. He had called the local authorities earlier and decided that had been a mistake. They would not hesitate to fry him for his neighbor's murders, he had no doubt. No justification in either of the killings. He decided Mike Briggs was the best person to admit guilt to. Jack dialed Mike Brigg's cell number and listened to the phone ringing. Again, a voice told him to hang up, but it was not in his head. The voice had come from the next room. Jack refused to hang up, but as soon as Detective Briggs answered, the voice demanded. "Hang up now or die!" Jack grabbed the phone and jerked it so the plug popped out of the socket in the wall, he sat there breathing heavily. He was slowly and surely losing his mind. The Demon in his head or in the next room was taking over his life in a very bad way. What had once been anxiety and depression was replaced with insanity and lunacy. Now several voices were talking all at once and he couldn't make out what they were saying. He held his hands over his ears, but he could still hear the voices. Jack began talking out loud reciting everything from the pledge of allegiance to the words of the Papa Roach song. Eventually the voices subsided. He had Susan's journal with him, she had written her name on the front, but she had never written a word in it. Jack thought of Susan and heard a voice that sounded like his own say I don't care for that bitch and what she has done to me. Lately he had bad thoughts of his former wife. He opened the journal and tried to read what was inside but his writing the last few days was just gibberish. Jack started writing more.

> ***Things have become so sordid for me. The Devil is in total control of me. Five times he has visited me and five times I accepted what he told me. My name is the word, and my word remains the same. He is with me. He is me. Death comes every time I think of Him. Susan is of the devil now, and death must come to those who abandoned me. The Devil was a murderer from the beginning, not holding to the truth, for there is no truth. When he lies, he speaks his native language, for he is a liar and is the father of lies. Susan was a liar also. The Devil pulls the strings that make us all dance. We delight in loathsome things, and yet we feel the horror of the ranks and legions. I wake and see the face of the Devil and I ask him why me? But he just sneers and stares. His glowing eyes resemble the embers of the fires we have caused, the lives we both ended and can never get back. Come to me and whisper things to me and mine. I live for you but one more will die because of me.***

Jack drew five stick figures standing beside six crosses. They represented Chucho Valdez, Vincent Beneventi, Allie Simmons, Bradley White and Dave Holloway. The sixth cross stood and waited for the sixth and final victim. Jack looked at what he had drawn and smiled. "Soon there will be one more for you Dark Lord!" Jack signed the page, ***Gad, Son of Jacob***. Jack closed his journal, knelt beside his bed and started praying. "Satan, I bow to you, for I am your blood stained, servant. You are a roaring lion. Your evil washes over me and fills me. The serpent called on me and talked of your power and successes. I have become your unlikely beast and join the other unlikely beasts who came before me and those who will come after me." Jack stripped naked and laid on his bed. "I will take one more life for you, Satan. One more soul will raise up to the heavens because of you, oh Lord. You are the master!" A voice called out from somewhere in the basement, "She must die, Jack!" Jack asked "Who?" But he was certain who the voice was talking about.

Susan Johnson met her friend Jane for an early dinner at a nice little restaurant in Old town Arvada, Jane had a coupon for a buy one get one free and pulled it from her bum bag. The two of them talked and they both laughed when Susan told Jane about Carla's 'R' rated story. They had a lovely late afternoon dinner together and after dinner Jane insisted on paying, despite Susan's arguments. They walked to the parking lot and hugged before getting into their cars and driving away in opposite directions.

Mike Briggs had just hung up from talking to Karl who wanted him to call Jack Martin's ex again, when his cell phone rang three times before he could grab it and answer. He recognized the phone number but couldn't place it so he answered, "Briggs, how can I help you?" But there was no one on the other end. He checked the phone number again and it hit him whose number it was, so he pulled his car over and made sure. "Holy Shit!" He exclaimed. It was Jack Martin's home phone number, the one he had been calling for a week. Apparently, the guy he had been trying to contact was home now and wanted to talk. He redialed the number, but it was busy. He waited several seconds and redialed again with the same results. Mike called Karl who answered immediately.

"What's up Mike?"

"Karl, Jack Martin just called me from his home and when I answered he hung up. Now the line's busy."

"Okay." Karl said. Mike was already loaded down with things to follow up on so he decided he would take over calling Jack Martin.

"Mike, give me Martin's home phone number and let me try to contact him. He doesn't know my number he may be more apt to answer me."

"Sounds like a good idea, I'll text it to you."

Karl waited for the text. It took several seconds to show up. When it did Karl, dialed the number and heard a busy signal. He googled Flights to Denver from Laughlin, Nevada. There was one early the next morning so he booked it. Sandra may not be happy about him leaving the state, she never felt comfortable when he did that, but he'd smooth it over with her tonight. Karl dialed Mike and his partner answered on the second ring.

"Mike, I just booked a flight to Denver at 7:00 am tomorrow morning. I just have a feeling this guy is at home now. You know me, I'd rather interview people face to face than on the phone."

"Me too, Karl. You've trained me well. Okay, well keep me in the loop, please?"

"Will do, have a good night big guy."

Susan got home from dinner with Jane and opened a bottle of Schmitt & Sohne wine, grabbed a wine glass and stepped out onto her balcony. The sun was setting, and she stood watching it. She had started writing, again, after divorcing Jack. It was always a passion of hers. It was something she had always wanted to do since graduating College. She grabbed her latest journal and began describing what she saw in front of her.

> ***Through misty eyes I watch the gold orb slip behind the horizon. That place where heaven and earth meet. Threads of light linger mingling with the cotton candy clouds, dyeing the Heavens first gold, then subtly changing to orange, then bright red until all that is left is a light mauve, melting away to be replaced, eventually, by darkness and sparkling diamondlike stars.***

She read it back to herself. She liked it. She found it descriptive and moving, not prosaic at all. She poured herself a glass of the Riesling and sat there enjoying the warm evening. Her thoughts shifted to Jack. She had gotten a second phone call from the Laughlin Police Department. The Detective that called had her wondering if Jack was in some sort of trouble. He said he wasn't able to say what the call was about he just needed Jack to call him as soon as possible. He asked her if Jack knew anyone near Lake Tamarisk between Indio and Blythe in California. "Not Lake Tamarisk but Jack has a younger brother in Cathedral City who owns a consignment shop in Palm Springs." She told him.

Mike Briggs was quiet, Susan knew he was writing all this down. He asked her if she had an address or phone number for Jack's brother.

She said, "I'm sorry, I don't have an address, all I have is a phone number and hopefully it's still a good one. Let me check my phone. Hold please."

Mike waited as she searched her phone. She gave him Joey's cell phone number and he added it to his notes. Detective Briggs thanked her and hung up. Susan sat and thought about the phone call. She wondered how Jack was doing. She thought about Jack's accusations, earlier in their marriage, about her and Mark Griffin. She had never fooled around on Jack with anyone, let alone Mark from the gym. Last she heard Mark was living with Stephanie, one of the Aquacise instructors at the gym. Susan had dated a few men, that her friends had set her up with, but nothing came of it. She was happy being by herself. She had her family and friends and now she had her writing. Writing came so natural for her. She wrote a novella, about her friend who died of Cancer, and submitted it to a publisher. They liked it and sent her a check for $1000. The publishing company signed her to a contract, and she began receiving royalty checks. They weren't huge but they were steady. Steady enough that she was able to quit her job at DiSanto & Anderson. When she left, Walt Anderson gave her a check for $5,000 and wished her luck with her writing. He told her that there was always a job for her, with their firm, if the writing didn't work out, but he was certain she would succeed as a writer. Susan was a smart woman and Walt told her the same. Her thoughts drifted back to Jack. She had loved him so much when they were in their twenties. She decided she would drive over to the Wheat Ridge home, tomorrow, Sunday, and see if he was home. She had a hair appointment early, but she would definitely go over to Jack's after the appointment. She pictured his surprised face when he opened the door. She hoped he would be happy to see her. She took a sip of the fruity white wine and smiled to herself. She was very anxious to see Jack again.

Mike Briggs kissed his wife goodbye and headed Southwest towards Cathedral City. He had called Joey and talked to him for half an hour, but, like Karl, he preferred to interview people in person. He felt he could pick up certain nuances face to face that wouldn't be as apparent over the phone. Joey wasn't a lot of help on the phone, he said Jack was too timid to hurt anyone. He talked about Vincent Beneventi for a while and Mike had interrupted him and asked if he could drive there and talk to Joey and his husband face to face. "Of course, Detective Briggs. Anything we can do to help but again, Jack couldn't hurt any living thing."

Mike got to the small home in Cathedral City about three and a half hours later. Joey answered the door and invited the detective in. There was another man there and Joey introduced him as his husband, Aidan. Mike shook his hand and the three of them sat at the kitchen table. Mike started the conversation, "Joseph, tell me again about your interaction with Vincent Beneventi, please." Joey took a deep breath and said, "That horrible man started extorting money from me many months ago. The first time he came in he tried to buddy up to me telling me there was a big mob community in the Palm Springs area and he could keep them away if I gave him $400 a month. If I didn't agree to that someone else would come by and possibly ask for twice that amount. I talked with a few other people who have stores in the area, and they have been threatened as well. I figured $400 was not a large amount, I did fairly well when I first opened, and that much money was a drop in the bucket. Within a few months the fee was doubled, and it was harder to come up with the money."

Mike was furiously writing notes. He asked, "And when did Jack first hear of Vincent Beneventi?"

"Middle of March, maybe the 18th, I don't remember."

Mike looked at the couple, they both seemed a bit scared. Mike asked, "When Beneventi showed up at your store a few days after Jack had been staying with you, the two of you said Jack disappeared and followed the gangster to his home in Indio?"

Aidan nodded yes, "That's correct detective. Jack said he followed that beast and confronted him in his garage. He took his gun from him and scared him so badly he soiled his pants. Vincent Beneventi hasn't shown up here since."

Mike rested his head on his left hand while he continued writing. He was tired from the long drive. He finally stopped and asked, "And you're sure Jack said Indio?" They both nodded yes to Mike. Mike shook his head, "Did either of you ever see Jack with a gun?"

They both shook their heads and answered, "No." In unison. It had been nearly an hour since Mike first started asking the two men questions, he was certain Jack was responsible for Vincent Beneventi's murder at the house in Lake Tamarisk. The detective hurriedly gathered his notes, thanked the concerned couple and headed to his car to call Karl.

Jack looked at his watch. 11:32 am, Sunday, April 3rd. He had been writing in his journal. Satan had visited Jack last night in a nightmare and ordered him to sacrifice another victim. Jack was certain who that someone was going to be. He pulled the gun and ammo, he bought at Cabela's, out and inserted about a dozen bullets into the weapon's magazine. He then popped the magazine into the grip of the weapon. He cocked it and was satisfied it was ready for when he needed it. Growing up in rural Minnesota, Jack had learned about guns at an early age. Jack and his father had gone hunting many times together, mostly for birds, some for sport and some for food. Jack especially liked quail, they were very small but very delicious. Jack placed the semi-auto on the desk and opened his journal and began writing, again. There was a knock on the door. A voice from somewhere in the basement, or possibly in Jack's head said, "Knock on the Devil's door and he will slam you through the wall." Jack answered the voice, "This is my last victim, no more killing after this one." He added another entry, he drew a stick figure next to the sixth cross and closed the journal. He grabbed the pistol, tucked it in his waistband and went upstairs to greet his visitor while a demonic voice laughed loudly somewhere behind him.

-Chapter 17-

Karl arrived in Denver on time and walked to the Budget desk, his rental car was ready to go. He climbed into the silver Chevy Malibu and typed Jack Martin's address into the GPS. It told him he was 29 miles and 49 minutes from Jack's home in Wheat Ridge. He dialed the Wheat Ridge Police Department, told the woman dispatcher who he was and why he was headed to their city, and asked her if she could send an officer to meet him at Jack Martin's house. She agreed and told him about the recent tragedies that had happened on Everett Court in the past week. One of the neighbors had been crushed under his girlfriend's car and another neighbor had died in a gas explosion. Karl was stunned. He made the woman on the other end of the phone repeat everything she had just said and give him some specifics. He knew the man he was heading to interview and possibly arrest, Jack Martin, was involved, somehow in the small neighborhood's recent tragedies. Too many bad things had happened to the homes adjacent to Jack Martin's house for him not to be involved in some way. As soon as Karl hung up, his cell phone rang, he answered and Mike was out of breath, "Boss, Jack Martin is our guy. Vincent Beneventi was extorting money from his younger brother. His brother and his brother's husband, both, said Jack just threatened Beneventi but I got a strange feeling from the interview. Jack Martin is our killer I would put money on it."

Karl told Mike he was on the highway minutes away from Jack Martin's home.

Mike cautioned his partner, "Karl, please be careful! This is it! Jack Martin is a killer and he's dangerous!"

Karl told his concerned partner the Wheat Ridge Police were meeting him.

Mike was adamant, "Do not confront this guy alone without back-up! Call me when you get there."

"Yes Sandra!" Karl retorted and hung up. Karl went over everything in his head, Jack Martin murdered Vincent Beneventi, and now Karl wasn't heading to interview a witness he was heading to arrest a murderer. The hair on his neck stood on end.

Wheat Ridge Police Officer Mel Pearce got the call to assist a detective from Nevada at a home on Everett Court. The dispatcher said the detective was at least forty minutes away. The subject at the address was going to be interviewed by the detective and he had requested someone from the local P.D. to be there, as well. It was a courtesy that most law enforcement people did when they were in another agency's jurisdiction, especially out of state. Officer Pearce was in the middle of a traffic accident investigation and decided the Nevada detective would have to wait at the location for his arrival. He was busy for at least forty minutes and he was about six miles from that address.

Karl drove over the speed limit the whole way to Jack Martin's house. It was a straight shot down Interstate 70 so he arrived within thirty minutes, way before the Wheat Ridge Police. He parked the rented Malibu in front of the burnt remains of Dave and Jen Holloway's home and climbed out and surveyed what was left of it. There couldn't be much left of Dave Holloways body, he thought, looking at the destruction left behind. He opened the trunk and slipped his Kevlar vest on, looking at the five other homes on Everett Court. On top of the vest he put a jacket on that said ***Big River Construction, Co***. on the left breast. He pinned his badge to his vest in front by his belt and checked his service revolver before returning it to the holster. He also grabbed a clip board with some papers clipped to it. He wanted Jack to think he was a Contractor soliciting work. Perhaps this would get him in the door, and Jack wouldn't be suspicious. He wasn't sure what would happen after that. He knew he should wait for the Wheat Ridge P.D. to show up, protocol and all, and Mike had scared him a little with his concern. Karl just had a strange premonition that he needed to get into the house as soon as possible. He walked quickly towards Jack Martin's house, watching the windows for any sign of life. He noticed all the Security cameras around the house. Not good, he thought. If Jack Martin wanted to harm him, he would have the upper hand on the detective for sure. He stepped onto the porch, felt for his revolver and knocked, hard, on the door. He waited a few minutes. Finally, he saw a shadow block the peep hole and knew there was someone inside sizing him up. He raised his hand and smiled, hoping to look as harmless as possible to the person behind the door, but the door never opened. Behind him a Police cruiser pulled up and parked. A uniformed officer got out and headed towards Karl. Karl pulled his jacket aside and showed his badge to the approaching man. The officer nodded and put his hand up as a greeting. "Mel Pearce." He said to Karl.

"Karl Schulz." Karl replied.

Officer Pearce asked Karl, "What are we getting into here?"

Karl said, "The owner here is a suspect in a couple murders and is most likely armed and not in the mood to talk to us."

This was different than what the dispatcher had told him, but Pearce nodded, and rested his hand on his weapon. Karl started to say something else when suddenly, a gunshot rang out from inside the house. The two startled lawmen ducked, pulled out their service revolvers and raised them pointing at the front door. Karl tried the door, it was locked. He backed up and slammed his shoulder into the door as hard as he could, it didn't budge. Again, he backed up and on the second try the wood of the doorframe splintered and the door flew open. The two lawmen burst in with their guns at the ready. The house was silent. They searched the main floor for nearly five minutes without finding anyone. Karl looked at the other officer and nodded towards the basement stairs, the Wheat Ridge policeman shook his head, yes, and they entered the stairway, Karl in front, Officer Pearce close behind. They slowly made their way down into the dimly lit basement. They both paused to allow their eyes to adjust. Karl saw the motionless form lying face down on the floor, he thought it might be a woman. A crimson liquid was pooling around the still body. Karl bent down and felt for a pulse, there was none. Whoever was laying there was dead. The two men continued searching every nook and cranny. The door to Jack's Spy versus Spy room was closed. The two men burst in, but there was no one in the small room. After about ten minutes of searching they agreed they were alone with the dead body in the dark basement. Karl walked to the unmoving figure lying in the, still growing, pool of blood. There was a huge hole in the victims back and blood oozed from the wound. Karl slipped on a pair of rubber gloves and turned the body over. He squinted trying to decipher who it was. It was Jack Martin, he recognized him from a photo Mike had dug up somewhere. Jack had shot himself in the chest. A large caliber pistol lay under him. Officer Pearce got on his radio and requested a Sergeant and the County Coroner. Within minutes the house was swarming with Police personnel. Karl wandered into Jack's Spy versus Spy room, again, and studied the TV monitors and the DVR security system. He went over some conclusions in his head, Jack had killed Flavio Valdez, for an unknown reason, possibly to help Victoria. If that was the case, Karl was thankful for that. Then Jack had driven to Lake Tamarisk and incinerated Vincent Beneventi for extorting and beating up his little brother. The empty gun and lack of bullets puzzled the detective, but that puzzle would eventually be solved when everything shook out, he was certain of that. Karl was also certain, after he and Mike went through Jack Martin's security recordings, they would most likely have answers to the neighbor's deaths. One of the neighbors was crushed to death by his vehicle and the other was killed in a gas explosion. Both incidents had a few possible causes and were still under investigation, but Karl suspected each was a homicide perpetrated by the dead man on the floor.

Susan's hair appointment had run late, she had it dyed to eliminate several gray hairs she had noticed in the mirror. Susan had planned on being at Jack's house at least an hour earlier. She turned her Jeep South on Everett Court, and immediately saw the remains of Jen and Dave's house. It was just a pile of burnt rubble. Their large garage and another building were still standing. "What in the world happened?" Susan gasped out loud. The street was full of emergency vehicles. Susan pulled over and watched what was going on. The house she and Jack had bought together years ago was swarming with uniformed men. What did it all mean? Were Dave, Jen and especially Jack alright? One of her questions was answered when two men in dark suits wheeled a gurney out the front door of Jack's home with a body in a black zippered bag. Susan put her hand over her mouth. "Oh my God, Jack!" Who else could it be? Tears welled up in her eyes. She thought of all the good times they had had together all those years ago, she and Jack. She decided she would walk to the house, explain who she was and hopefully someone would tell her what had happened.

Karl had called Mike Briggs and filled him in on everything that had happened since he arrived at Jack Martin's house and told his partner about the DVR in the basement. Mike was happy Karl was okay. Karl stood outside talking to the Sergeant in charge about contacting Fred and Gladys Martin of Brainerd, Minnesota, when his phone pinged indicating a text message had come in. He looked at his phone, the text was from Victoria. He looked around, a woman was getting out of her Jeep and heading towards the crime scene tape. He was afraid the woman was with the press and pointed an officer towards the woman to intercept her. Karl walked to the side of the house where he had some privacy, and, looked at the text. Victoria had texted these words to him.

> ***Hi Detective Schulz, Hector came early he was born this morning. He's healthy. 7 pounds. I need to talk to you. Please call.***

Karl dialed Victoria's number immediately.

She answered and he congratulated her. "Congratulations Mommy!"

She thanked him and said, "I don't know how to say this, but Hector and I are ready to become Schulz's."

Karl couldn't believe his ears. He thrust his fist into the air and said excitedly. "Sandra and I are ready for that, too!"

Victoria's Mom had signed the required papers, she finally accepted that the white couple would be the best thing for her young daughter. Sandra and Karl could begin the adoption process as soon as possible. He felt tears welling in his eyes and told the new mother, "I'm in Colorado but I'll call Sandra and give her the good news. Tell me what hospital you're in and the room number." He pulled a pad from his pocket and wrote down everything the teen told him. He was ecstatic, "Oh, Victoria, I can't begin to tell you how happy we are right now!"

Victoria started crying, "Thank you for inviting the two of us into your life Mr. Schulz, uh, I'm sorry I don't know what I should call you. Is Karl okay?"

Karl asked her what she called her dad when she was younger.

She said, "Papi."

Karl said, "I'm good with 'Papi.'"

Sandra was standing in the kitchen staring into the open refrigerator trying to decide what to make for the evening's meal. Karl should be home by then and would be tired and hungry. The phone rang, the Caller I.D. said K. Schulz. She answered, "Hi honey I'm so glad you called,".

He said "Hi, love."

She always worried when he was away from home, especially when he was out of state, "How is Colorful Colorado?" She asked him.

"It's fantastic!" He gushed, "But not as fantastic as it is there, in Laughlin!"

She was stumped. "Okay, I'll bite. What does that mean?"

Karl blurted out, "Victoria just texted me, Hector arrived this morning, a few weeks early. He's a healthy Seven pounder. Victoria's in room 212 at Laughlin Medical. But, even better," He paused a few seconds, for effect.

Sandra asked excitedly, "Yes, what is it? What could be better than a new baby boy? Don't leave me hanging!"

Karl gushed the news to his wife. "Victoria has decided to allow us to adopt her and Hector! Her mom signed the papers."

"OH, MY GOD!" Sandra yelled into the phone so loud he had to pull the phone away from his ear.

Karl yelled back at his wife, "Congratulations Grandma! I'll be home later this evening. I love you!"

Sandra excitedly said back, "I'll get some champagne and put it on ice. I love you, too." Karl hung up his phone. Sandra sat down on a kitchen chair, still holding the phone's receiver, overcome with emotion.

The next day, back in Laughlin, Karl and Mike went over the recordings in the DVR they had found in Jack Martin's basement. They saw Jack knock the jack out from under the Porsche resulting in Bradley

White's demise. Later in the recording they saw Jack run from Dave Holloway's house holding a small white dog, about forty minutes before the large home exploded. It took several days of sifting through the rubble but forensic people with the Wheat Ridge Fire Department finally found a ribbed gas line with the saw cut in it. Jack had killed his neighbor who, most likely had seen Jack kill Bradley White. Dave Holloway, despite being one of Jack's best friends had become a liability to Jack and he took care of the liability.

Karl visited Joey Macklin and gently gave him the bad news about his big brother. He re-interviewed Jack's brother and his husband, and they repeated what they had told detective Briggs, that Jack had helped them with a mobster, Vincent Beneventi, who was shaking them down for protection money. But neither of them thought Jack was capable of torturing someone and then setting them on fire. "Oh my God, my brother just threatened him, detective. Jack couldn't kill anyone." Joey sobbed while Aidan held him. Joey was overwhelmed by the news his brother was dead of a self-inflicted gunshot wound. Karl knew that Jack was involved, somehow, in Chucho Valdez's murder also, but he couldn't prove it. The surveillance recordings from the casinos along the river didn't reveal the crime. The Highwater was missing a camera in the back and Karl was certain that is where the murder of Chucho had happened. He and Mike had talked to all the dealers at the casino and they had told the detectives that Jack was aware there was no camera back there, he had sat in the back with them on a few nights. One of the dealers, Amber Tilly, asked the two detectives, "Was Jack involved in the biker's death?"

Karl told her that seemed to be the case at present but they were still gathering evidence and talking to witnesses.

Miss Tilly said, "Oh my God, he seemed like such a nice guy, a true gentleman."

The three young thieves who happened to be in the wrong place at the wrong time were charged with the murder of Allie Simmons, based solely on circumstantial evidence. All the DNA evidence came back and none of it matched any of the three teens. They all broke down and sobbed when the sentence was handed down. Their families in the court room did the same. Thirty-five years, each, in an adult penitentiary. Their lawyers vowed to appeal the verdict. "These boys are innocent of murder they are only guilty of theft. What about the DNA? It doesn't match any of these boys!" The news stations intimated the three were, indeed, capable of murder. They all had records, it seemed like a no brainer. Pictures of the three teens in red jumpsuits being led out of the courtroom in handcuffs were plastered all over the local Denver papers, their faces blacked out. Public sentiment sided with the news stations and the local papers. Everyone decided these three teens were, indeed, murderers and got what they deserved.

A full week later, Karl and Sandra were sitting in the living room with Hector in his baby bouncer chair. The sweet, happy little boy was smiling and making gurgling noises. Sandra got on her knees in front of Hector and started making silly faces for him. Karl sat on the couch smiling at his wife and the baby. He opened Jack's journal to the last entry. It was rambling but revealing. He apologized to Sandra for breaking the happy mood in the room and read it aloud so she could hear the strange words.

> ***I've given in to the Dark Lord. I have killed five times and today will be my sixth. I never intended to become this horrible unlikely beast. Susan was the love of my life. I failed her. Satan entered my soul at some time after she left me and ultimately divorced me. I have seen him. He is very real. There is no way to defeat him other than ending my life.***

Below this Jack had drawn the sixth victim standing next to the sixth cross. The drawing represented Jack.

Sandra gasped, "Oh my god Karl. This man went completely mad at the end, didn't he?"

"He really did. It's as if some evil entity was controlling him."

Karl closed the journal and thought about the drawings. Jack had drawn six victims, but Karl only knew of five of them. He held his hand out and counted them. Chucho Valdez, Vincent Beneventi, Bradley White, Dave Holloway and Jack, himself. Yes, he was correct. That was only five victims. Out there, somewhere was a sixth victim that had eluded him and Mike. He promised himself he would search murder files around the U.S. until he knew who the other victim was. He and Mike would start in the Palm Springs area, and then check for unsolved deaths in the Denver and Wheat Ridge area. This case was not yet closed in his mind. He and Mike still had some work to do, there were definite loose ends.

Victoria came bounding down the stairs in one of her new dresses looking pretty as a peach.

"Come on Papi, the movie starts in twenty minutes."

Karl jumped up, kissed Sandra and their grandson and followed his daughter out the front door.

— The End —

CPSIA information can be obtained
at www.ICGtesting.com
Printed in the USA
LVHW082005020920
664873LV00016B/331

9 781634 989213